DARK TIMES IN THE CITY

Danny Callaghan is having a quiet drink in a Dublin pub when two men walk in with guns. On impulse, Callaghan intervenes to help the intended victim, petty criminal Walter Bennett. Who sent the assassins? With a troubled past and an uncertain future, Danny Callaghan finds himself drawn into a vicious scheme of revenge. The police grope for answers, and a gang war moves towards a bloody showdown. In a city on edge, affluence and cocaine fuel a ruthless gang culture, and a man's fleeting impulse may cost the lives of those who matter most to him . . .

GENE KERRIGAN

DARK TIMES IN THE CITY

Complete and Unabridged

CHARNWOOD
Leicester

First published in Great Britain in 2009 by
Harvill Secker
The Random House Group Limited
London

First Charnwood Edition
published 2010
by arrangement with
The Random House Group Limited
London

The moral right of the author has been asserted

British Library CIP Data

Kerrigan, Gene.
Dark times in the city.
1. Organized crime- -Ireland- -Dublin- -Fiction.
2. Suspense fiction. 3. Large type books.
I. Title
823.9′2–dc22

ISBN 978–1–44480–157–6

Published by
F. A. Thorpe (Publishing)
Anstey, Leicestershire

Set by Words & Graphics Ltd.
Anstey, Leicestershire
Printed and bound in Great Britain by
T. J. International Ltd., Padstow, Cornwall

This book is printed on acid-free paper

In memory of
Bridget Kerrigan and Eileen Kerrigan
and Larry McDonagh
and Thomas Daly

This is the dark time, my love.
It is the season of oppression, dark metal,
    and tears.
It is the festival of guns.
                            — Martin Carter

CONTENTS

The frightened man said, 'Please don't do it. He's just a kid.'

The thug said, 'This is the one I'll use.' He held up a small, blunt-nosed bullet, the hallway light reflected in the shiny brass shell.

'It wasn't his fault,' the frightened man said.

The thug was leaning forward, his face inches away. There was resentment in his voice.

'Hey, old man, I'm supposed to take the loss?'

'He hasn't got that kind of money.'

'You give it to him.'

'*I* haven't got that kind of money.'

'Everyone's got that kind of money. Sell something.'

'Look — '

'Not my problem.' The thug dropped the bullet into the breast pocket of his Hugo Boss jacket and began to turn away.

'Please.'

'Big boys' rules.'

'I'll sell what I can.'

'You do that.'

'But it's not — '

'He's got till the end of the week.'

★ ★ ★

From up here in the Dublin mountains, the lights of the city glowed like countless grains of luminous sand strewn carelessly in a shallow bowl. There were random patterns in the glitter — silvery lights bunched together, clusters of tall buildings, cranes topped by red hazard lights, curving lines of orange street lights heading out into the suburbs or marking where the coast road held back the black sea. Above, the lights of airplanes moved along an invisible path towards the airport. The sky was clear, the moon almost full, the air as sharp as broken ice.

The two men, one turned sixty, the other in his early twenties, paused at the edge of thick woods and looked down on their city. A lot of lights, a lot of people. Half a million in the city itself, another half-million in the surrounding area. Every one of them wanting things, needing things. Some of what they wanted couldn't be bought legally — other stuff, they'd rather not pay retail prices. Many of them were wealthy and wealth is detachable. In that shallow, glittering bowl there were a million opportunities.

Some of the cranes were decorated with coloured lights, to celebrate the impending Christmas. It used to be that the chattering classes were never done boasting about how many cranes there were on the Dublin skyline. The cranes were badges of national pride, and they talked about them in the same respectful tones that the old folk used when they remembered the sacred patriot dead.

Not so much boasting these days.

'What do you think?' the younger man said. 'This the place to do it?'

The older man looked away from the city

lights. He switched on his small flashlight and led the younger man a couple of dozen yards into the woods, to a small clearing. There he used a heel to probe the ground.

'Hard,' he said.

'Time of year.'

'Doesn't have to be deep.' He gestured around the clearing. 'When it's time, you'll be able find your way back to this place?'

'No bother.' The younger man buried his hands in his armpits. 'Jesus, it's cold up here.'

The older man tapped the ground with his foot. 'It'll have to do.' He grinned. 'Anyway,' he said, 'we won't be doing the digging.'

On the way back to the car, from somewhere down there in the city the older man listened to the wavering sound of a distant siren. Police, ambulance or fire brigade — someone was in trouble.

Part One
Impulse

Day One

Chapter 1

On that part of the street, at this hour of the evening, only the pub was still open for business. Near the middle of a row of shops, between the flower shop and the hairdressers, it offered the street a welcoming glow on a chilly winter's night. There were two entrance doors, one to the bar and one to the lounge. The windows were small, high on the wall and barred. The pub front had been recently painted off-white. The blue neon decoration high on the wall was a bog-standard outline of a parrot. The pub was called the Blue Parrot. It was owned and managed by a man named Novak.

This was a neighbourhood place and most of the younger set travelled into the city centre or favoured local pubs that featured entertainment. Novak didn't believe in pub quizzes, pub bands, comedy nights or DJs. He just sold drink and provided a venue for companionship.

On the other side of the street, it was all terraced houses with well-tended front gardens. They were of a standard municipal design that was duplicated throughout the Glencara estate and across similar council-built estates throughout Dublin — Finglas, Cabra West, Drimnagh, Crumlin, Ballyfermot. Small and narrow, most of the houses now bristled with extensions. Many had colourful cladding or fanciful embellishments — columns flanking the front door or tiled canopies overhanging the windows.

From the far end of the street a motorbike made its way towards the pub. Traffic was light here, far from the main routes through the estate, but the motorbike was taking its time, easing gently over the speed bumps installed to discourage joyriders.

The passenger was first to dismount at the pub. He took something from a saddlebag. At the entrance to the lounge he paused and gestured to the driver to hurry up.

★   ★   ★

When the man in the black motorcycle helmet came into the pub, Danny Callaghan slipped down from the bar stool and looked around for anything he might use as a weapon. His hand grasped the only possibility he saw within reach — his half-empty beer glass.

A few feet inside the entrance the assassin paused. The helmet hid most of his face, with just a gap behind which his eyes glanced from table to table. He had a revolver in his right hand, held casually down by his side. Behind him a second man in a matching motorcycle helmet came in, cradling a sawn-off double-barrelled shotgun. Both men wore dark blue boiler suits.

Most of the drinkers were seated at the tables and booths around the edges of the pub, half a dozen of them sitting or standing at the bar.

The first assassin spotted his target and began to move forward.

By now, most of those in the vicinity knew what was happening. The motorcycle helmet indoors, the armed minder watching the killer's back and the quick stride towards the intended victim — in recent years, a routine as recognisable as a Riverdance twirl.

The panic subsided in Danny Callaghan's chest.

Not me.

He relaxed his grip on the beer glass and put his hand in his pocket, to try to stop it shaking. The assassin was walking towards an alcove over by the large fireplace, where three men were now white-faced and standing up.

The man in the middle — small, middle-aged, grey-haired — was named Walter Bennett. Where his companions' expressions were a mixture of fear and bewilderment, Walter's pinched face was all dread.

Danny Callaghan felt the Swiss Army knife in his pocket. It had a small pliers, with a screwdriver, a bottle opener and a two-inch knife blade. A hopeless weapon, but he held onto it anyway. He used a fingernail to pick at the knife blade.

Just in case.

Less than ten seconds had passed, and by now even the dimmest customer in the Blue Parrot knew the score.

The noise from the fifth-rate soccer game on the sports channel continued, but much of the pub chatter had been replaced by the coarse sounds of startled men releasing gasps and swear words.

Several just turned their faces away, crouched or ducked. Some stared open-mouthed, not wanting to miss a thing.

'Ah, come on, fuck off.'

Novak, the pub owner, was behind the counter, sucking in his gut, holding up an open-fingered hand towards the first gunman. The man, almost at the alcove now, ignored him.

From across the pub floor, Walter made eye contact with Callaghan.

'*Help me, Danny!*'

Four feet from his victim the gunman raised his arm, aimed the revolver at Walter's forehead, paused a second, then squeezed the trigger.

It didn't even make a clicking noise.

Nothing.

No sound, no recoil, no wisp of gases. Just a gun not working.

The gunman ducked when Novak threw a bottle of gin. And Walter moved, one foot stepping up and backwards onto the seat behind him, his other foot up and forward onto the table, the table lurching, drinks falling over. He hit the floor running.

The gunman turned, crouched, arm extended, revolver pointing at the moving figure. A clamour of shouts and screams from the customers was followed by the loud, flat sound of the gun going off.

Walter, unhurt, was coming Callaghan's way.

'*Help me, Danny!*'

One hand clutching at the lapels of Callaghan's jacket, Walter paused a moment and then he was past, head twisting from side to side as he sought a way out.

'Danny!'

The fuck does he think I can do?

Callaghan released his grip on the Swiss Army knife and took his hand out of his pocket.

Walter turned towards the toilets, but even in his panic he knew they offered only an enclosed place to die. No time to get across the counter, through the archway and out into the bar. He turned to the approaching gunman, then twisted and crouched sideways, as though he could shrink his body beyond harm's way.

Grunting a warning as he passed Callaghan, the gunman pointed his revolver at Walter and Callaghan hit him square across the back with the bar stool. The gunman went down, landing heavily on his side. As the gun flew from his hand, Callaghan dropped, one knee pinning the gunman to the floor.

Walter ran forward and kicked the gunman hard, connecting with his ribs. He bent and snatched the gun, a small grey pistol, and before he could do anything with it Callaghan's left hand gripped both Walter's hand and the revolver itself. With his other hand he unpeeled Walter's fingers from the gun and looked around.

There wasn't a customer above table level.

Novak was out from behind the counter, standing with his back to Callaghan, one hand held up, palm towards the gunman at the front

11

door, the other hand holding a hammer. The gunman waved the shotgun and shifted from one foot to the other.

'Anybody hurt?' Novak shouted.

Silence.

Then the man with the shotgun let out a hoarse roar. 'Let him go!'

Novak lowered the hammer, his voice unnaturally calm. 'It's over, okay, just take it easy.'

Callaghan bent down, bunched the prone gunman's boiler suit under his chin and pulled him up. The gunman was heavy, but Callaghan took him easily. He heard a satisfying gasp as he twisted the man's arm up behind his back, a squeal as he pushed him past the bend in the bar and around towards the front door. The gunman's movements were awkward, his vision limited by the helmet.

Novak's voice was strained. 'Take it easy, no harm done.'

Holding the gunman in front of him, Callaghan moved alongside Novak. The one with the shotgun was a dozen feet away. Callaghan said, 'Don't be stupid, okay? You piss off, and we let him go.'

The one with the shotgun hesitated. Callaghan pointed the pistol at him and said, 'Leave that and go.'

The would-be killer put the shotgun down on the floor and backed away, pushing the door open. He called back, 'Come on, Karl, come on!' Then he was gone.

Callaghan reached around and pulled the

helmet off the gunman. Karl was about twenty, bulky little guy with hair cut tight to his skull and the shadow of a moustache above his quivering lip. Callaghan's hold on his arm was solid, but he could feel the strength there.

'Toddle along, Karl — you come back here, you'll get your pimply arse kicked.'

Callaghan jerked the gunman forward, leaned him against the front door and pushed. Outside, the second gunman was astride the motorbike, the exhaust already belching. His partner jumped onto the pillion and the harsh revving noise the motorbike made as it carried them away was maybe meant to be aggressive but it came off like a petulant bark.

Novak was standing beside Callaghan, watching the motorbike accelerate towards the far end of the street. 'Jesus, Danny,' he said.

Callaghan nodded. 'Jesus.'

In the distance, the motorbike passed through an orange beam from a street light, then jumped and wobbled as the driver forgot to slow for a speed bump. The tyres screeched as the motorbike turned sharply into a side street. In seconds even the noise of the engine had disappeared.

Novak was breathing as though he'd done a couple of laps around the block. 'This bloody city.'

Callaghan said, 'Recognise anyone?'

Novak shook his head. 'Someone'll tell the cops — I'll have to call it in.' He raised an eyebrow. 'Were you in tonight?'

Callaghan just looked at him.

13

Novak said, 'You better go, so.' He nodded towards the shotgun down by his side. 'What should I do with this?'

'Raffle it.'

Holding the revolver with the hem of his brown suede jacket, Callaghan used the front of his black T-shirt to wipe it. He offered it to Novak. 'Raffle this too.'

Novak said, 'This is going to screw the place up for a couple of days, with the coppers making a fuss.'

Walter Bennett came out of the pub in a hurry, brushed past Novak, and began the jerky stop-and-start lope of a man unused to such exercise.

Novak and Callaghan watched him go. Novak snorted and said, 'You're welcome, Walter.'

Chapter 2

In the ten minutes it took Danny Callaghan to walk to his apartment he sought to keep thought at bay by repeatedly cursing his own stupidity.

Fucking idiot.

That's how it happens — one moment —

He cursed himself again and realised he'd said it aloud.

'Fucking idiot.'

There was no one to hear him. The air was cold enough to show his breath and the street was deserted. Callaghan was tall, with the build of someone capable of making a living with his hands. He had an unfinished look about him.

His hairstyle was an old-fashioned short-back-and-sides that might have been done by a third-rate barber in a hurry. The peppered grey of his hair aged him beyond his 32 years.

The roar of a boy racer announced the arrival of a young man in his early twenties, in a light blue Ford Fiesta. The car came to a too-abrupt stop at the T-junction just ahead. Windows darkened, decorative blue lights reflected from the road underneath the chassis, the entire body of the car seemed to throb with the hip-hop beat of the pulsing music. The night was cold but the driver's window was rolled all the way down. Nothing to do with ventilation, all about youth and image and the insistence that everyone should listen to his chosen music. Callaghan remembered the feeling.

The kid might well be on his way home from a job that paid under the minimum wage, in some kip where the manager didn't bother to ask his surname. In his head, though, he was motoring through the 'hood on his way to score a couple of keys of blow, ready to get down and dirty with a bitch or two and waste any muthafucka that got in the way. The kid gunned the engine, leaning forward as he glanced to his left, then turned right and kicked off, the screech of the tyres almost as loud as the scream of the engine.

The first time Callaghan had got that buzz he was fifteen, and behind the wheel of a stolen Lexus. Fifteen and immortal, fifteen and in no doubt he was a natural-born driver who could fishtail his way out of the tightest corner. And so it was, until two years later, lost in the

15

wagon-wheel layout of Marino, with a squad car somewhere behind, he cut a corner too close and ended up clipping a lamp-post. When the ambulance crew took him out of the wreck he was smiling, his head still full of that buzz.

Callaghan felt a shiver now, remembering. There was no cure except time for that mixture of testosterone, arrogance, courage and stupidity.

He walked through a narrow passageway and out into a wide and overgrown area of green stretching across a dozen acres. With a bit of work it might make a nice little park, but that wasn't in anyone's budget, so it wouldn't get done. The landscape was uneven, full of hillocks and hollows. The tarred surface of the pathway that cut through it was encrusted here and there with sprinklings of broken glass.

Who'd want to kill Walter Bennett?

One man with a gun could be a personal grudge. Two — main man and backup — that had the smell of a drugs gang solving a problem.

Hard to believe, though, that Walter Bennett had graduated to that level of action. They'd met in prison during the final year of Callaghan's sentence, when Walter came in to do five months for breaking and entering a car showroom. Since Callaghan got out, they'd bumped into each other a couple of times, had a drink once. Walter's life had been repeatedly interrupted by prison terms, leaving his ageing face with the perpetually resentful look of a loser. Callaghan couldn't imagine how such a small-timer fitted into the quarrels of young men with serious weapons, and he didn't care.

16

Fucking idiot.

Whatever he'd got himself into, Walter couldn't help being a fool, but Callaghan ought to have known better. If heavies with guns wanted Walter dead, for whatever reason, he was going to die. Interfering in that kind of squabble was pointless.

That was the logic of it, but logic didn't allow for impulse. It was impulse that made Novak get involved, defending his pub and one of his customers. It was impulse, fuelled by his friendship with Novak, that drew in Callaghan.

Near the centre of the green there was a mound covered with bushes, behind which stood some kind of municipal storage shed. As Callaghan approached, three teenagers, wearing the hoodies of their tribe, emerged from the bushes. One of them saw Callaghan and gave him a nod, which Callaghan returned. The kid — his name was Oliver — shared a flat with his grandfather two floors above the apartment that Callaghan rented. They'd met on the first floor landing, on the day Callaghan moved in. Shuffling up the stairs with a suitcase in each hand, Callaghan had cursed as an uncooperative travel bag slipped from one shoulder. It wasn't the kind of area where you could leave a case on the street for a couple of minutes while you carried the rest up. Oliver, coming down the stairs, paused, then nodded and reached for one of the suitcases. 'Fucking lift,' he said, 'it goes dead every second week. And it takes them a couple of days to get it going.'

He carried the suitcase up to Callaghan's

17

floor. He said he lived two floors up, then he nodded at Callaghan's thanks and set off down the stairs, whistling. He didn't seem to have regular work and spent a lot of time hanging around the area. Danny saw him a couple of times in Novak's pub. The kid was right about the lift.

Oliver was one of a group of local kids who regularly used the bushes in the centre of the green to store their booze, bought earlier in the day from a supermarket. The bushes were visible from the apartment block and apparently no one had ever been stupid enough to risk stealing the drink. Later in the evening, the kids would come back and cluster in some hollow with their bottles of cider and cans of beer and build a fire to keep warm while they drank.

In his apartment, Callaghan poured himself a Scotch. The five-floor apartment block was known to its tenants as the Hive. There were bars on the windows of all the ground-level flats. Callaghan's third-floor bedroom was just about big enough for a bed and storage for his clothes. It was slightly smaller than the space that served as combined living room, dining room and kitchen.

Having sipped at the whisky for a while, Callaghan decided he wasn't enjoying it. He poured what was left in the glass down the sink.

Fucking idiot.

He'd switched on the boiler but it would be a long time before the radiators had an effect on the icy air. He put his hands in his jacket pockets and hunched his shoulders against the cold. Finding the Swiss Army knife in his pocket he took it out and opened the blade. He used it almost daily for one chore or another, but in a fight it might as well be a toy.

What kind of fool goes up against a handgun and a shotgun with no weapon to hand except a bar stool?

Dumb.

Maybe it was a mistake coming home so early. He didn't want to be with anyone, but the apartment had few distractions and he could feel the thoughts he'd so far kept at bay, fluttering around his mind, making only occasionally painful raids but aware of their power to dominate.

One moment you're alive. The next — and Callaghan knew the arctic chill that seized his scalp had nothing to do with the temperature of the apartment.

★   ★   ★

The policeman knew Novak was lying and Novak didn't care.

'No way you don't know him.'

'I'd tell you if I knew.'

'According to two of your customers, the intended victim is a regular. Name of Walter something.'

'No, sorry, doesn't ring a bell.'

The few customers still there when the police arrived had already been interviewed. After the police questioned the two bar staff and allowed them to take off, Novak cashed up and put the money in the safe.

The policeman said, 'Shut that thing off.'

On the television screen high on the wall, a bald man with a lined face was leaning forward, his eyebrows agitated. One hand hammered into his other palm to emphasise every third or fourth word as he warned that too drastic an approach to tackling global warming would have adverse effects on competitiveness. Novak told the policeman, 'I like to keep up with what's happening.'

There were three other policemen in the pub, two of them examining the bullet hole in the wooden panel on the back wall. The third had bagged the shotgun and the pistol and was now sitting at a table, phone to his ear, having an animated conversation with his wife.

Novak said, 'How long is this going to take?'

'That depends.'

This policeman had introduced himself as Sergeant Wyndham. A big man, taller than Novak, big as Callaghan. Where Callaghan was lean, though, the sergeant's 36-inch belt strained to hold an overhanging 40-inch belly. The page of the notebook he'd opened when he approached Novak was still blank.

'It's a neighbourhood pub. This Walter guy drinks here two or three times a week and you don't know him?'

'Like I say, first I heard of his name was when you mentioned it.'

It didn't really matter. Once they had Walter's name they'd find him. They'd get Danny

20

Callaghan's name and find him, too. But Novak had principles about this kind of thing. A man in his position, if he started talking to the bluebottles they'd keep coming back. Soon they'd start thinking of him as a source of tips about the less socially committed of his customers. And every time some local put a dent in the law the police would call around and Novak would get the kind of reputation that wasn't good for his kneecaps.

'The man who stepped in, the one who prevented the killing — I'm told you and he were talking, before this thing happened?'

'I'm friendly with all my customers. That guy — I never got around to asking his name.'

Novak's tone was flat, his jowly face expressionless, the greying stubble a contrast to the shaven head. His face made no attempt to corroborate his lies.

'And the gunmen — recognise anyone, hear any names?'

One of the pub customers, under questioning, had said that one of the gunmen had used the other's name, but he'd told the police it had all happened so quickly that he didn't register it.

Novak said, 'I was kind of busy, trying to keep everyone calm.' 'The guns.' The policeman pointed to the shotgun and the pistol, on the counter in separate evidence bags. 'I suppose you got your fingerprints all over them? Anyone else touch them?'

'It got a bit hectic. I wasn't taking notes.'

'Only stupid people make an enemy of the police.'

21

Novak stood up straight and looked the policeman in the eye. 'I'm just about to make a fresh pot of coffee. You and your mates, would you like to join me?'

Wyndham said nothing for a moment, like he very much wanted to remain aggressive. Then he sighed and said, 'Why not?'

Chapter 3

The way the receptionist at the shabby little hotel smiled, Karl Prowse knew she wanted him. She was in her late thirties, almost twenty years older than Karl, but he felt the hunger surge. It wasn't the dyed blonde hair or the tight purple dress, it was the frank look-over she gave him, like she was mentally assessing how his weight would feel against her braced thighs. He savoured the thought while the receptionist nodded to the whore by Karl's side. The whore had an account with the hotel and the cost of the room was included in the price she'd quoted Karl. As they went up the stairs, arms linked, Karl looked back. The receptionist had returned to her magazine.

Karl remembered something from a television movie, about how a brush with death stokes the sex drive. He understood that. Once the fear and the tension goes, the juices all flow back and you need to connect with life and that means you need to fuck something. He could still feel the adrenalin.

Back in that shitty pub, when the job went

sour, there was just one moment when Karl Prowse felt fear. The rest of the time, he was on top of things. Even after that fool butted in, even when Karl felt something hard smash into his back and he went down, the gun jolting from his hand, he was in control. His confidence assured him that within seconds he would hit the floor, roll over and come up, the gun in his hand again. Even when the interfering bastard came down heavily, his knee pinning Karl to the floor, that was something he could deal with. His mind was instantly assessing weights and angles and forces, his muscles tensing — then, from the corner of his eye he saw a hand reach down and take the gun and he felt something lurch inside his body. It was Walter, the piece of crap that he'd gone there to flush, it was his fingers taking control of the gun. Karl knew there was nothing he could do in those next few seconds that could stop that gun punching a hole in his head. And for those seconds, even as his body heaved against the weight of the bastard who butted in, he accepted that he was about to die and it drained his mind of thought. Then he saw the interfering bastard's hand take the gun away from Walter, easily pulling the weapon from his fingers, and his fear gave way to rage.

Where the fuck are you?

By now, Robbie's shotgun should have sorted this out. The interfering bastard should be jam on the floor. And Walter — soon as Walter reached for the gun, his blood should have been decorating the walls.

Where the fuck?

23

Pulling Karl to his feet, the interfering bastard jerking his arm up behind his back. Unsteady on his feet, the pain didn't matter — the humiliation fuelled Karl's rage.

'Let him go!'

Robbie, goddamn retard, holding the shotgun like he was afraid it was going to explode in his hands.

'It's over, okay, just take it easy!'

Guy from behind the bar, he was trying to make it all go away.

Fucked up. It's done. Over.

For now.

Then the one who was holding Karl, the interfering bastard, was telling Robbie not to be stupid and the interfering bastard took Karl's helmet off and he was pushing him towards the door and the whole thing was almost finished, and Robbie the retard went so far down the stupidity scale they didn't have a number for it.

'Come on, Karl, come *on!*'

No names.

First principles in a job like this — no matter what happens you don't use names.

Stupid bastard.

Karl was pounding the whore, her face pushed hard into the pillow, his fingers gripping her hips, his thrusts making the bed shake. She made gasping, moaning noises, as though she was contractually obligated, and after a while Karl remembered he'd had her before. He closed his eyes. He was thinking of the receptionist.

When they'd got clear of this evening's operation, Karl didn't say anything to Robbie about the fuck-up. No point.

'Karl, I'm sorry — '

Robbie Nugent was a good kid — they'd known each other since primary school, and it was Karl who'd recommended him to Lar Mackendrick. Maybe a mistake. This was Karl's big chance — maybe, when Lar Mackendrick asked if he knew another guy who could handle himself, maybe he should have nominated someone harder. But Robbie was a pal — a goddamn retard, but a pal.

Karl swore at the whore, told her to shut up, then he bent forward and made small grunting noises as he came, his lips pressed against her back, her scent filling his lungs.

Once they'd got away from the pub, and Karl had changed clothes at a safe apartment and told Robbie to stay there, he'd taken a taxi the couple of miles into the city centre. There, in a pub dominated by grey and chrome surfaces, with a huge neon flower decorating the wall behind the bar, he found a phone.

'It didn't happen.'

'Why?'

'A civilian stepped in, threw his weight about.'

'And?'

'We cut our losses. The way it went, it was the right thing to do.'

'And?'

Karl felt his face flush. Something in his voice had told Lar Mackendrick there was more. Screwing up a job was bad enough. Leaving behind the revolver and the shotgun — *Jesus*. Karl hated the timidity in his voice but he couldn't do anything about it. 'We lost the tools.'

Silence from Lar.

Karl said, 'I'll explain when we meet.'

Lar said nothing, just clicked off.

Now, in the shabby little hotel, Karl found his jeans on the floor and paid the whore, then told her to fuck off. After dozing for an hour or so he felt hungry, so he got up and got dressed and went downstairs. There was a buck-toothed young Chinky boy behind the counter in reception. Karl found a pub, had a beer and a sandwich and when he was done he went home.

★ ★ ★

Sergeant Wyndham could hear laughter in the background. It sounded like there was a dinner party at the Chief Superintendent's home. The Chief Super said, 'You don't think it's connected, then?'

Four gang members dead in less than two weeks, all public executions. Tit gets his head punctured, so Tat gets his balls blown off. None of the murders happened in the Glencara area. If this thing at Novak's pub was connected, it could mean the feud was spreading out from the inner city.

'Doesn't look like it. We have a first name — Walter — we'll trace him. Middle-aged man, local, doesn't sound like any kind of a major player.'

'Personal, then?'

'We'll probably find out he groped someone's

kid, or maybe he took someone's parking space.'

The Chief Super sounded relieved. 'Maybe it's over, then. Two dead on each side. Could be they're getting war-weary.'

'Could be.'

'You don't think so?'

'Hope for the best, expect the worst.'

'Say a prayer.'

★ ★ ★

When Danny Callaghan slipped between the cold sheets and lay down he smelled his own sweat from the pillow. He hadn't taken anything to the launderette for a couple of weeks. He hadn't had a woman back here for over a month. It took a moment to cast the pillow aside and find a spare blanket to roll up to serve as a pillow.

That's how it happens — one moment —

When he decided the thoughts were too strong to suppress, he turned on his back and stared at the ceiling.

One slip.

Maybe, instead of taking him down, the bar stool glances off the gunman's shoulder and the guy — Karl — he stays on his feet, holds onto the gun and Callaghan takes a bullet in the chest, then one in the head as he lies on the floor of Novak's pub.

Or the gunman's minder wasn't so sluggish, he moves in quickly, pulls the trigger when the shotgun is a foot from Callaghan's head.

All over.

And since Callaghan is 32, that's maybe fifty years of life flushed down the pan in an instant.

Fucking idiot.

It should be a big thing, dying. It should come with some warning, a little time to take a breath, to recognise the significance of the moment. It should be about something more than a loser like Walter Bennett.

In the decade since Danny Callaghan had killed a man, there hadn't been a day when he hadn't thought about it. Remorse rubbed shoulders with anxiety about the probability of retribution. When he saw the helmeted man come into the Blue Parrot, a gun in his hand —

Callaghan kicked the blanket off and let the air chill his body. The cold was an efficient distraction. Out on the street, three floors down, someone was cursing someone else. Callaghan listened, letting the sounds draw his mind away from tonight's foolishness. The male voice was repeating '*Always!*' over and over. The yelling stopped and the object of derision made a crying sound. The voices continued for a while, alternately harsh and mewing, fading into the distance.

Callaghan picked up his Nokia from the bedside table. He opened the contacts list and scrolled down through the names. He stopped and stared at Hannah's name. His thumb caressed the centre button in a random pattern. When the light on the screen dimmed he put the phone away. After a while, he pulled the blanket up and rolled over, waiting for the heat to build up inside the cocoon.

His hand was resting on the pillow, inches in front of his face. In the dim light from the window he stared at his fingers and imagined them now, if things had gone the other way. Right now, he'd be lying on the floor of Novak's pub, blood pooled beneath his body. A policeman, maybe a doctor, staring down at something that used to be Callaghan. His hand not a hand, just cooling flesh, with no more life than an empty glove.

Callaghan flexed his fingers.

He closed his eyes and when the first wisps of sleep began to fog his mind, he welcomed them and let himself slip away. He woke to the distant sound of music and laughter. Still dark, the noise coming from another apartment. He looked at his watch — not yet midnight. Hunger pangs reminded him he hadn't eaten, but he shied away from the thought of getting dressed and going out. After a minute, he rolled off the bed, went into the toilet nook and emptied his bladder. Then he stood by the bedroom window and looked out across the green in front of the Hive. He could see flames from the hollow where the neighbourhood kids were drinking, maybe ten or twelve of them. One of them was dancing around the fire, his arms waving, his body swaying.

Chapter 4

The little prick should have been here by now if he'd done what he was told. Detective Garda

Templeton-Smith glanced at the door of the pub, then back to the coffee on the bar in front of him. Usually Walter was sensible enough, but the panic Templeton-Smith heard in his voice might have driven him into some little bolt-hole where he could curl up.

'Freaking out won't help. Calm down.'

'Two of them, *two* of them! With *guns*! *Jesus!*'

It took a while before Garda Templeton-Smith got the story of the two assassins and how the gun didn't fire first time and then it did but the guy missed and how Walter used the confusion to make his getaway.

'What the fuck are you going to do?'

'Calm down.'

'Easy for you to say — what are you going to do about making me safe?'

Garda Templeton-Smith named a pub on the south side of the city centre. 'Go directly there, soon as you hang up. I'll meet you there.'

Walter's voice went up a pitch. 'I'm not going near that shithouse!'

'Twenty minutes from now, I'll be at the bar, waiting for you. Take a taxi — shouldn't take you much longer.'

'You people going to put me somewhere, keep me safe?'

'We'll talk.'

'I'll need stuff. I can't just — '

'Don't go home — go straight to the pub.'

'I'll be there.'

That was ninety minutes ago. Still no sign of Walter.

The pub walls were lined with sporting

30

memorabilia. Not just programmes and photo-graphs but jerseys and signed balls, an oil painting of a cup-winning team, a large photograph of the pub owner with his arms around the shoulders of two grinning sports heroes. The pub was fairly busy, mostly men. Garda Templeton-Smith went through two Ballygowans before he switched to coffee.

There was always a possibility that the people who wanted to kill Walter had come upon him by chance on his way to the pub. Unlikely, if he did what he was told. Walter would be next to invisible travelling in a taxi. This pub was far removed, in every sense, from Walter's usual haunts.

The barman was pouring a fill-up when Garda Templeton-Smith saw Walter come in. The policeman said, 'Pour us a second cup, please.'

Walter waited until the barman had finished and moved away. 'This is where the queers drink.'

'Soon as you walked in the door, you set their pulses racing.'

'Fuck off. I don't drink in places like this.'

Garda Templeton-Smith took a sip of his coffee and said, 'Did you have any warning?'

'I told you, they just came into the pub waving cannons.'

'No one said anything to you over the past few days? Nothing to make you wonder? Anyone act strange — maybe someone shut up as soon as you came into the room, that kind of thing?'

Walter was staring at two men further down the bar, their heads together, their voices low. He

31

said, 'Nothing like that.'

'You piss anyone off — take something, maybe grope someone's missus?'

Walter said, 'That's not me.'

'You into anything where you might hold back someone's share?'

'No, nothing like that.'

Garda Templeton-Smith took Walter through the attempted killing, move by move.

'You sure you didn't see any faces, no names?'

Walter shook his head.

'It's best you move on, so.'

'What the fuck do you mean?'

'It's not safe for you, this city. Someone knows you've been yapping to me, probably. Probably you've been careless.'

'And that's all you can say — jack it all in, leave Dublin?'

'Or stay, take a chance — your choice.'

'What are — you've got witness protection, you've got places — '

'You're not a witness, Walter, you're a tout. And now that you've been blown you're an ex-tout.'

'Fuck that.'

Templeton-Smith smiled. 'You play this the wrong way, you're a dead tout.'

Walter's expression flickered between anger and panic. 'I can't go home, I need somewhere.'

Templeton-Smith took an envelope from an inner pocket. He gave it to Walter, who looked inside and then slapped the envelope against the bar. 'That's less than — *Jesus*, in this town, that wouldn't buy me a good meal. How am I supposed to survive?'

'We don't do pensions.'

One of the two men further down the bar turned and looked their way. Walter stared until the man turned back.

'How can I move — where can I go?'

'You'll get by, Walter. You're a practical kind of guy.'

Walter made a contemptuous noise. 'Word gets around — people hear how you treat people who work for you — '

'You're threatening me now, Walter?'

'I'm just saying.'

Garda Templeton-Smith nodded. He leaned closer. 'We get into a pissing match, Walter, who do you think's going to get wet?'

Walter just sat there.

Touts have a short-term view of life. They sign up because they're looking for a quick way out of trouble — like Walter had been when Templeton-Smith caught him driving a BMW X3 he'd just stolen to order for a northside outfit.

'No way — no way,' Walter said when Templeton-Smith first made him the offer.

'Your choice,' Templeton-Smith told him. 'Judges identify with people who get their BMWs stolen. This isn't a month or two sitting on your arse while the screws prepare breakfast. Three years, minimum, at a guess. You got three years to spare, Walter?'

It took ten minutes. Walter said the people who commissioned him to do the BMW X3 were off-limits, and that was fair enough. 'And I won't give evidence against anyone,' which was as much as could be expected.

Garda Templeton-Smith gave him a pass on the BMW and Walter began dropping titbits. Disappointing stuff so far, but he might have coughed up some more useful information in the long run. Should have lasted more than seven weeks, but those were the breaks.

Who?

Someone in the station, probably. Over the seven weeks, Templeton-Smith met Walter just once, in a pub. He'd rung the tout once a week. Should have been safe enough, but there was no telling. Someone saw or heard something, yapped about it. It happened.

Walter tapped the envelope. 'You can afford more than that. Please.'

'I have to go.' As Garda Templeton-Smith stood up he put a tenner on the counter. 'You stay, have a drink on me.'

Walter shook his head. He picked up the money. 'I wouldn't be caught dead drinking in a place like this.'

'Fair enough, you've got standards.'

Walter gave it one last try. 'Look, Jesus, there's got to be more you can do — if not more money, somewhere to go — '

'I'm a policeman, Walter, not your guardian angel.'

'You don't care, do you? You don't care what happens to me.'

Garda Templeton-Smith thought for a moment, then he nodded. 'Don't give a fuck.'

Day Two

Chapter 5

The kettle plugged in, switched on, Danny Callaghan took down his mug and reached for a spoon, his hand knocking against something. When the jar of instant coffee hit the floor, Callaghan barked an obscenity.

Great start to the day.

After he'd cleaned up the coffee and the broken glass, he did the washing-up — the glass from which he'd drunk his orange juice, the bowl from which he'd eaten his microwaved porridge. He put them in the cupboard with the coffee mug he hadn't used. One bowl, one glass, one mug — and, in the cabinet, one plate — all bought at Tesco the day he moved in. He washed the two spoons he'd used. Part habit from prison, part the urge to keep things simple. Clean as you go, that way a little place like this stays liveable.

Callaghan set out for the local shopping centre. He passed a petrol station and shop that used to serve as a neighbourhood convenience store. It had already closed down, bought by a developer, when Callaghan moved into his flat. The intention was to build another apartment block, with retail units on the ground floor, but the developer killed the project when the property market collapsed. Now there was no local shop and there wouldn't be one while the developer awaited a new property boom. Meanwhile, the garage had become an eyesore, the pumps vandalised, the abandoned car wash a haven for teenage lovers in search of ten minutes of frantic privacy.

It took Callaghan twenty minutes to reach the shopping centre. He bought two newspapers, then he went to the coffee shop and took a black coffee to a seat by the window. This time of morning the shopping centre had yet to come fully to life. Mostly old people and young women with buggies.

One bowl, one glass, one mug in his kitchen. In the seven months he'd been out his life had remained small, bare, cramped, not much in it beyond the things that met his immediate needs. Living within a prison routine for eight years, it never occurred to him that life outside might contract into a routine just as narrow.

He'd had a general intention, when freedom came, to return to some variant of the business he'd set up before he went inside — interior fittings for kitchens, apartments and shops. Throughout his sentence, the country had been full of chatter about opportunity. Once he got out, he recognised that he simply didn't have the interest in the constant planning and assessing involved in running a business.

'Take control,' Novak told him. 'If you're not in control of your life, someone else will be.' Which was when Novak offered him the driving job. 'Until you pull things together.'

The driving ate up hours, the routines of sleep and food and drinking slotted into the spaces around the work. Much of the rest of the time just seemed to evaporate. There were times, here at the coffee shop, when he'd be staring at something innocuous — an old man leaning on his cane, a dog waiting outside the shop for its owner to return — and he'd take a sip of coffee and find the remnants had gone cold. He couldn't tell if ten minutes or an hour had passed.

Two Asian waitresses, barely out of their teens, were cleaning nearby tables. During Callaghan's eight years inside, a lot of things had changed. All the talk was of money, opportunities and the nervous prosperity. And it was like every hotel, pub and café and most of the shops had become a mini-United Nations, staffed by Asians, Africans or Eastern Europeans. Despite the low pay, the loneliness and the racial insults, they seemed to burn with a sense of purpose. Watching the girls, Callaghan tried to imagine them making their way across the world, each probably alone, determined to survive and prosper. He envied their passion.

His mobile rang.

★   ★   ★

'You okay?'
'Fine.'
Novak said, 'I called last night.'
'I'm fine.'
'Must have had your phone off. You haven't forgotten you've got a pick-up this morning?'

37

The silence said that Callaghan had forgotten.

Novak said, 'I can get someone else — it's not a problem.'

'No, it just — it slipped my mind. You know how that goes.'

'Fine.'

'Tell me again.'

'The airport, two people — take them to Northern Cross, the Hilton. Then on to the financial centre. They're due in mid-morning, wait a minute — ' Novak checked a sheet of paper and said ' — eleven-forty. Aer Lingus flight from London. They've got a working lunch with the people picking up the tab for this. Then — whatever. Their schedule's a movable feast.'

'Until?'

'Whenever. Today, tomorrow morning, depends how today goes. You have a pen there?'

'Go ahead.'

'Rowe and Warner — R-O-W-E.'

Novak gave him a flight number, then waited a few moments before he said, 'The police been around?'

'No.'

'Most likely someone will give them your name.'

'Yeah.'

'Will you be dropping by tonight?'

'Depends what time these people finish their business. Probably not.'

'Tomorrow, then.'

'Yeah.'

'Take care of yourself.'

'Yeah.'

It was mid-morning when Karl Prowse woke. He could hear his wife making baby talk with the kids, down in the kitchen. When he came down he kissed her, then kissed the baby attached to her right tit.

'You working late tonight?'

Karl poured a coffee. 'Depends. You know how it is.'

Sitting on the floor in a corner, the two-year-old was complaining about something, so Karl put his coffee down and spent a few minutes hunched down with her, playing 'A Sailor Went to Sea-Sea-Sea' until she started laughing. He went to the local Centra for the *Sun* and the *Mirror*, but there was nothing about the shooting.

Karl was upstairs, texting a friend about a cancelled trip to Amsterdam, when his phone rang.

'Outside, now,' and the call ended.

He went to the window and moved the curtain enough to see down into the street, where a green Isuzu was parked across from his house, Lar Mackendrick's shape recognisable behind the wheel.

★ ★ ★

Danny Callaghan drove his Hyundai to Novak's garage off the North Strand, parked it and picked up the VW Tuareg he'd use for his driving job. He spent a couple of minutes checking it out. It was clean, a full tank, everything in order. He adjusted the driver's seat, then spent a minute tweaking the side mirrors. He popped a mint into his mouth and started the car. The morning traffic was heavy as usual, but he allowed for that. At the airport, he took a rectangle of white cardboard from the boot, used a black marker pen to write the names *Rowe* and *Warner* in neat block letters and went to stand in Arrivals.

Rowe had long fair hair in a ponytail. Jeans and a white waistcoat over a light blue T-shirt. Warner wore a dark suit and a white shirt, but no tie. Their only luggage was one overnight bag each. On the way to the hotel the one with the ponytail asked Callaghan what he knew about the nightlife.

'There's a place or two.'

'Maybe we'll have time later — you can show us around?'

'My pleasure.'

It was going to be a late night, then.

Traffic was light enough on the short drive to the Hilton at Northern Cross. After a brief stop at the hotel, the two gave Callaghan an address in the financial centre. From their conversation, it seemed that Rowe and Warner had something to do with marketing. Apparently some outfit had called them in to try to rescue a new product that was failing to take off. At first, Callaghan thought the product was some kind of food, then Rowe said something that made it sound like a range of clothes. Warner was doubtful that the project was doable, given that the client had spent five years making a balls of securing his customer base. It sounded to Callaghan like maybe he was talking about financial products. When they got to where they were going, the small black lettering on the wide glass door said the company was called 257 Solutions.

Rowe said the working lunch would tie them up for a couple of hours, then they had a meeting — he read aloud an address, in another part of the financial centre — and they needed to be there by four. Back to the hotel by six, and by then they'd know where they'd be eating, and after that they'd play it by ear. 'Okay, driver?'

'Sounds good.' The office building had an underground car park and Callaghan said he'd get something to eat and be waiting in the lobby within the hour, in case their working lunch ended early.

After he parked, he sat in the car for a couple of minutes. He wasn't hungry and as the day went on there'd likely be lots of breaks to grab a sandwich.

Less than a hundred yards from Hannah's office.

When he got out of the car Callaghan still wasn't sure what he intended to do.

Don't be pathetic.

He closed down the thought and began walking.

★　★　★

'If the gun had worked first time,' Karl Prowse said, 'we'd have got the job done and been away within thirty seconds.'

Lar Mackendrick said nothing. In this part of Santry, the houses had narrow streets and shared driveways, and the developers had crammed in as many units as the land would take. Lar might have been focusing on the driving, or he might have been angry. Karl couldn't tell. Lar had the kind of face that remained the same no matter how he was feeling — like he was trying to remember what it was about you that most pissed him off.

They turned in to the indoor car park at the Omni shopping centre. Lar pulled in behind a large green SUV and switched off the engine.

'Tell me.'

There were still moments when Karl Prowse felt a ripple of disbelief — three weeks ago, the thought of chatting to Lar Mackendrick, alone, almost as an equal, would have been fantasy. If he'd got a shot at something like second-string muscle on a minor Mackendrick operation, that would have been the height of his ambition. Then, out of the blue — a phone call, a visit, a blunt offer — and now it was like he was Lar's right hand.

In a business dominated by psychos with short tempers and long memories, you needed luck as well as balls. The most Karl Prowse had imagined for himself was the occasional dangerous job with a reasonable cut of the proceeds, along with an occasional stretch in Mountjoy. Now he had a shot at something that mattered, shoulder to shoulder with Lar Mackendrick, with maybe his own outfit

42

somewhere down the road.

And the first serious job he got to do went down the toilet and Karl was trying to explain why.

'From the beginning.'

Karl decided the best thing was to give it straight, no spin. Lar had contacts all over the place — in other gangs, in the police, in the newspapers. Since last night he'd probably made some calls, picked up the basics of what happened. Karl kept it short, straight, no messing. The gun misfiring, Walter screaming for help, the interfering bastard.

'How did Robbie perform?'

'There wasn't much he could do. He didn't have a clear shot.' Karl tried to sound calm, to play it like a professional. 'It happened so quick. The gun doesn't fire, I'm chasing after Walter, this bastard steps in, just knocks me down, Robbie is way back at the front door. He doesn't have a clear shot — not with a shotgun. Might have taken out half the bar.'

Lar Mackendrick nodded.

For Karl, there was no upside to ratting out Robbie. Make Robbie look dumb, it would reflect bad on Karl. And, besides, Karl knew where he stood with Robbie. Without Robbie, Lar would bring someone else on board, someone Karl didn't know, someone who might pull rank.

'It was just the way it worked out — the gun, the bastard who stuck his nose in.'

Lar Mackendrick didn't say anything for a while. Then he said, 'Who was he, this fella?'

'Walter said his name — Danny something.'

'You're sure about this — it was a civilian?'

'Yeah.'

'It wasn't like Walter had protection?'

'No, it was just — it didn't look like that. I don't think so — it wasn't like Walter expected — I don't think so.'

'That would change things.'

'It didn't seem that way.'

Lar Mackendrick nodded. 'That's what my sources say — just a smartarse sticking his nose in. The police don't know yet who he is.'

Karl nodded. 'I'll ask around.'

'No, you won't. I've got people who charge good money for that.'

'What about Walter?'

'Gone to ground. Probably he's not sure what we know, why this happened. The danger is, eventually he decides there's no way out of this, so he coughs everything he's got. My guess is he's a couple of days from that — maybe less.'

'I'm sorry, Mr Mackendrick.'

Lar leaned closer. 'Things go wrong, Karl — it happens. But it's not a good sign. You and Robbie, first job I give you.'

Karl waited in silence, trying to think of something to say that might impress Lar. He decided to keep his mouth shut.

'You and Robbie, you get your shit together, you fix this Walter thing. Or this whole project, we have to think it out again.'

Karl wanted to say he understood, but he didn't trust his voice to work without a quiver, so he just nodded.

Chapter 6

The gift shop was in a wide pedestrianised side street in the financial centre, a street where every building and artefact had a sheen suggesting it had been installed within the past twenty-four hours. Behind the glass-topped counters, the shelves were filled with trinkets, gadgets and novelties. Crystal embellishment or a veneer of semi-precious metals justified a premium price for otherwise standard pieces of tat.

In the ten minutes that Callaghan had been here, the first signs of the lunchtime trade had arrived. The shop was convenient for office workers who needed acceptably expensive gifts but didn't have time to shop around. Two men and a woman customer pondered overpriced knick-knacks.

Hannah's print shop was directly across from the gift store. This was the fourth time that Callaghan had made his way down to these streets since his release from prison. Intending no more than a quick glance from across the street while he walked past, Callaghan had panicked when Hannah came out the doorway of the shop next to her own. He quickly found refuge in the gift shop. He let a minute pass before he chanced a glance across the street, more than half expecting her to be still standing there, staring at the gift shop. There was no sign of her and a minute later she came out of her own place carrying a large cardboard box of lever arch files and brought them into the vacant shop next door.

He cursed his foolishness.

'Perhaps I can help, sir?'

It was the second time the sharply dressed shop assistant had asked. The shop was now empty apart from Callaghan and the assistant's expression suggested a vague discontent. Callaghan was neatly dressed in the suit he kept for chauffeur duties, but this kind of shop always made him feel like he'd been instantly identified as a potential shoplifter by an exceptionally hi-tech CCTV camera.

'A bit pricey, this stuff,' Callaghan said.

The assistant nodded, like something had just been confirmed. 'You get what you pay for, sir, that's what I always say.'

Across the street, Hannah was coming out of the vacant shop. Callaghan had his phone out and his thumb was working the buttons. By the time Hannah answered his ring she was back inside her own shop.

'Hi, I'm in the neighbourhood.' It came all in a rush. 'Thought you might have time for a coffee?'

'Hello — of course.' She seemed pleased to hear from him. 'Drop in.'

'Be right there.'

Callaghan felt the shop assistant's gaze on his back as he left.

* * *

They went around the corner to a mock Italian restaurant where the waiter who took their order

46

knew Hannah and spent a while bent over her side of the table, chit-chatting and exercising his smile. Callaghan forced himself to resist repeating the order. Finally, the waiter said, 'That was two regular coffees, right?'

'Fine,' Hannah said.

'I can't tempt you with a little snack?'

Callaghan wanted to tell him to get lost.

'We're fine,' Hannah said.

The waiter said it was lovely to see Hannah again, then he went away.

'Well,' Hannah said, 'what brings you down among the temples of mammon?'

He sensed the same lift he'd felt the first time they spoke, a dozen years back — a chaotic mesh of delight and anxiety, curiosity and simple pleasure in looking at her. There was lust and hope in there, too, but only small remnants, scorched dry by the events of the past decade.

'I've got a couple of clients — picked them up at the airport, they've got a meeting nearby.'

'Novak still has you behind the wheel?'

'I like the work — it changes all the time.'

One day he was looking after the transport needs of visiting businessmen, the next day he'd be collecting packages from one side of the city and delivering them to another. All of it pleasant, demanding no great effort of mind or body, just the kind of work with which Callaghan felt most comfortable these days. People needed to get themselves or something else from one place to another, reliably, safely, and that was a good thing to do with his time. Callaghan was one of four drivers working for Novak, whose transport fleet consisted of two small vans and a large one, the VW Tuareg and a Volvo. So far most of the work came out of the overspill from larger firms, but Novak reckoned it was a growth market. Callaghan's favourite work was a country run, delivering or collecting outside the city, which allowed him hours of mindless driving.

Hannah told him about how her firm was expanding, taking over the premises next door. She was a freelance typesetter when they'd met — by the time they married she'd linked up with a designer, secured her first few contracts and was outsourcing the printing. Two weeks after the divorce she opened her first print shop. Callaghan was well into his prison sentence by then. Now her main print shop was in the financial centre, with two smaller outlets elsewhere in the city. She had recently been approached by a major graphic imaging company with a view to a buyout.

'Business has been crazy these past few weeks. Early starts and late finishes — there's times I feel I should set up a bed in the office.'

The decision to call her, to suggest they meet for coffee, came out of a sudden panic. Had she seen him from across the street? For fear she might think he was stalking her, Callaghan suddenly wanted to announce his presence, and before he had time to think he was making the call.

One thing leads to another.

The driving job that took him to the financial centre, the impulse to walk towards Hannah's workplace, the sudden sight of her across the street, his panicked reaction and now his joy and unease in her presence.

She sees through it all.

Knows I didn't just turn up.

Feeling sorry for me?

Afraid of me?

Just embarrassed?

'It's really good to see you.' There was no hint of anything patronising in her words or her smile. Probably she hadn't noticed him, standing across the street.

Probably.

'How's Leon?' It would be churlish not to ask, and Callaghan tried to make it sound like he wanted to know.

'He's fine, everything's fine.' He was glad she didn't offer him any examples of exactly how fine her husband's life was. She told him a story about a carpenter who'd been hired to fit shelves in the new shop, a perfectionist who insisted it wasn't good enough that the shelves be strong enough to hold things up, everything had to be rebated or bevelled or dovetailed. 'The difference between ordinary and extraordinary is that little bit extra.' She imitated his avuncular tones and his knowing nod. 'He's a charmer. Before we knew it, a three-hundred-euro job was looking like a bargain at twice the price.'

Callaghan was smiling. 'Some genius hired him on an hourly rate, right?'

Hannah nodded. 'I fired him this morning.' She smiled. 'This afternoon, I'm firing the genius who hired him.'

Same old Hannah.

More than a decade earlier, when Callaghan had quit college and set up his cabinet-making business, Hannah had acted as an unofficial, unpaid back office, hustling for work for him and chasing debtors. It was like she pulled on a new personality when she was doing business. No mercy, no limit, forever thinking five moves ahead, anticipating sharp practice and prepared to respond in kind. Callaghan had never grown used to the contrast between that Hannah and the woman who could make his blood flow faster just by showing up. She smiled at him now, aware that he was appraising her. Her dark hair was shorter than it had been the last time they'd met, otherwise she was the same as ever. Her clothes expensive, conservative, mostly dark colours, her skin pale, a minimum of make-up, and the small smile that peeled him open and left him deeply aware of his vulnerability.

She asked him about the training course he'd mentioned the last time they met and he said he'd decided to give it a miss. 'The driving, for now, that's the kind of work I need.' There was a time when she would have insisted on discussing that, gently nudging him one way or another, but for now she seemed to accept that what he needed was work without pressure, life without ambition.

'Made up your mind about the takeover offer?'

She said, 'Almost. Soon as the print shop's up and running, I'll appoint a manager and move on.'

'Congratulations.'

Hannah made a small pumping gesture with a

fist, a triumphal signal that she used to mark a victory. It was one of the countless minor intimacies he remembered from their time together. He'd long accepted the finality of his detachment from her life, at the same time aware that for him the sense of their intimacy had never faded. He didn't know if it was affection or a sense of obligation that moved Hannah, and now it didn't matter — he accepted things as they were. His remoteness from her life seemed to exist comfortably along with the elation he still felt when he saw, heard or thought of her.

'Anything else?'

The waiter was back. The lunchtime trade was drifting in. Hannah had taken only sips of her coffee. Callaghan hadn't touched his.

As Callaghan paid, Hannah leaned forward and said, 'You probably think I've forgotten — Saturday night?'

Callaghan said, 'Saturday — what?' He tried to sound puzzled, but he knew he wasn't convincing.

'Dinner party?'

The phone call from Hannah had been ten days ago. 'I'll let you know,' he'd said. Now, as they emerged onto the pavement outside the restaurant, Hannah raised her eyebrows and waited.

Callaghan shrugged. 'What I said — it's really not my kind of thing.'

'What you said was you'd think about it.'

Callaghan said, 'I've never been a big fan of dinner parties. Dinner's something you eat — and what I remember about parties is they're

51

places where you drink a lot and make a show of yourself trying to get off with someone.'

'We're not teenagers any more. Besides, how many parties have you been to, the last seven months?'

There were three men standing several feet away, the two younger ones seemingly awed as they watched an older man swear viciously into his mobile, telling someone that was fucking *it*. 'Too *late*, old flower. The deal's done and you're *out*. You've just destroyed yourself.'

Callaghan said, 'Some people love their work.' He and Hannah began to walk towards her office.

Hannah said, 'What about Saturday?'

'You really don't have to organise my social life.'

'Come for my sake, then — I'd love to see you there. Just a couple of hours with pleasant people, no pressure.'

'I'll see.'

Her smile said she knew he was saying it to shut her up.

Chapter 7

When they came out of the casino Rowe was sober, Warner was mildly pissed, but the guy from 257 Solutions was walking like his legs had been disconnected from his brain. Pissed or stoned, more probably both. His expression was tight, worried, as though he'd just begun to wonder if he was making a fool of himself.

Callaghan had spent the afternoon ferrying Rowe and Warner to and from their meetings, and waiting in between. Then he dropped them back to the hotel at Northern Cross and had a couple of hours off. He went home, cooked his first real meal of the day and watched something mindless on television. When he got back to the Hilton he found he now had three passengers. The 257 Solutions guy — name of Costigan — had volunteered to take the visitors on the town. The private casino, widely touted as the coolest hang-out for the financially overconfident, was the final stop. The kind of place it was, the drink was sold at a discount, ensuring that idiots like Costigan swallowed enough alcohol to boost their self-belief in direct proportion to the rate at which it dimmed their judgement. An evening of showing off meant that Costigan would spend the next few months clearing his credit card bill.

Callaghan had the rear kerbside door open when they reached the Tuareg and he helped Rowe ease the drunk inside. 'We'll drop him off first,' Rowe said. Callaghan nodded. When he got behind the wheel he looked back and Rowe was helping the drunk into his seat belt. Warner slid into the front passenger seat.

'Where are we off to?' As Callaghan eased away from the kerb the drunk moaned. Callaghan was already pushing his door open as he braked, then he slid out of the car and was reaching to open the rear right passenger door when a blue Ford van coming from behind almost clipped him.

Shit.

As Callaghan pressed himself back against the car to avoid the blue van, he figured the delay might well make his effort pointless. After the van was past — dark blue with white writing on the side — he jerked open the door, then stood back as the drunk's upper body flopped forward and vomit splashed onto the road.

Getting the door open in time made the difference between going straight home after he'd dropped his passengers and spending an hour in Novak's garage, ridding the car of the stains and the smell.

'He needs a minute,' Rowe said. He got out of the car and lit up a cigarette. Callaghan shook his head at the offer of a smoke.

'You work for that idiot?' he said. Costigan from 257 Solutions was taking long, noisy breaths.

'We're freelance consultants,' Rowe said. 'We work for a lot of people, most of them far more clueless than our friend. He's kept that company alive single-handed for the past year.'

'You give advice?'

'Mostly we take the blame. These days, the world's full of corporate heroes who're paid so much they're terrified to make a decision in case it's the wrong one. So they hire consultants to draw up reports and recommendations. Then they make a wild guess. If things go well they take the praise. If things go wrong they blame the consultants.'

'Professional scapegoats?'

Rowe smiled. 'Very highly paid scapegoats.

Consultants are God's way of telling a company it has too much money.'

'You get much work over here?'

'Dublin's been a gold mine for years. Things are tighter now.'

An advance party of raindrops danced on the car roof. Callaghan leaned into the car and asked the 257 Solutions guy if he was okay.

'I'm fine, I'm fine.' There was an edge to his voice, as though the question was preposterous and offensive.

Rowe took a last drag on his cigarette. 'I'll give you warning if there's a problem.'

Callaghan said, 'Thanks.'

★ ★ ★

When the phone rang, Lar Mackendrick ignored it, his attention focused on the book he was reading. *The Art of War*, written by a Chinaman named Sun Tzu. It wasn't an easy read. Mackendrick was rereading a paragraph that had puzzled him first time around. He let the phone ring, as he took his time with the troublesome paragraph.

The phone finally stopped.

Three minutes later it rang again.

Lar put down the Chinaman's book.

'Mr Mackendrick?'

'Who is this?'

'Walter Bennett, Mr Mackendrick.'

For a moment Mackendrick didn't register the name. Little over twenty-four hours since Walter had survived Karl Prowse's best efforts. The last thing Lar expected was a call from the little fucker.

'Walter, how the hell are you?'

Mackendrick wondered had the little man gone to the police after all, and was the phone call being recorded.

Bennett paused, as though surprised by the warmth in Mackendrick's voice.

'I did nothing, Mr Mackendrick, nothing to deserve this.'

'What?'

'Please, Mr Mackendrick — '

'Is everything okay, Walter?'

'I want to know why Karl Prowse tried to kill me.'

'Jesus Christ!'

'I did nothing wrong — '

'Walter, what's this about?'

'I did nothing — '

Mackendrick applied a layer of shock to his voice. 'Please, Walter — from the beginning — when did this happen?'

★   ★   ★

Bullshit.

No way he didn't know.

'Walter?'

Walter said nothing.

'Please, Walter, what happened?'

It was misting rain and Walter leaned back against the steel shutters of the flower shop. A couple of teenage girls, both slightly drunk, came chattering past. They went into the café next

56

door. Walter had been having a late-night snack when the anxiety became too much. On an impulse he went outside to find privacy for the phone call. No answer. He felt relieved and went back into the café and ordered another pot of tea. He'd hardly sat when the anxiety propelled him back outside, making the call again.

'There's no way Karl — you *had* to know!'

'Walter, I swear — obviously someone's got hold of the wrong end of the stick. Whatever's happened, we can sort it out. Now, *please*, Walter, what the fuck *happened?*'

Mackendrick sounded pissed to be in the dark about this. Maybe —

Karl — the shithead —

If Mackendrick doesn't know what happened, that means Karl's been afraid to tell him. Fucker's running a thing of his own.

'Swear to me, Mr Mackendrick.'

'I swear to you, Walter, on my mother's grave, that I've no idea what you're talking about.'

'Karl and someone else, I think it was Robbie Nugent, I didn't see his face but it had to be — look, Karl's always — '

'What did he do?'

'They had guns, Mr Mackendrick, they came into a pub, both of them — I was fucking lucky to get out of there alive.'

'Walter, I'll come round to your place — we need to — '

'I'm not at home.'

'Where are you staying?'

Walter shook his head. He kept respect in his voice when he said, 'Mr Mackendrick, it's not

57

that I — I just don't want to say.'

'That's fair enough. A thing like this — look, Walter — whatever happened, it had nothing to do with me and I'm really angry. You know I'm depending on you, Walter, and — I swear to you, whatever caused this balls-up, nothing like this will happen again. *Ever.*'

Walter opened his mouth, desperately needing to believe in Mackendrick, and closed it again, afraid of his own need for reassurance.

'You ring me back tomorrow, Walter, or the next day, whenever you feel okay with that. I won't sleep on it — tonight, soon as I hang up, I'm going to find out what the hell's going on. When you're ready, we'll meet, we'll sort this out.'

'Thanks.'

'I can't imagine what it's about, but — Jesus Christ — '

Walter had never heard Mackendrick lose his composure. Where there had only been dread, there was now a sliver of hope.

'Leave it with me, Walter, leave it with me.'

When the call ended, Walter stood in the street, holding the phone down by his side, wondering if he dared go home after all. The rain was heavier now and his jacket was soaked. He decided going home would be stupid. It'd have to be Sissy's sofa again tonight.

* * *

Danny Callaghan was on his second Scotch, standing at the window of his apartment, the lights out. He let his tongue play with the taste, then let the liquid down.

A good day.

Behind him, the radio was playing something soft and melodic. It was a classical station he'd listened to a lot in prison. Callaghan didn't know any of the composers, he hardly ever registered the titles of pieces. He just liked the feeling that came with the music. In prison the radio had been important, and it remained a part of his day. Mostly music, usually switching to RTE to get news on the hour. He listened to most of the news shows and the phone-ins. When he was inside, news of the real world had been important. If he knew what was happening he could have opinions about it, he could feel like he was still part of that world. He read a couple of newspapers each day, the real ones, the ones you could almost believe were telling something close to the truth.

In the seven months since he'd left prison, there'd been a lot of days that dribbled to an end in the small hours, his tiredness a consequence of nothing except squandered time. He had the liberty he'd longed for, year after tedious year, and he was doing nothing with it. Days like today made him feel like he had some control over his time. Driving a couple of businessmen around wasn't what he'd pictured himself doing with his freedom, but it gave a structure to the day. He was doing something useful. And earning money. On top of the wages he'd get from Novak he got a sizeable tip from Rowe and

Warner when he dropped them off at the Hilton. And another bonus was that the guy from 257 Solutions hadn't soiled the car on the way home.

A *good day*.

The soft music ended and something different started. Jerky, noisy shit, like someone was trying to get a military band to put a nightmare to music. He crossed to the radio and tried the pre-sets. After surfing past a couple of pop stations he found a talk show he'd often listened to in prison. Sometimes it seemed as if the city was full of lonely, angry headbangers.

'We don't clutter up their country, do we?'

The radio hack said, 'Can't argue with that, Barney.'

The caller's next sentence was a succession of obscenities. The radio hack emitted a prolonged chuckle. 'Now, Barney, there's no denying you've a way with words — '

Callaghan switched off. He wondered if he'd ever care enough about anything — or be lonely enough or desperate enough — to make a phone call to tell strangers how he felt about anything. Maybe the Barneys were even less connected to the world around them than Callaghan was.

He finished the Scotch, considered pouring a third and decided against. A drink or two topped off the day. Go much further and it'd feel like he was giving in to something.

On the green, across from the Hive, he could see the abandoned embers of a fire the kids had built earlier. The cider party was over.

60

Lying on the bed, Callaghan let himself surrender to his tiredness, the noises from the apartments above and below and from each side combining into a comforting kind of low-level hubbub.

A *good day.*

★   ★   ★

These days, Lar Mackendrick seldom drank alcohol. After his brother Jo-Jo's death, when Lar took on the burden of running the business, the pressure and the drink and the grief almost killed him. He'd got through that, thank God, and now that he was secure in his health and his fitness he allowed himself just the occasional drink, late at night.

May was in bed, the house was quiet. Lar sat by the large gas-flamed fireplace, in his white leather armchair, a glass of Merlot in his heavy John Rocha crystal. Thoughts of Walter Bennett hovered, but Lar dismissed them. He was satisfied that Walter hadn't gone to the police, wasn't wired for sound. Too cowed. Little man, drowning in fear. He'd get back to Lar, looking for hope. Now that he had made contact, he was just one small part of the problem — and one not too difficult to fix.

Lar found the page in his book with a corner turned down. He opened *The Art of War.*

When able to attack, we must seem unable; when using our forces, we must seem inactive; when we are near, we must make the enemy believe we are far away; when far away, we must make him believe we are near. Hold out baits to entice the enemy. Feign disorder, and crush him.

Day Three

Chapter 8

Noise.

Stopped now, but the memory echoing.

His eyelids heavy, his mouth dry, Danny Callaghan heard the thudding noise that was pulling him into consciousness, but he didn't know what it was. In the dark he could see the luminous numbers on the clock beside the bed, but his mind was too clogged to register what they meant.

Thump — thump — thump.

Callaghan sat up. Then another trio of thumps, loud and slow and evenly spaced, a fist on the door of the apartment. It was the sound of someone who wasn't going away. Up on one elbow, Callaghan leaned forward and squinted at the clock.

6.22.

Again, the *thump, thump, thump.* Then the doorbell, three jabs, then someone pressed the button and kept it pressed for at least ten seconds, followed by a repeat of the thumping.

Before the bell stopped ringing Callaghan bent over, reached down under the bed and grasped the hammer lying on the carpet. His heels off the floor, trying for stealth, arms wide to compensate his uncertain balance, he moved as quickly as he could across the room and stood off to one side of the door.

'Who is it?'

'Come on, open up. Police. *Garda Siochana.*'

Possible.

Maybe.

Maybe not.

Sooner or later the police would catch up and start asking questions about what happened in the Blue Parrot. Maybe this was it, maybe it was the other thing. It had been like this the first few weeks after he got out of prison. Always alert, always half expecting. Then, when nothing happened, he relaxed a bit. Now it took something real, like a couple of guys walking into a pub wearing motorcycle helmets, to bring the edge back.

Or someone thumping on the door in the night.

'Show me some identification.'

'Christ sake.'

A second voice. 'Police. We don't have all night.'

'I'm not opening up until — '

A small white card appeared on the floor, pushed underneath the door.

Callaghan used a toe to pull the card away from the door, over to the side. When he bent to pick it up he noticed a trembling in his legs. Maybe the after-effects of suddenly broken sleep, maybe fear. Maybe just the cold.

'Come on, open up.' The first voice again.

The card had the Garda insignia on the right, printed in gold, and *An Garda Siochana* along the top, with *Michael Wyndham* printed underneath and below that *Detective Sergeant*.

'I could get a thousand of these run off in ten minutes. Not good enough.'

'Maybe I should call the Commissioner, ask him to get out of bed and come down here and hold your hand.'

'Or you could just fuck off.'

After a few moments, a pale green laminated ID card was pushed under the door. This one had the same name and rank, with a photo of someone Callaghan had never seen. Could be anyone. Unlikely, though, that the kind of people he feared would go to the bother of having two kinds of cards made. People like that, they didn't do subtle. People like that, chances were they'd have been blazing away already.

Careful not to make any noise, Callaghan slid the oiled bolt open. He took a deep breath and hefted the hammer, moved sideways a step to make room to swing his arm, then unlocked the door and jerked it quickly open. One of them matched the photo on the ID card, fat-faced, pursed lips. The other was a balding older man. Both of them stood casually, hands in the pockets of their overcoats. It was Fatface who nodded at the hammer. 'Strange time of night to be doing a bit of DIY.'

The older one said, 'You going to ask us in?'

★ ★ ★

The cushion Walter Bennett was using as a pillow had an embroidered map of Gran Canaria

65

on it and when he woke up he could feel the pattern mark on his cheek. He held up his wrist to the faint light from the window.

Nearly half-six.

Too early and too cold to get up, too late to try to go back to sleep. The sofa was old and sagging and he knew his back would hurt when he stood. He lay there for almost half an hour, twisting this way and that, before the discomfort of the sofa won out against the coldness of the room. Walter shuffled towards the kitchen. The air there was even more chilled, the tiles arctic under his bare feet. He filled the kettle and switched it on, then went back to the living room and hurriedly got dressed. The kettle was one of those rapid-boil ones and when he returned to the kitchen it was making a racket, so he closed the kitchen door to keep the noise from disturbing Sissy. She'd be up soon enough, hassling the kids to get ready for school.

Walter made a cup of tea, then checked his jacket. It was still damp.

Get going soon.

Another hour or two before he could ring Mackendrick, but pretty soon two moody teenagers would be shuffling around the house and he didn't want to get under Sissy's feet. He'd do better to find a breakfast place where there was some warmth and wait there until it was time to ring Mackendrick.

One hell of a sister, Sissy. Gold dust.

Didn't take a feather out of her when he turned up last night, shivering and sniffling.

'I don't want to be trouble, Sis.' Standing in

66

the doorway, rain seeping down his face.

'Get out of that jacket, it's saturated.'

She was a dozen years younger than Walter, her husband long gone, the two boys entering the awkward stage. She treated Walter like she was the big sister. Since she'd been in her late teens she'd mothered him, though she was ten times the woman that bitch could ever have dreamt of being.

Before she went to bed Sissy ran the iron over his shirt, to get the dampness out, but the jacket was too soaked to do anything except leave it across the back of a chair, near the living-room fireplace. Sissy gave him her dressing gown to wear and he fitted into it comfortably.

Then, the house quiet, the boys in bed, they shared a soft conversation over the kitchen table. This was the second night he'd stayed here and sometime that day someone Sissy met had told her about what had happened at Novak's pub, the real reason why Walter hadn't been able to go home. He'd used the excuse that he was having landlord trouble.

'Why did they try to shoot you?'

'Complicated.'

'Jesus, Wally.'

'Please, Sis.'

'You're too old for that crap.'

Walter shook his head. 'This has nothing — look, it's a misunderstanding. Some people, they've got their wires crossed, they think — it's not what — ' He made a dismissive gesture. 'Anyway, it's over now, I talked to a guy, I'm gonna to talk to him again, it's gonna get sorted out.'

Sissy put her hand on Walter's forearm. 'I'm scared for you, Wally.'

Walter smiled. 'I promise — I'll sort this out. If I think I've still got anything to worry about I'll be in Glasgow within twenty-four hours. Two days at the most. Stay there until this blows over.'

'You have enough money, if you need to get out?'

'I'm fine.'

Sissy looked at him like she wanted to believe him. Walter said it was time to get some sleep. She stood up and kissed him on the forehead, something she'd done since she was a kid. She was still standing there in the kitchen when he patted the Gran Canaria cushion and put his head down, Sissy's dressing gown still wrapped around him under the duvet cover.

Seven-twenty.

Should be plenty of breakfast places open by now.

Time to go.

Damp as it still was, the jacket would have to do. Once he'd sorted this out with Mackendrick he could go home, get changed. Walter swallowed the last of the tea. Jacket on, he patted his side pockets, then fingered the lapels near the collar and adjusted the jacket on his shoulders.

Wrong pocket.

He patted the left side of his chest — nothing. He was right-handed, always put the wallet in the left-hand inside pocket. The wallet was in the right-hand inside pocket. Someone had moved it.

He took it out, opened it. Tucked into the front flap he found four fifties, folded in half.

Jesus, Sissy.

Walter felt a wave of gratitude and love and shame at his own need. This wasn't spare money. Sissy's part-time work didn't bring in much more than her weekly expenses. She never had any cash left over to splash out. This was money accumulated for a purpose — a bill or maybe something the boys needed. For a few moments Walter stood there, wallet in hand. Then he opened the top drawer beside the cooker, where Sissy kept a ragbag of little-used kitchen implements and coins and batteries and bottle openers and rubber bands and bills and assorted pieces of stationery. He found a sheet of writing paper and an envelope and in his best handwriting he wrote *THANKS*, added *love you SIS* and signed it *W*. He put the paper in the envelope and slid the four fifties in alongside, sealed the flap, wrote his sister's name on the front and left it propped up on the kitchen counter.

The streets were still wet, but the rain was soft, no more than a mist, as Walter Bennett closed the door of his sister's house behind him.

Chapter 9

Detective Sergeant Michael Wyndham wiped condensation from the window of Danny

Callaghan's apartment. On the green down below, the grass was coated with morning frost. Wyndham kept his hands in his pockets and flexed his shoulders a few times in a pointless effort to generate heat. Must be depressing to live in a dogbox like this, with walls like cardboard. Apartment blocks all over the place, these days, populated mostly by the young and the eager. Weaned on *Sex and the City*, impatient to sample the supposed sophistication of Manhattan on the Liffey, using their own money to rent, or daddy's money to buy. During the late lamented boom, it had seemed like it took some builders no more than a long weekend to throw an apartment block together.

Sergeant Wyndham said, 'Jesus, it's cold in here. You got something to warm the place up?'

Danny Callaghan was slumped in one of the apartment's two chairs, yawning. 'Your choice, knocking on my door before dawn.'

Wyndham smiled. 'They tell us that's the best time to do it. People are at their lowest ebb. Makes them more likely to blurt out the truth. You going to tell us the truth, Danny?'

'Depends on the question.'

'We came here twice yesterday, looking for you.'

'I was working.'

'Working by day, scrapping with gangsters by night.'

Wyndham's partner, Detective Garda Jeremiah Harley, grinned.

'Danny's a tough guy.'

Callaghan crossed to the wall beside the door

and pressed a button on a timer. A small red light came on and from inside the kitchen there was the dull *whump* of the gas boiler starting. He said, 'You'll be long gone before the radiators take the chill off.' Callaghan sat down again, his face resentful but resigned. The kind of expression, Wyndham thought, that convicts get used to wearing.

Wyndham pulled the second chair around and sat down facing Callaghan. 'The Blue Parrot. Walter Bennett. I think we know the score — just need you to tell us the way you saw it.'

Callaghan ran a middle finger along his lips, like he was wiping away something invisible. 'I was having a drink, two guys came in the pub carrying guns. Pistol and a shotgun. It just happened. It wasn't like I wanted to get involved — but the guy with the pistol walked right past me, he was chasing Walter. That's it.'

'That's what we heard. What I don't know is why some heavy mob would be gunning for a little creep like Walter.'

'Beats me.'

Harley said, 'You sure you weren't on duty that evening?'

'And that means what?'

Harley said nothing, just stood by the window, leaning against the windowsill and watching Callaghan.

Sergeant Wyndham said, 'We've got witnesses who say Walter Bennett called out to you for help, like maybe he expected your protection. In which case, whatever he's involved in, maybe you've got a piece of it.'

71

'Don't be silly. I've got a piece of nothing. I work for a living. And I don't do bodyguard.'

'Your record says you did a lot of things.'

'You know I did time, you know I haven't put a foot wrong since I came out.'

Over at the window, Harley said, 'Five convictions — probation twice and three sentences.'

'I was a kid. I stole a few pairs of jeans from Roche's Stores.'

'You were eighteen. You got probation for shoplifting. You did time for burglary and stealing cars.'

'It was kid stuff, in and out in a few weeks.'

Wyndham kept his voice level. 'Murdering Big Brendan Tucker — that was kid stuff too?'

'I'm not a murderer.'

Harley levered himself away from the window-sill and leaned forward towards Callaghan, his face showing mock surprise. 'I should maybe tell Big Brendan's family he's not dead, he's just — what? — been having a wee rest beneath the sod in Glasnevin for the past few years?'

Callaghan leaned back in his chair. 'You came here in the middle of the night to talk to me about things that happened years ago — fifteen years ago, some of them?'

Wyndham said, 'Look at it from our point of view. Why would a hard man like you put himself on the line for a piece of nothing like Walter Bennett?'

'What makes you think I'm a hard man?'

'Apart from the fact that you greet visitors with a hammer in your hand? Or maybe because you spent most of your twenties behind bars for murder?'

'Manslaughter.'

'Same difference. In your case, the way I hear it, manslaughter was a jury's way of saying you murdered someone but that's okay because he was a scumbag, anyway.'

After a few moments' silence, Callaghan said, 'You done here?'

Wyndham said, 'Couple of people carrying guns waltz into a pub — that usually means the gangs are sorting out a problem. Drugs, family feud, protection, whatever.' He pointed to his colleague. 'Detective Harley, he's got a point of view on gangland murders.'

Harley nodded. 'The more of them the better. Dumb fuckers take each other out, saves us a lot of work.'

Wyndham stood up. 'Detective Harley and me, we have a difference of opinion on this. I think that when dumb fuckers get the habit of using guns to solve their problems there's no telling where they'll stop.'

★   ★   ★

There was misty rain in the icy wind and Lar Mackendrick quickened his pace as he neared the shelter. The few walkers and joggers on the Clontarf seafront had bundled up against the weather. The morning rush hour had started and traffic on the road that paralleled the seafront crept impatiently towards the city centre. Mackendrick wore a red anorak, a tweed cap and soft leather gloves. The figure waiting in the shelter wore a dark green waxed coat and a leather homburg hat.

'Bracing weather,' Declan Roeper said.

He was about the same age as Lar Mackendrick, with the face of someone who had become used to disappointment. 'Wonderful public amenity, this. Green space on one side, the sea on the other — the sweep of the bay, the sea air, a long, clear path to walk on. Relief from the mundane.'

Mackendrick said, 'Not in this fucking weather.'

'Rain or shine, seven days a week, I take advantage of it — keeps old age at bay. I'm surprised they never sold it off to a developer with connections. You could fit in any number of apartments if you didn't mind spoiling the view.'

Mackendrick grunted. 'Don't give them ideas.'

A young woman, soaked through, in red shorts and a white Nike top jogged past towards the Bull Wall. Roeper watched her go.

'I can't stay long,' Mackendrick said.

'You're ready to take the material?'

'Almost.'

Roeper nodded, as though this was the answer he feared.

'Not good enough. I brought you down here to set an unbreakable deadline.'

Brought me down here?

Who the fuck do you think you're speaking to?

Lar Mackendrick kept his expression calm.

'Declan, it's not as though — '

74

'The pick-up was supposed to be immediate.'

'Something serious came up — '

'That's your problem.'

'There was a time, Declan, in the years before peace and brotherhood became all the rage, and your people needed a place to stay or something delivered — many's the time I did what I could, and damn the risk.'

Roeper stretched his legs out and crossed one foot above the other. 'You were well paid.'

'It's a short, unavoidable delay.'

Roeper looked directly at Mackendrick. 'If you don't take possession of the material within the next forty-eight hours, we'll have to dispose of it. And we don't give refunds.'

'We're not ready.'

'Get ready.'

'Declan — '

Roeper turned his gaze back towards the sea. 'We don't provide storage. We sourced the material, prepared it for use — now it's sitting in a lock-up and every day that goes by is another twenty-four hours of risk we didn't agree to.'

'Be reasonable.'

'Forty-eight hours. The clock is ticking.' There was deliberate insult in the abrupt way Roeper stood up. Watching the slight figure hunch against the cold wind and walk with head down towards the bridge to the Bull Wall, Lar Mackendrick let the restrained rage of the past couple of minutes show on his face. Then he spat on the wet ground.

★ ★ ★

From the window, Danny Callaghan watched the two detectives cross to their unmarked car. The older one took the passenger seat, Fatface got behind the wheel. Beyond the waste ground he could see the slip road that led out of the estate. It was already busy, feeding into the main road, with the city's day shift flowing towards their workplaces. His own work — picking up Rowe and Warner and taking them to the airport — would start late and finish early.

He yawned. It was inevitable that the police would come asking silly questions, but they could have picked a civilised hour.

'Why didn't you hang around the Blue Parrot, wait for the police to arrive? Why didn't you come forward?'

'Mostly, I try to avoid you people — and I'd nothing to say that someone else couldn't tell you.'

They took him through the incident and Callaghan avoided any detailed description of the gunmen. He didn't need to be caught up in witness statements, identity parades or anything else that would draw him further into something that was none of his business. By the time the cops left, they'd probably accepted that he had nothing to do with whatever Walter Bennett was involved with.

The policemen's car turned off the slip road and settled into the creeping traffic. It was unlikely that Callaghan would get back to sleep now, but if he lay down he might get an hour or so. He was about to turn away from the window when he saw the blue Ford van.

Shit.

In a parking bay just across from the apartment block, thirty yards down to the left.

It's the same van.

Hurrying to open the door before the guy from 257 Solutions spilled his guts in the car. Callaghan stepping back to avoid being creamed by the passing blue van, something white written along the side.

It's just a blue van — how many of them are there in this city?

From up here he couldn't read the white writing along the side. The misty rain on the window didn't help. The angle of the windscreen made it impossible to tell if there was anyone in the van.

No one's going to park down there at dawn, sitting around, watching an apartment block. It's someone's work van. Someone who lives around here, maybe someone visiting. He was letting the cops rattle him. It was what they'd intended.

'Stupid thing to do, sticking your nose in?'

'I was hyped up — the guy crossed in front of me, I reacted.'

There was a tiny smile around Sergeant Wyndham's lips. He leaned forward and spoke quietly. 'Maybe you were hyped up because when you saw them coming in you thought they were coming for you? Big Brendan's family?'

'No.'

'The way I read it, after the trial Frank Tucker made it clear he was going to have you. Blood for blood — that was the phrase, am I right? You killed his cousin, you'll die screaming, that's

77

what he said. Frank is more than a big mouth.'

'If that was going to happen he could have had it done in prison.'

'Maybe he wanted you to have the pleasure of slopping out for eight years before he finished you off.'

'I've been out for months — nothing's happened.'

'Could be Frank decided to let you stew.'

Callaghan said nothing. It was as if Wyndham had been reading his mind.

Now Callaghan stared down at the blue van.

The radiators had started to take the chill out of the air. When Callaghan looked at his watch he saw that twenty minutes had passed since the cops had left and he was still standing at the window. No sign of life from the blue van.

Two days, two blue vans.

Who knows how many blue vans there are?

Hundreds.

With white writing along the side?

Why not?

He made a cup of coffee and when he came back to the window the blue van was gone.

Chapter 10

'Mr Mackendrick?'

'Walter, thanks for calling back.'

'What's the story, Mr Mackendrick? Why did those bastards — '

'It was a mistake, Walter, a bloody awful mistake. And it's my fault.'

Mackendrick put some remorse in his voice. A touch of guilt.

'I'm sorry, Walter — all I can do is hold my hands up and apologise. And I've made damn certain nothing like that will ever — *ever* — happen again.'

Walter said, 'What happened?'

'I spent three hours last night, after you called — half the night — getting hold of those gobshites, finding out what went wrong.'

'What went wrong?'

Keep it simple.

'My big mouth. A few days ago — this had nothing to do with you — a few of us were talking about something, about a problem — I'd rather not go into it on the phone — I made a remark. Like I say, my big mouth, just something off the cuff about something that had nothing to do with you, someone else altogether. By the time it got to Karl, it was — there was a fuck-up — that's the best way to explain it.'

'This was no fuck-up, Mr Mackendrick, those two bastards, they knew what — '

'Wrong place, Walter, wrong man. My fault. I don't want you to blame Karl — he was doing what he thought — it was *my* fault, I should have been clearer — my responsibility. I swear to Jesus, last night we went through it, it's all been straightened out — I mean, what can I say, Walter, all I can do is — '

'It's not good enough, Mr Mackendrick.'

'I know that, Walter, and I'll see that we make it up to you. All my fault.'

Silence. MacKendrick wondered if he'd

79

sounded too contrite.

He won't buy too much meekness.

He put the slightest edge into his voice.

'Be reasonable, Walter — a right royal fuck-up on my part, but I've made it clear to everyone — this was my fault, no one else's, and you're an innocent party. You're an important part of the team.'

'Fuck that, Mr Mackendrick — they almost killed me.'

'Let me make this up to you, Walter. Wherever you're staying, you know now it's safe for you to go home. Home ground, Walter, you and I can — '

'No.'

'Wherever you say, we'll meet wherever you say, the two of us, we'll sort — '

'No, no meeting.'

'Whatever you want. But you have to be reasonable. Give me an address, so we can send — I know, I know, it won't make up for what happened, but some compensation is on the cards, just a token of — '

'This isn't about fucking compensation.'

Mackendrick said, 'I know you're upset, Walter, you've a right. Fuck sake, *I'm* upset, and I won't be happy until we put this shit behind us.'

Put it up to the little bastard.

'I hope you accept that, Walter.'

'I want to believe you, Mr Mackendrick.'

Silence again.

'I hope you do, Walter. I really hope you do.'

Mackendrick paused, as though searching for

the right words. 'I need to show you — I'm really, there's no other way to say it, Walter, I'm embarrassed, really embarrassed. I want you to know that. I want you to see that. In person. When you feel comfortable. Tonight, maybe.'

Walter didn't respond.

'Or maybe tomorrow — maybe you can ring me again?'

'Tomorrow,' Walter said, 'I'll ring you again, Mr Mackendrick, and we'll arrange something.'

★   ★   ★

It's not what he said.

What Mackendrick said, it made a kind of sense, it might be true.

Except for what happened when Walter lost his temper.

'*This isn't about fucking compensation.*'

Walter felt an immediate surge of regret and fear. He'd never dared display such irritation with Mackendrick. And when the reply came back instantly, Walter knew it was all bullshit.

'*I know you're upset, Walter, you've a right.*' Calm, sympathetic, understanding. No matter what the circumstances, Mackendrick wouldn't take cheek from anyone, least of all someone he usually treated like a halfwit. He was being too understanding.

'*You're an important part of the team.*'

How fucking dumb does he think I am?

This wasn't about a mistake, about compensation or wanting to make things right — this was about Mackendrick getting his hands on Walter.

81

Fuck that.

The offer of money was tempting, but money wouldn't keep you warm if you were face down in the Dublin mountains.

'Tomorrow, I'll ring you again, Mr Mackendrick, and we'll arrange something.'

Yeah, right.

The sensible thing to do was to get out now. The money from Garda Templeton-Smith, the couple of hundred that was all he could get from an ATM, that would be enough to get him to Glasgow. He had a few hundred in a bank, some more in the Credit Union, but his account books were in his apartment and he wasn't going there. The kind of money he'd need to keep him going in Glasgow — he'd need Dessie Blue to cough up. Once that was sorted — he had friends in Glasgow, from the old days, people he could trust. A thing like this, it would sort itself out in a few months, he could come back.

Or not.

Bugger-all reason to stay in this crummy town, apart from Sissy.

Today, touch base with Dessie Blue, pick up that eight hundred — with that kind of money in his pocket, this Glasgow thing could work out not too bad.

He looked at his watch. Gone half-eleven. *Time to wake up Dessie Blue.*

He found a crumpled piece of paper in his wallet and checked the number.

⋆   ⋆   ⋆

Christ.

It was the third time Lar Mackendrick had tapped out Karl Prowse's number and the third time he'd got the engaged signal.

We don't have this kind of time to waste.

Everything was already on hold until Walter Bennett was replaced. Now his elimination — just a piece of necessary housekeeping — had turned into a project all of its own.

Again, Mackendrick tapped out Karl Prowse's number. Again, the barren sound of the engaged signal made him frown.

★   ★   ★

'Well? Have you got it?'

'I've got it.'

Got it.

Walter Bennett tried to keep the hope out of his voice. He gently swayed forward and back, his stare fixed on the ground at his feet. 'Great. I can meet you now.'

Dessie Blue said, 'Not now. Tonight.'

'Now.'

'Tonight.'

'This afternoon, then.'

'Tonight. Maybe first thing tomorrow — at the latest.'

Shit.

'You don't have it.'

'I have it. I just need to get my hands on it — just a matter of arranging things.'

'Arranging things?' Walter's voice was tighter, the pitch higher. 'What does that mean?'

'Getting the money actually into my hands.'

'You're fucking me around.'

'I swear.'

'This is *important* to me! I *need* it, you *owe* *it* *to* *me*, you bastard!'

Dessie Blue broke the connection.

Shit-shit-shit-shit.

Shit.

Walter ground his lips together. After a few seconds, he hit the buttons on his phone.

'Fuck off.'

'Please, Dessie — you've no idea, man, this — '

'You call me a fucking bastard, then you — '

'I'm under pressure, Dessie, the worst kind.'

'Tonight, then.'

'Thank you — thanks, *Jesus*, man — '

'Half.'

'Half what?'

'Half the money.'

'Ah, fuck that, Dessie, please, please.'

'I can get you half — you want to take half, or you want to wait a while?'

'Half now, half later.'

'You want this in a hurry, Walter, you take half. *Finito.*'

'Fuck you.'

'Whatever.'

Silence.

'You settle for that, Walter, right? Half?'

'It has to be tonight, though.'

'You working tonight? Anthony's place?'

'No.'

'Be there. Nine-ish.'

'Dessie — '

He was gone again.

★   ★   ★

This time, no engaged signal from Karl's phone. Lar Mackendrick was standing by his dining-room table. One hand holding the phone to his ear, the other silently tapping the table top in time with the distant ringing.

Come on.

'Yeah?'

Mackendrick said, 'It's me.'

'Everything okay?'

'You're free today?'

'I'm busy this afternoon,' Karl Prowse said. 'Family stuff. Free this evening.'

'Good.' Mackendrick spoke evenly, as though passing a comment on the weather. 'I've talked to our friend. He insists on staying out of touch. I spun him a yarn, but I don't think he's buying. So we've got to find him, urgently.'

'Any idea where he's staying?'

'Probably a B&B, maybe he's got family.'

'Okay.'

'Use your initiative.'

Chapter 11

This was the time Danny Callaghan liked best. Alone in a car, a straightforward task to perform, no time pressure. The motorway was busy — the afternoon light fading, endless streams of cars

85

mostly driven by tired, edgy people, in too much of a hurry to get somewhere that might make up for the long hours of work they didn't much enjoy. But Callaghan liked the calming effect that came with emptying his mind of everything except the mechanical routine of calculation, adjustment and response involved in driving on a busy motorway.

The drive to the airport, in the early afternoon, had been mostly silent. He gathered from their infrequent remarks that Rowe and Warner weren't too confident they could offer a cure for the problems of 257 Solutions. Rowe suggested a holding memo, as soon as they got back to London. Before heading home they were off to another job, this time in Frankfurt.

On the way to the airport, Callaghan caught himself yet again glancing in the mirror, not just routinely checking traffic but scanning the road behind for a glimpse of blue.

Stupid.

Once, he caught a hint of something blue and looked again but couldn't see it. When he got too close to the hatchback in front he gave up the vain search in the mirror.

Stupid. The notion of looking for a blue Ford van. Whoever it was — if there was anyone to worry about — could be driving any kind of car.

He glanced in the mirror again.

If it was just about the blue van he could write it off as paranoia. But this afternoon, an hour before he was due to pick up Rowe and Warner at their hotel, Callaghan had been getting ready

86

when the doorbell rang.

Shit.

The police did things like that. Figured the time most likely to mess you up, then came to collect you for a wholesome chat down the station, and you didn't get to leave until they'd screwed up your day.

His hand on the lock, Callaghan drew back.

Don't assume it's the police.

He fetched the hammer from under the bed and when he opened the door the kid from two floors up was standing there.

'Someone's looking for you.'

The kid, name of Oliver, was wearing the same hoodie outfit he'd been wearing when he'd nodded to Callaghan a couple of nights back, out on the green in front of the Hive.

Callaghan waited.

'Couple of fellas, they were asking around last night.'

Callaghan said, 'The police. They were here this morning. It's nothing.'

'Not the cops. I saw these guys. These weren't cops.'

'These days, they're recruiting all sorts. It's not just mountainy men in long overcoats — long-haired men, little chirpy women.'

The kid said, 'I know cops. These weren't cops.'

Callaghan said, 'Two fellas, right? Both of them wearing anoraks. One was fat-faced, the other — '

'No.'

'What did they look like?'

87

'Nothing special — jeans, I think, heavy jackets.'

'Fat-faced fella, big?'

The kid shook his head. 'Nothing like that. These weren't cops,' he said for the third time.

After a few seconds, Callaghan said, 'Okay.'

The kid pointed to the hammer. 'You expecting trouble?'

'I don't know. Thanks.'

The kid nodded. He said, 'See you, then,' and he turned and left.

★　★　★

Callaghan was south of the airport on the M1, having dropped Rowe and Warner at Departures, when his phone rang. It was Novak. 'Any chance you could handle another job?'

'That's fine. I've just dropped — I'm free for the day.'

'It's way out west?'

'No problem.'

'From there on to Celbridge?'

'No problem.'

'Thanks, Danny — we're stretched this afternoon.'

Novak said the job came from a larger transport firm, embarrassed by a limo breakdown that threatened to leave three clients stranded at the Citywest Hotel.

'I'm on it.'

There were a lot of SUVs in the car park of the Citywest, and helicopters lined up in the grounds. Legions of primped and burnished middle-aged men hanging about in expensive casual wear. The three clients were from that tribe, and they talked about golf all the way to Celbridge. Danny Callaghan tuned them out. The last time he'd held a golf club had been almost a decade earlier and there'd been blood on the clubface then.

At Celbridge the three golfers asked to be dropped at their local pub, where they gave Callaghan an extra-large tip.

On his way back now, Callaghan was in no hurry. His glance instinctively found the mirror again, and he cursed himself.

Do something.

Find out.

It had become too much of a habit, this checking the mirror and expecting the flash of blue. The blue van might have something to do with what had happened in Novak's pub. Or maybe Frank Tucker was finally looking for payback for his cousin's death. Perhaps it was the police, still looking to link him to whatever Walter was into.

Or maybe it was nothing at all — just two blue Ford vans with white writing along the side. A coincidence, and not all that big a one.

Find out.

Kill the fear.

All around him drivers radiated intensity from within their speed-pods, every one an isolated unit in a regimented herd, aggression sustained by anonymity. Behind and to Callaghan's left a four-year-old I Series BMW, the cheapest in the range, was playing silly buggers. In the mirror, he'd watched it jigging from lane to lane, the driver pushing the nose of the car into lane gaps, laying down the challenge — *Hit me or fuck off* — and always getting what he wanted, surging across the line, into the new lane, immediately searching for the next gap. Callaghan glanced across at the BMW, now passing on his left. The driver was in his thirties, shirt-sleeved, leaning forward, his lips tight. Whatever the rest of his life was like, out here in his speedy bubble on the M50 he knew himself to be a Spartan engaged against terrible odds in a fight for all that mattered. As the BMW surged forward again, Callaghan eased back. The best place to be when that type was around was anywhere else.

His life was like that now — quiet, limited, safe. His irregular work kept him well within the borders of his small ambitions. In his earlier life such limitations would have chafed. When he'd met Hannah, a dozen years back, he was exuberantly open to whatever life brought along, whether business or personal.

'You don't recognise me, right?'

When Hannah asked the question, Callaghan was in her kitchen, measuring an oven housing that turned out to be an eighth of an inch too narrow for the oven it was supposed to house. A nuisance, but not a problem.

'No,' he lied, and the way Hannah smiled told him she knew he was lying.

'The face is familiar,' he conceded.

'I was a year ahead of you — UCD,' she said. And he said, 'Really?'

What he remembered was a woman with

swaying dark hair, the centre of a crowd of loud types, mostly male, always boisterous at social or sporting occasions. Collectively they made the kind of noise that told the world to stand back and pay attention. A woman he'd watched from a distance, acknowledging to himself a mixture of interest and desire, but disinclined to do anything about it. Her smile, her bursts of enthusiastic chatter, the intensity she exuded, usually seen from across a bar or a canteen, at a debate or passing in a corridor.

Callaghan was wrestling with a decision at the time, having long decided that university was a mistake. He knew what he wanted to do and he wanted to do it now. And that meant he needed to smother the assumption his father had drummed into him — that to get anywhere you needed a passport in the shape of a degree. At that time, his pull towards a woman he didn't know was a distraction he couldn't handle.

'You disappeared.'

Callaghan was surprised that she'd noticed.

'I dropped out. Got into this game.'

He hadn't seen her again until that day in her new apartment. By then, his small custom cabinet-making business was motoring merrily along. Hannah was recently graduated, working part-time with a PR firm set up by a friend. Callaghan had installed a kitchen for a colleague of hers, who'd passed on his number.

'I knew you as soon as I saw you,' Hannah said. It was a couple of weeks later and they were lying in bed. Callaghan grinned. 'Obviously I made a big impression.'

91

It was dark now, so when Callaghan glanced at the mirror all he saw behind was the array of headlights on the motorway. No detail. Still, looking for a glimpse of a blue van was now a habit.

Do something.

He fished a Bluetooth headset from his pocket, adjusted it on his ear and hit Novak's number.

'Yeah?'

'You doing anything tonight?'

'What's the problem?'

'No problem. Just, you know, you busy?'

Novak laughed. 'You want to take me bowling, right?'

'I need you to do something, set something up. I want to talk to you about it.'

'Okay.'

'There's something — there may be something happening, whatever, I need to check something out.'

'This about what happened with Walter?'

'Maybe, maybe not.'

'Drop by later.'

Chapter 12

Right mess, this is.

Pamela took two handfuls of shredded cheese, scattered them across the pizza base, checked the order and reached for a handful of pepperoni.

She worked at her usual snappy pace, but tonight there wasn't much point.

The trouble with this place — no coordination.

Tonight, for instance, there were plenty of staff to put the pizzas together, not enough delivery people. Two guys had quit yesterday, another was out sick, everything was backed up. The orders came in, the pizzas got made, everyone was waiting for the two delivery guys who'd turned up tonight to get back, but they were each working two vectors instead of one, so it was twice as long before they returned to collect for the next run.

The shop was called Anthony's Pizza Place and the guy who owned it, Anthony Mohan, was spending half his time tonight on the phone, having no luck rustling up some more delivery guys. He considered shifting some of the pizza makers into delivering, but most of them were too young to have driving licences — the one who had a licence couldn't find his arse with both hands and a mirror.

The shop looked like a cartoon version of old Chicago, the pizzas had gangster names, and the delivery staff wore silly gangster uniforms. 'Nice guy, Anthony,' Pamela told her boyfriend. 'Pays more than the minimum wage — never pushes anyone around. Just hopeless at organising.'

'Hey, Walter!'

Pamela looked up and saw that Anthony had a big smile on his face, his voice with an edge of pleading. 'An answer to prayer, that's what you are.'

Rubbing his hands from the cold outside, Walter Bennett shook his head. 'Sorry, Anthony, the reason I'm in — '

Pamela liked Walter. Little old guy, a gloomy look about him, but he called her 'dear' and he never leered at her tits, not like some his age.

'Come on, man, it's an emergency.'

'No,' Walter said.

And, from the other side of the open kitchen, sprinkling cheese across the twenty-third pizza she'd handled since her shift started, Pamela could tell he meant it.

* * *

Okay, so Anthony Mohan was a nice guy, but Walter was buggered if he was going to waste one of his last evenings in Dublin delivering pizzas for loose change.

'Where've you been the past few weeks?'

'Busy,' Walter said. 'Anyone asking for me tonight? I'm expecting — '

'Two hours,' Anthony said. 'That's all, just to get us out of a hole.'

'Sorry, Anthony, no can do.'

Anthony's Pizza Place meant handy pocket money on a slow week, but Walter reckoned it was demeaning, a man of his age. Work like that was for students or Chinks. He did it when he was especially short of the readies, but just about anything else was preferable. Which was how he'd got into that thing with Dessie Blue.

It'd been a month, now, waiting for Dessie to come through. Dessie ran a small rental business

94

on the fringe of the music industry — amps, mikes, that sort of thing.

Mean bastard.

Could have come up with the money straight off. It wasn't like that kind of money was a lot to Dessie. It was like he enjoyed being a mean bastard.

A month back — Walter's phone rang. Dessie Blue said he knew that Walter knew people who could get him what he needed. That time Dessie paid upfront and gave Walter two hundred just for making the connection and bringing the stuff round. Two hundred on top of the grand the stuff cost from the wholesaler.

Walter wasn't personally into nose candy, had never even tried it. And he'd never got into moving it in a serious way — but he knew people and this thing with Dessie Blue was just about making a connection.

Two days after that, Dessie Blue rang again.

'Something similar.'

'Come on, Dessie — you got enough marching powder to keep a regiment going for a month.'

'Some people I know. How about it?'

Dessie was a consumer, now he wanted to distribute, that way he could subsidise his own use.

Walter said, 'Same deal?'

'Half — five hundred's worth. And a hundred for you.'

'Two hundred, same as before.'

'One-fifty, and they want it tonight.'

'Bring the money around.'

Which was when Dessie Blue had said it'd be

quicker if Walter financed the deal himself. 'You can put the five together — for a start, you've got the two hundred I gave you for the last deal. Bring the stuff here, I pay you the five, plus your one-fifty.'

Walter thought for just a second, then he said, 'For that service, two-fifty's my price.'

Dessie Blue said, 'That's fair enough.'

And the fucker said, when Walter brought the stuff around, expecting his two-fifty fee and the five hundred for the product, 'This is embarrassing, Walter. The people I'm talking to — they came to me, it was their idea. Now the bastards say it's okay, someone's made them a gift of a goodie bag, they don't need any more right now.'

'That's not my problem,' Walter said.

'Don't worry, Walter, I can shift the stuff — these days, no problem finding buyers. What I'm saying is, I can't pay you tonight, it'll take a day or two.'

'Fuck that.'

Which was when Dessie Blue had said that was okay — if Walter wanted to hold on to the stuff, retail it himself, that was fine with Dessie. But if he wanted to offload it right away and he was willing to wait a day or two for payment — certainly by the weekend — Dessie would have no problem finding a market.

'I'll round it up, your fee, from two-fifty up to three, to make it up to you. Wait a day or two, I give you an even eight hundred.'

That had been a month, and a lot of futile phone calls, ago. If Dessie was still using, if he was selling on to his friends, he'd cut out Walter

Bennett and he was sourcing the stuff through someone else.

'*Be there. Nine-ish.*'

Walter looked at his watch.

Eighty-thirty give or take.

Come ten o'clock, the latest, and Dessie Blue or no Dessie Blue, he'd be out of here.

'A straight fifty, Walter — whether it's two deliveries or twenty.'

'I'm busy, Anthony.'

'A guaranteed fifty — this isn't about money.' Which was true. What Anthony didn't want was to piss off regular customers. You delivered late, you screwed up people's evenings, they remembered, and next time they ordered from someone else. So, instead of paying Walter the delivery charge, he offered a guaranteed fifty.

'I'd love to help out, but — '

'Just two hours, a guaranteed fifty. With tips you maybe double that.'

'I'm expecting someone, Dessie — I've got an appointment.'

'Do a run while you're waiting. And if some-one comes in looking for you, and you're out on a run, I'll keep them here until you get back.'

'Look — '

'Okay, sixty, Walter — two hours, easy money.'

With tips, maybe double it.

Not to be sneezed at. There was more than a chance that Dessie Blue was fucking around again. No guarantee he'd show at all. This way, Walter for certain would get something out of the evening.

'Sixty?'

'Jesus, Walter, thanks.'

'One thing,' Walter said.

'Sixty, I can't go more than that.'

Walter shook his head. 'I don't have to wear the shitty gangster uniform, right?'

*   *   *

From inside, Pamela watched Walter stash the pizzas in the van and drive away. She was taking a break, getting a can of Coke from the machine. She popped it open and took a slug. She took out her mobile and made a call. It went straight to voicemail. Karl must have had his phone switched off.

*   *   *

Karl Prowse took a bottle of formula from the fridge. His wife had made up four of them that afternoon. The baby was making the little twitchy movements that meant he was about to wake and begin testing his lungs.

Tonight could go either way. They had a few hours to get hold of Walter, and if that didn't happen there was no telling in which direction Lar Mackendrick would explode. Karl hadn't seen that happen, but he knew Lar's reputation, and he didn't want to satisfy his curiosity. This afternoon he'd spent over an hour on the phone, asking around about Walter Bennett. So far, the best lead he'd had was an address for Walter's sister. Maybe later tonight he'd drop around there.

Just sixty seconds in the microwave, then Karl put the nipple on the bottle, shook some of the liquid onto his forearm to check the temperature. *Fine.* Twenty minutes later he switched on his mobile and saw he'd got a voicemail message, to call Pamela.

★　★　★

'Yeah?' Pamela said.

Sitting by the window of Anthony's Pizza Place, her mobile to her ear, she watched Walter's delivery van arrive back.

'Hiya, Pam, how you doing?'

Long time since Pamela and Karl had had a thing — lasted no more than a week or ten days, nothing special. When Pamela had found out he had a wife it wasn't like a big surprise, and it wasn't as though the thing was going anywhere. Nice fella, Karl, but dull.

Pamela felt the cold air waft past as Walter came through the doorway. He dumped the delivery pouch on the counter and said, 'Anyone looking for me?'

Anthony shook his head and checked the order slips.

Pamela said into the phone, 'That old guy you asked me about — Walter whatsisname?'

Karl said, 'You seen him?'

All he'd asked Pamela was did she know Walter. *Greasy little geezer, works part-time for Anthony?*

You want me to tell him you're looking for him?

No, Karl said. *Just, you know, if he comes into work, let me know. I've got some money I owe him*. She knew that was bullshit — more likely it was Walter owed Karl money.

Into her mobile she said, 'Anthony's got him working tonight. Took a little persuading but the way things are here — '

'What area's he delivering?'

Vectors, Anthony called them. The pizza shop in the middle, one *vector* to the north-west, one to the north-east, two more south-west, south-east.

'South-west vector.'

'Where the fuck's that?'

'Runs from here up to Carndonagh Road, across as far as the Mansfield estate.'

'You're a star, Pamela — thousand per cent.'

'*No problemo.*'

⋆   ⋆   ⋆

Robbie Nugent was up a ladder, changing a fuse in a circuit board. An old woman, a few doors down from his home, a right pain in the arse, but he liked her. His dad was a handyman and he'd rewired her front room, free gratis. Robbie helped out and since then the old dear had called on Robbie and his dad whenever she needed something done. No question of paying, and she never even said thanks. It was like she saw it as her right.

It amused Robbie that this old wagon, half dead as she was, had that kind of spunk. Must have been a kick-ass bitch in the old days.

'That's done, now,' he said, speaking loudly because she was a bit deaf.

'Right,' she said, and she opened the front door to show him out.

Robbie was almost at his house when Karl rang.

Chapter 13

The Blue Parrot wasn't busy when Danny Callaghan came in. He nodded to a barman and arched an eyebrow — the barman waved a thumb towards the back office and Danny went through.

Down the short corridor, a tap on the varnished door, and when Novak said 'Yeah?' Callaghan went in.

'I need you to do something, set something up. I want to talk to you about it.'

'Drop by later.'

Dropping by to see Novak in the back room of the Blue Parrot — for a word of advice or the kind of practical help that made a difference — had become a habit since Callaghan had got out of prison. Novak had been there all along, even before the trouble that led to those years in a cell.

★   ★   ★

It's almost a decade back and Danny Callaghan, age 23, is very serious about mastering his golf swing.

He's got the grip right, he knows that. And he's spent a lot of time getting the correct angle between his forearm and the shaft of the club. But somewhere in the downswing, while he's keeping his hip movement under control, the angles slip and he loses power and accuracy.

Identify the problem, that's half the job. The rest of it, all it takes is practice until you do it without thinking.

Almost seven-thirty in the morning, more than half the stalls in the driving range are occupied. All male, in a line of 26 stalls, each of them blasting one ball after another out onto the range, each working to master his own little glitch. Danny Callaghan, with not enough time in the day to do all he needs to do, is trying to tune out the chatter from the fools two stalls across on his right. Three kids, students, who sound like they've been celebrating since the previous evening. Almost sobered up, they've come here to wring the last few drops of pleasure from their overnight adventure. They've hired one driver and a bucket of balls between them and they take turns hacking balls into the distance. Every swing, every mistake, every remark, creates a chorus of hooting.

'Cool!'

'Go for it, baby!'

'No way!'

One of the kids says, 'Just as long as you're back by Thursday!' and the others go into spasms of chortling. It seems to be some kind of punchline they picked up during their revels, because he says it again and again, each time provoking a gale of laughter that's louder than it needs to be.

'Shut the fuck up.'

The fat guy to Danny's immediate right is squeezed into jeans and a red check shirt. He stands facing the kids, gesturing with his club. 'Christ sake.'

'Sorry,' one of the kids says. The fat man turns away, lowers his club to the ball.

The laughter is muted for a while. The only noise is that of golf clubs cutting through the air, the *thwock!* of the clubfaces connecting with the balls, and the distant sound of a golf cart, far out across the range, the driver protected by a net as he scoops up the used balls.

After a while, the kids forget the fat man and when one of them tops the ball and it hops ten feet, then dribbles to a stop, all three of them erupt in quaking howls of laughter.

'*Shut* — the *fuck* — *up!*'

The big fat man, in his mid-thirties, as tall as Callaghan but lots of blubber around the middle, flesh billowing beneath his chin, has dropped his club and he's standing to one side, hands on his hips, facing the kids.

'Hey, look, we're sorry — '

Two of the kids are still laughing, the third is holding his arms out, palms up, head tilted to one side, apologetic. 'Really — we didn't — ' He turns to his friends. 'Okay, lads, let's not make pricks of ourselves, right?'

The laughter of the other two has subsided to grins, and they're nodding and making diffident gestures.

'Little bastards.'

The fat man turns and picks up his club, bends again to place a ball and as he does so a prolonged, very loud fart escapes from his arse.

He turns around at the flare-up of uncontrolled laughter. He faces the kids again, his chin bobbing, his cheeks roiling as he chews gum and seethes. The kids can't stop now, they're still laughing when the fat man comes around the barrier into their stall. The one who apologised is the first to recognise that the game is over. One hand raised in appeal, he says, 'Listen, man — ' His hand is brushed aside and the fat man is right up in his face and his head snaps forward and the kid goes down, his nose a rosette of blood.

Danny Callaghan makes a disgusted sound.

The fat man kicks the fallen kid, not too hard.

One of the other kids, a thin, pale-faced youth, says something to the fat man and the fat man uses one chubby finger to poke him in the chest. 'You his boyfriend?' He keeps at it, poking, taunting, 'You his boyfriend?' and the kid's eyes are pleading and the kid says, 'Mister . . . ' and the fat man grabs the kid fast by the front of his shirt, pulls him forward, holds him there and raises his other fist. He shows the cringing kid the big fist for several seconds, then he draws the fist back and punches the kid unconscious. It's a boxer's punch, the fist, arm and shoulder snapping into alignment so the blow has the weight of the fat man's body behind it.

Everything has stopped. The one kid still on his feet is visibly trembling. All along the length

104

of the driving range no one's moving, no one says anything. There's just the *phut-phut-phut* of the golf cart in the distance, the guy down-range, scooping up the balls.

The quiet is broken by Danny Callaghan's impulsive shout. 'You fat fuck!'

★ ★ ★

Novak said, 'Thanks for picking up those three gents at Citywest.'

Callaghan said, 'No problem.'

Novak said, 'The outfit that passed the job on to us, they're good people — we got them out of a hole, they'll remember that.'

The back office of the Blue Parrot was dominated by a big oak desk. Novak was in the leather swivel chair behind the desk. Callaghan sat in one of the two standard chairs on the other side of the desk. Brushed aluminium laptop on the desk, along with a penholder, a small calendar and a large hardback notebook. In one corner of the office, three filing cabinets, a small Bose sound system on a shelf behind Novak. Three large photos on a far wall. Novak's two kids, Caroline and Jeanie, both in their teens, both wearing party dresses, then Novak and his wife Jane at Caroline's wedding. On the right, Novak shaking hands with Terry Wogan, both of them young, both of them showing their biggest smiles to the camera. This was where it all came together, what Novak called his business empire — the pub and the transport firm and a specialist bread shop run by a cousin of his.

105

Novak was 58 and the empire was the proceeds of forty-five years' work, and this office was the controlling centre of it all.

Callaghan said, 'The other night, those two guys, I thought at first it might have been me they were after.'

Novak said nothing.

'I think I'm being watched. A blue van, it's turned up a couple of times, then someone's been asking questions about me, around the Hive.'

'You think it has something to do with what happened to Walter?'

'Maybe so.'

'Or the Tucker thing?'

'Maybe so. Since I got out, it's been like waiting for the other shoe to drop.'

'And you want me to — ?'

★ ★ ★

Novak didn't come every week, but two or three times a month for eight years when Callaghan was called to the prison visitors' room it was his smile he saw at the other side of the barrier.

It was Hannah who got Callaghan the job fitting out the kitchen in Novak's pub, just as Hannah did most of the hustling for business in those days. 'Good job, son,' Novak said, and he recommended Danny to a bookie-shop owner who needed someone reliable for a mid-sized renovation. And after what happened at the driving range, when Callaghan's whole life was going down the toilet, it was Novak who

106

arranged an efficient lawyer who did what he could against an overwhelming case.

At his lowest, Novak whispering, 'What happened, Danny, it was just the way things went. Sometimes people figure out what they have to do to get somewhere else — they walk over anyone in the way. People like that, the hell with them. What happened with you — it was just one thing leading to another.'

After the trial, it was Novak — even more so than Hannah — who was his link to the outside. And when Callaghan came out of prison it was Novak who gave him work and arranged the apartment, Novak's wife Jane who bought the sheets and the towels and stocked the fridge.

'Look — I don't want you to think I'm taking all this for granted.'

'All what?'

'I can't imagine a better friend.'

'You got a bad break.'

'I fucked up.'

★   ★   ★

Danny Callaghan, age 23, is six feet away from the big fat man in the red check shirt. The one kid still on his feet has taken advantage of the distraction, and all that's left of him is the fading sound of his running feet. The kid who's been punched out is on his back, still and pale. His friend is on the ground a few feet away, half-sitting, one hand held to his nose, failing to staunch the flow of blood from his nose.

'Be smart,' the fat man is telling Callaghan.

The way the fat man is standing, the kid with the bloody nose can't stand up without risking a kicking. The fat man looks like he's savouring the prospect.

'They're kids,' Callaghan says.

'Walk away.'

The first blow is the one that counts. If it's fast and hard and accurate enough it can settle everything right off.

Trouble is, throw a sucker punch and if it's not fast or hard or accurate enough there's no going back from what follows. And that's going to be nasty and dangerous. Every fight hurts, even the ones you win.

In that silent moment, Danny Callaghan knows that if he waits too long the chances are that the fat man will start it and maybe finish it right off.

Move now or he will.

Which is when Callaghan feels a hand grip his left forearm, another hand grip his left bicep, just a fraction of a second before the same thing happens to his right arm. He instantly lunges to elude the grasping hands, jerking his left shoulder, then his right shoulder, but the men he can see on either side are big, their hands are like steel grips on his arms, and his struggle lasts just a few seconds. The fat man is smiling. 'I told you to be smart.'

He looks first at the man on Callaghan's right, then the other one, and he says, 'Hold tight.'

His arms held firm, his body tilted off balance so he can't lash out with his feet, Callaghan's belly and chest are totally unprotected. The first blow feels like the fat man's fist has punched right through to Callaghan's spine. Callaghan needs to go down, curl up, protect himself, but the hands on his arms hold him in place.

★   ★   ★

The judge looks down from the bench. The distaste in his features is not for his task but for the defendant below him, convicted and awaiting sentence. Danny Callaghan looks up and sees a smug man who has never felt pain or humiliation. All through the trial Callaghan has felt like he's been describing what happened in a language that makes no sense to the judge or the lawyers or the jury.

'Your able counsel made the case that when you went to Mr Brendan Tucker's apartment two evenings later you intended nothing except to remonstrate with him. In the alternative, he argued, you sought at worst to deliver an appropriate physical response to the beating you had received. I cannot — as the jury did not — find the former explanation credible. You don't bring a golf club to someone's home in order to give him a piece of your mind. And while you'd been subjected to a vicious assault by Mr Tucker, the extent of your retribution went far beyond any notion of a manly physical rebuke.'

He outlines the medical evidence — that at least one blow to the victim's abdomen, from the golf club, had been so severe as to penetrate to his pancreas, pushing the organ against the spinal column and causing a bleed that later contributed to Mr Tucker's sudden death.

The judge leaves a moment or two of silence, and when he speaks again his voice has dropped a couple of degrees. 'Your claim that you did not bring to the scene the golf club with which you struck the fatal blows — your assertion that it was produced and waved about by the victim — seems to me fanciful. We heard from police witnesses that the victim owned a full set of golf clubs, none of which matched the make of the driver used to deliver the fatal blows. His fingerprints weren't on the club. We heard persuasive evidence from the victim's cousin, Mr Frank Tucker, that he partnered the deceased in regular golfing sessions and the fatal club didn't belong to the victim. The victim's father gave similar evidence. This cowardly effort to evade responsibility for your actions speaks volumes.'

From the corner of his eye, Callaghan can see the radiant green of Hannah's outfit. Despite him asking that she stay away, she's been here every day. Novak too. Callaghan's father hasn't made an appearance.

The judge speeds up as he notes the long record of offences accumulated by Big Brendan Tucker during his 34 years — two holdups, a fistful of assaults and one conviction for drug possession for sale or supply. 'While the victim was undoubtedly a man of questionable character, that doesn't excuse the defendant's actions — the cold-blooded decision to seek out

Mr Tucker, to bring a golf club as a weapon, the clear intent to do him harm and the ferocity of the assault which resulted in his death.'

Twelve years.

As Danny Callaghan is taken out of the court, Big Brendan's cousin, Frank Tucker, holds aloft a fist. 'Dead man, Callaghan — blood for blood.' His voice is strained, his face red, his eyes alight.

★ ★ ★

'And you want me to — ?'

'Set up a meeting with Frank Tucker.'

Novak raised an eyebrow. 'I don't think — Danny, that could — '

'I've been looking over my shoulder since I got out. The last couple of days, maybe you're right, I'm being spooked by nothing much — but I need to know what's real. Either I'm a target for Tucker or there's something else — or there's nothing.'

'You go see Frank, maybe you stir things up, things that calmed down over the past eight years.'

Danny Callaghan slumped in the chair, hands in his pockets, long legs stretched out in front. 'I need to know.'

'You want me to go see him?'

'No — I mean, thanks, but — '

Silence while Novak thought it through.

'Yeah, if it's going to be done, best you do it yourself.'

'Yeah.'

111

'I'll call him in the morning. Clear heads in the morning.'

'Thanks.'

'Soon as I know, you'll know.'

Chapter 14

It came to twenty-seven-fifty and the Polish guy gave Walter Bennett a twenty and a ten. Standing on the doorstep, Walter took his time counting out the change — *one, another one, fifty cents* — and when the three coins were laid out on the palm of Walter's left hand the Pole reached over and took two of them and gave Walter a big smile and said thanks.

Jesus.

Walter turned and walked away. When the door shut behind him he looked at the euro in his hand and he said aloud, 'Cheap bastard.'

Up to now he'd done well in tips. Two more stops, all deliveries within a couple of roads from here, then back to Anthony's place and the way things were going maybe he might offer to work an extra hour. He'd left his mobile number at the pizza place, and Anthony had agreed to call him as soon as Dessie Blue appeared. 'Believe me, I won't let him leave until you get back.'

That was if Dessie Blue showed — which Walter by now was reluctantly beginning to accept was more a hope than a belief. At least he was clocking up a little extra for Glasgow. As

112

long as he didn't come across too many of those Polish bastards.

He started up the van.

It wasn't that Walter had anything against Poles. 'It's just that they don't understand freedom,' he used to tell Sissy. 'Not used to it. Don't know how to behave. In this country, we were born free and we know how to handle it.'

Sissy gave him another of her smiles.

'No, really,' he said.

Walter checked his mobile — just in case he'd missed a call.

Nothing.

Briefly, Walter wondered if maybe before he headed off to Glasgow there might be something to be done about Dessie Blue. By way of revenge, and maybe a small financial return. A call to Detective Garda Templeton-Smith, one last bit of business.

Not worth it.

And if Dessie didn't cough up tonight — and he probably wouldn't — when Walter eventually came back to Dublin it might be no harm to have a debt that might still come through.

Live in hope.

Walter slid around a small roundabout that led into the Mansfield estate. A wannabe neighbourhood, Walter reckoned, and very nice too. On the other side of the river, in the days of the boom, these houses would go for an arm and a couple of legs. And they looked after their houses, the people around here. Some of the front lawns looked like they hadn't been mown, more like shaved. Walter reckoned, what with the way the economy had been going, a lot of people in places like this had trouble meeting their mortgage payments — and that meant before too long a house in a place like this might be halfway affordable.

Walter kept an eye on that kind of thing. 'You're mad,' Sissy laughed at him when he talked about house prices. 'You stand in the middle of your bedroom, the only kip you can afford to rent, and when you stretch your arms out you can touch both walls.'

'You never know when you might get a lucky break,' Walter told her. 'It's all about watching the market, seizing your opportunity. And if you don't keep up to speed with these things you never know what you might miss.' Sissy just looked at him, a smile on her lips, and after a while Walter started grinning and the two of them had a good laugh.

'Three twelve-inch pepperoni, three Cokes,' Walter said when his next customer opened the front door. Karl Prowse showed him a big smile and a small gun and said, 'That's right — won't you join us?'

★　★　★

Lar Mackendrick had several mobile phones, all off the shelf, no contract. The Sony Ericsson had two numbers keyed in — one each for Karl Prowse and his buddy Robbie Nugent. Those were the only numbers the phone had ever called, and the only numbers from which it had received calls. Once the phone was destroyed,

114

there would be no record linking it to Lar Mackendrick or anyone else.

Lar was pouring a sherry for May when the Sony Ericsson beeped notice that a text had arrived. He finished pouring the drink and brought it into the living room, where May was sitting in front of the television. She was halfway through a boxed set of the fourth series of *ER*, the final series in which George Clooney appeared. She limited herself to one episode per night, eking out the series over almost a whole month. Lar thought George Clooney was an asshole.

'Thanks, love,' May said, and as Lar left the room she pressed the button that brought the menu up on the screen.

Back in the kitchen, Lar took out his Sony Ericsson and checked the text message.

Our friend is leaving. Any last requests?

Walter had twice called Lar at home and Lar had already stressed to Karl Prowse the importance of not leaving that kind of evidence lying around. No harm giving Karl a reminder.

Remember to get his phone.

It was a big room and mostly white. Two smaller rooms converted to one. The carpet and the walls were white with a slight golden tinge. The large fireplace was white marble. There was a painting over the fireplace that was all white except for a small swirl of red in the lower-right corner. Against one wall a tall white vase with purple flowers stood on a black marble sideboard. The three-seater sofa, where Walter Bennett was sitting, was white, matching the two armchairs.

Walter sat with his knees together, his hands clasped in his lap. He had given up trying to control the quivering of his lower lip. His forehead and scalp felt icy, his insides had turned hot and liquid.

'Please.'

The word was a breath, and he doubted if Karl and Robbie heard it.

'Not hungry?'

Karl spoke through a mouthful of pizza, Robbie was swigging a can of Coke. Both of them, sitting in the armchairs facing the couch, were more than halfway through their pizzas. The third pizza sat untouched in front of Walter, the flat box open on the white marble coffee table.

'That's good pepperoni,' Robbie said.

'Why?' Walter said.

Karl said, 'The cheese is a bit rubbery.'

They each wore tight white surgical gloves.

Walter could feel a drop of sweat on his jaw. He wanted to wipe it away but he knew that his hand would shake and he didn't want to draw attention to the depth of his fear.

'Why?' he said again.

Karl rose from the white chair, then squatted in front of Walter. His voice was gentle. 'We know things, Walter.' He flicked away a tiny piece of cheese from the corner of his mouth.

'Please, Karl.'

'We hear things. And what we hear is that you've been cosying up with a certain copper — name of Templeton-Smith. Is that right?'

When he spoke, Walter knew how it sounded. 'What it was, it was other stuff, nothing to do with you, nothing to do with Mr Mackendrick.'

'I should hope so, Walter.'

'He offered me money.'

'Of course he did.'

'Nothing to do with you, Karl, I swear.'

'I believe you.'

'I know people, just small-time — mostly knocking off cars, burglary, a bit of cocaine, that kind of thing. Nothing to do with anything.'

'And he paid you money.'

'He caught me, it was a car thing. Few weeks ago, he makes me an offer — I hardly told him anything about anyone. Nothing about this, about you, about Mr Mackendrick. I swear.' Walter heard his voice turn squeaky. 'I *swear*, Karl, I swear.'

Prowse said, 'We know that, Walter, we know all about it. We have our sources.'

'Then why — you tried to kill me.'

'It's not what you told the cop, Walter, it's what you *might* tell him. You're a tout, and touts sell information. Maybe one of these days your back's against a wall and someone offers you a way out if you've anything heavy to sell. Once you start touting, Walter, who knows where it'll end?'

'Ah, Karl, I'd never — '

'So you say, Walter. And you expect us to take

a gamble on your good character?'

Karl stood up and took his car keys from his pocket. He tossed them to Robbie, who was chewing pizza as he left the room.

'Karl.'

'No point, Walter.'

Karl sat down in one of the white armchairs.

They sat in silence until Robbie came back. He was carrying a baseball bat and a heavy-duty clear plastic bag. He put them down neatly, alongside each other, on the white carpet. Then he reached down and took his last slice of pizza.

Walter didn't intend to make a moaning noise, it just came out.

Robbie stood there chewing for a minute. Then he put down the remains of his pizza slice and used his gloved fingers to wipe his mouth. 'That's as much as I can handle.'

Walter knew that if he tried to stand up his trembling legs wouldn't support him.

'Your phone,' Karl said.

Walter didn't know if this required a response.

'Give it to me.'

Walter's fingers trembled as he passed over his Nokia.

'This the phone you used to call Lar Mackendrick?'

'Why?'

'This the phone?'

'Yeah.'

'You sure?'

'Yeah.'

Karl slipped it into an inside pocket.

'Okay', Karl said. 'We don't have all night.'

Chapter 15

Pros and cons. Swings and roundabouts.

You lose a juicy murder case to detectives from another station — a pain in the arse, yes. But it's not all downside.

Truth was, when this thing started an hour ago Detective Inspector Dermot Leahy had felt a tension headache coming on. He'd been involved in two previous murder cases, neither of which led to a conviction, both of which did his career no favours. And his diary was quite full enough with assaults and burglaries and road accidents and teenagers staggering home from drinks parties and vomiting in their neighbours' gardens. The headache began to ease once he got the phone call from his chief superintendent. 'We pass it on. Ongoing case,' the chief super said. 'Someone had a pop at this guy three nights ago, tried to shoot him in a pub on the Glencara estate. Looks like they did a better job this time.'

So the Mansfield Close job was folded into the existing investigation.

'Sorry about that, Dermot.'

'Can't be helped, sir.'

Inspector Leahy waited in the hallway while the member from the Glencara case looked things over in the living room. When Detective Sergeant Michael Wyndham came out into the hallway he was trying to keep his face blank.

He said, 'They did a thorough job.'

'You could say that.'

Wyndham said, 'Who owns the house?'

'Couple out for the evening. Left around

seven-fifteen, got back almost midnight, found the lights on. Didn't come in — rang 999.'

'Good.' Too often, panicky civilians did a headless-chicken routine all over the crime scene.

Leahy said, 'I hear someone tried to kill this fella already?'

'Two or three nights back — he got lucky. We've pushed all the usual buttons, with no great results. Walter, God rest him, was into a bit of this, a bit of that. Petty stuff — no obvious reason someone would want him dead.'

The hall, long and narrow and done in various shades of brown, made Inspector Leahy feel claustrophobic. He nodded towards the front door and led Wyndham out into the garden. After the atmosphere in the house, the air outside felt pleasantly cold.

Wyndham said, 'Technical on the way?'

'Any minute. I've had a couple of members knocking on doors, no one heard a peep.'

There wouldn't be much from the neighbours. One of those keep-yourself-to-yourself neigh-bourhoods. Mansfield Close had about twenty houses ranged in a horseshoe layout, with a green area in the centre. Big houses, built in a style most often seen in 1950s Hollywood versions of Olde English villages. The name suggested the estate was probably built in the mid-1990s, when the money was starting to flow but the boom hadn't yet gathered speed. The North was still leaking blood, and the South's middle-class aspirations and distaste for the excesses of nationalism came together to create a fashion in housing estates with English labels — Sherwood Park, Tudor Heights, Balmoral Lawns. That was before the economic boom and the winding down of the Northern blood-letting encouraged the middle classes to adopt a bit of the old nationalist swagger.

On the green in the centre of Mansfield Close, where an English village might have had a war memorial, there was an outsize monument commemorating nothing in particular, with a clock on each of its four faces.

A white van was pulling up across the road. Technical was here.

'The house owners — where are they?'

Inspector Leahy pointed towards a squad car. 'Back seat, trying to keep their blood pressure under control. Name's Waterman. Roy and Denise.'

'They let anyone else have keys to the house?'

The inspector shook his head. 'Side window open, second floor — access from the garage roof.'

'So, what do you reckon — Walter's burgling this place with someone else — and what? Thieves fall out in the middle of a job? Doesn't look like a spur-of-the-moment thing.'

'He delivered the pizzas. The name is on the boxes — Anthony's Pizza Place. Seems this Walter fella did occasional work, delivering. They say the order came in, three pizzas for this address. We checked the phone in the living room, the pizza place is the last number dialled.'

'Someone broke in — '

'Picked an empty house at random.'

121

'And ordered pizza?'

'So it seems.'

'And how did the killers know Walter was working tonight, delivering to this area?'

Inspector Leahy said, 'I've got a member over there now, talking to the guy who runs the pizza shop.'

Wyndham went to meet the two technical people getting out of their van. He gave them the basics as they changed into their white Tyvek coveralls. 'And bag the remains of the pizzas. Just might get some DNA.'

He and the inspector watched the two technicians, mouths masked, hoods up, slowly mount the steps and enter the house.

'Not a job I'd fancy,' the inspector said.

Sergeant Wyndham said, 'It'd put you off pizza for a while, right enough.'

⋆   ⋆   ⋆

Roy Waterman said, 'Look's like someone's finally in charge. Back in a minute.' His wife, white-faced and murmuring into her mobile, nodded. Waterman got out of the back of the squad car.

The detective inspector he'd already met introduced him to the policeman who'd recently arrived. Waterman didn't catch the name, but he heard the rank.

'*Sergeant?* Has this case been downgraded already?'

'Don't worry, sir — we have a full team on the job, all ranks, and no effort will be spared.'

'How long are these people going to be crawling all over our house?'

'It's a murder investigation, sir. It takes as long as it takes — but I can assure you — '

Waterman wasn't listening. He turned and looked across the road to where he could see the outline of his wife's head in the back of the squad car. Months, this would take, before they got back to normal — if ever. Waterman could adjust. As long as the place was cleaned up he'd have no problem living there. Denise, though — she'd probably want to move out. And with the property market the way it was — and the added selling point that a man had been murdered in the living room — Jesus, this was just what he fucking needed.

The two detectives were moving away, head to head, talking. Roy Waterman turned and walked up the steps and into his hallway. He was halfway towards the living room when he heard the fat detective behind him.

'Sir, you — '

From the living-room doorway Roy Waterman hardly noticed the two policemen in their white coveralls. His gaze was immediately drawn to the figure on the floor. Everything about the body conveyed composure — arms crossed on the chest, feet crossed at the ankles — except for the large, shapeless, clear plastic bag tied around the head, the inside painted red with blood, and the red pool leaking out onto the white carpet from where the bag was bunched up, tied around the man's neck.

'Sir, you'll have to, sir, please — '

Waterman turned and shuffled down the corridor. In the open air he stared again at the figure of his wife in the back of the squad car.

'Sir?'

Waterman turned to the fat detective. When he spoke, he met the sergeant's gaze and his voice was quiet, his tone lifeless. 'What's this fucking country coming to?'

His eyes made it clear this was not so much a question as an accusation.

★   ★   ★

After the inside of the car fogged up again, Danny Callaghan had the chamois ready and he took his time wiping the moisture from every inch of the windscreen. Then the side windows. He brought the window down and wiped the rear-view mirror. The black Hyundai was parked midway between two street lamps. This time of night, after one in the morning, most of the houses were dark. The street was deserted, only the occasional car passing through to disturb the stillness.

Sleeping dogs.

Maybe he should have let things be. Arranging to confront Frank Tucker might be reckless. The blue vans were probably a coincidence.

Against that, there'd been that moment in Novak's pub when Callaghan saw the killers coming in, and the infinite feeling of helplessness that had swept through him before it became apparent that he wasn't the target.

The alternative to confronting Tucker was perpetual fear.

Callaghan stared again at Hannah's house, across the street and two houses down. Big detached house, painted yellow, set back from the road. The only sign of life a light in the hallway.

He sat still as a pair of headlights appeared in his mirror. As the car drew near Hannah's house it slowed down. Hannah's red Saab took a curving turn into the wide driveway, pulling up behind Leon's Nissan Patrol. Leon got out of the passenger seat, leaned on the roof of the car and said something to Hannah, who was locking the driver's door. Callaghan could hear her laugh from a hundred feet away. After they went inside, the hall light stayed on for just a few minutes, then the front bedroom lights came on. Someone closed the curtains. Callaghan couldn't tell which of them it was. All went dark after a few minutes. Another quarter of an hour or so passed before Callaghan switched on the engine, listened to it hum a while, then drove away.

Part Two
Entrepreneurs

Day Four

Chapter 16

After waiting almost an hour, Danny Callaghan stood up and crossed to the door of the interrogation room. He shook the handle until a uniformed garda came. The garda unlocked the door and told him to stop being a pain in the arse.

'I want to know why I'm here.'

'Because.'

The garda pulled the door shut and locked it.

Callaghan sat down at the scarred metal table. The room was bare, drab — whatever beige liquid they used to paint the walls, odds were that the sub-contractor had watered it down. After eight years inside, Callaghan had developed the patience necessary for coping with institutional timescales. You learn patience, or you grow yourself an ulcer.

After another forty minutes Detective Sergeant Wyndham arrived, his round face puffy and unshaven. 'Thanks for coming in.'

Callaghan stood up. 'Two of your flunkies pulled me out of bed this morning — it's not like I had a choice.'

'Won't take long.'

'I've wasted half the morning in this room.'

Wyndham sat down on the other side of the

table and motioned for Callaghan to return to his seat. 'Look — I've had four hours' sleep on a camp bed, so your troubles don't impress me. Where were you last evening?'

Callaghan took his time sitting down. Then he said, 'What time?'

'You tell me — whenever you finished work.'

'What's this about?'

'You finished work what time?'

'What am I supposed to have done?'

'You finished work what time?'

Callaghan said nothing for a while, then he said, 'Late — I had to pick up some people at the Citywest Hotel, bring them across the city.'

'Time?'

'I wasn't keeping track. Had something to eat, dropped in to my local, had a coffee, went for a drive.'

'Where to?'

'Nowhere, just around. I like to drive — maybe half an hour, maybe more, I don't know — then I went home, went to bed.'

'Did you see Walter Bennett, talk to him at all?'

'No.'

'He call you?'

'No.'

'You call him?'

'No.'

'After you helped him out the other night, did he say anything about why it might have happened?'

'I told you — we never spoke — I knew him briefly when I was inside, that's all.'

'You hear anything about what he's been up to these days?'

'Look, sergeant, it's not like I'm hanging around street corners, swapping jokes with the neighbourhood wiseguys. I get up, go to work, go to bed, get up again — I hear nothing about anything. I got into trouble a long time ago, I was a kid. Then the other thing happened and I went to prison. I don't steal, I don't hurt people — that other stuff, it's like it's someone else's history.'

Wyndham gave in to a long yawn, his head back, the back of one hand to his mouth. He flexed his shoulders, then he said, 'Later on, if we find out you knew something — '

'What's happened to Walter?'

'If I find out you've been hiding something, if it turns out you and he had something going on — ' He leaned forward, his voice hard. 'You never finished your sentence, sonny. You're on parole, which means you step out of line and we make a court application and back you go — no charges, no trial, just the stroke of a pen — four more years behind bars.'

'What's happened to Walter?'

Wyndham's face softened. His sigh wasn't all about tiredness. 'The other night, when they tried to shoot him? The way things turned out, it would've been a mercy to the poor bastard if you'd let them do it.'

Sergeant Wyndham left an *Evening Herald* behind when he went to take a leak. The front page headline screamed 'Mob Boss Torture Killing'. The story said that Walter Bennett, a

131

veteran gangster, was the latest victim of Dublin's gangland feud. It also said his throat had been cut.

'Bullshit,' Sergeant Wyndham said when he came back.

'How did it happen?'

'Mind your own business.' He stood, holding the door open. 'Off you go.'

' 'Mob boss torture killing' — it doesn't make sense. Walter wasn't anyone's boss.'

'There's a whisper, so they guess the rest. If your business is selling papers, one guess is as good as another. Walter's a mob boss today, and that sells papers. Tomorrow, maybe he'll be an innocent bystander — whatever — it'll sell more papers. It's show business. Cops and robbers, like on the telly, but with real corpses. Now, if you'll kindly toddle along, I've got work to do.'

'You believe me? I'd nothing to do with anything?'

'The warning stands — I catch you lying just a little bit, and you'll do four more years without even the benefit of a trial.'

★ ★ ★

Heavier than it looks.

'You're doing fine, lads — take it easy.'

Karl Prowse liked the way Lar Mackendrick didn't leave everything to the foot soldiers. He wasn't much help when it came to shifting things, but at least he turned up.

'Wait a minute,' Robbie said. 'My grip's a bit — ' He used a knee to take the weight while

132

he slid his fingers back a couple of inches along the steel pole.

The beer barrel was set within a rectangular metal frame. Two steel poles fitted into pairs of parallel slots in the frame. Robbie and Karl held the poles at one end, two of Derek Roeper's people held the other. Together, they had the barrel halfway towards the back of the white Ford Transit Connect.

The van, the back doors open, was backed up to the entrance of the lock-up.

Robbie took a breath. 'Okay.'

When they got the barrel into the Ford, one of Roeper's people went to work with a spanner and tightened the nuts that kept the metal frame immobile on the floor of the van.

Robbie sat on the floor of the van, just in front of the beer barrel, while Karl drove and Lar Mackendrick sat up front. It took half an hour to get to the street in Santry where Karl was renting a house with his wife and two kids. The house had a garage attached. When they parked the Ford Transit inside the garage there was just enough space to open the driver's door. As he climbed out, Karl looked back and saw Mackendrick leaning towards the barrel, giving it a gentle, affectionate tap.

Chapter 17

At the front desk of the police station Danny Callaghan asked a sergeant if he could get a lift home and the policeman just smiled. The

133

sergeant gave him his wallet, his money, his mobile, his keys and his Swiss Army knife. Outside, Callaghan crossed the car park and turned right and a car horn beeped from across the road. Novak's red Audi pulled away from the kerb, U-turned across the road and pulled up alongside Danny.

'Get in,' he said.

Callaghan climbed into the car. 'How the hell did you know I was here?'

Novak glanced in the mirror and pulled away. 'Kid named Oliver, he drinks in the pub — called me, said he saw the police take you away from the Hive this morning.'

'They tell you what it's about?'

'They didn't have to. When I heard about Walter, I knew that had to be it.'

'So you told them to let me out or you'd — what? — stamp your foot and hold your breath till your face turned blue?'

'I gave my fat friend Sergeant Wyndham a shout. Told him your solicitor was on her way to the station — they hate that — and he said not to bother, you'd be out by lunchtime. And here I am.'

'Thanks.'

'Wyndham's heart wasn't in it. If they thought you were involved, they'd have kept you for at least a couple of days.'

'Probably.'

'Lunch — I'm doing an omelette, that sound good?'

'I'm okay.'

'You'll sit and eat a mushroom omelette, and

when it's gone down you'll belch and say that tasted lovely.'

'Thanks.'

It took about fifteen minutes to drive to Novak's semi-detached in Glasnevin, close to the Botanic Gardens.

'We've got the best garden in Dublin on our doorstep. Any time of year, Jane and me get a spare hour — nothing like it, letting the colours and the shapes and the scents get at your head. Nature's detox.'

In the kitchen, Novak was all business, giving a running commentary as he cooked. 'What you don't want to do, when you make an omelette, you don't want to beat it to death. So you leave the whisk alone, you use a fork, right? You have the heat right up — get a pan like this, an omelette pan, otherwise it spreads all over the place and you're making a pancake.'

Quietly, Danny Callaghan said, 'I don't need cheering up. I'm okay.'

Novak dropped the mushrooms into the pan, flipped over one edge of the omelette. 'You're such a whizz in the kitchen, you don't need a cookery lesson?'

'Since you picked me up, you've been non-stop yapping. I'm okay.'

Novak nodded and concentrated on his cooking.

Eight years.

All that time ago, at the driving range, with Brendan Tucker beating up the kids, an impulse made Danny Callaghan shout at a bully and one

135

thing led to another, and he went into a box for eight years.

Quarter of my life.

And now, again, he'd crossed the border into territory where it wasn't possible to take the next breath for granted. At any moment, someone might point a gun at the back of his head and he'd die without an instant's warning.

The image of his life as a stunted thing, the greater part of it gone, closed down whole areas of Danny Callaghan's mind. Permanently standing on the edge, forever expecting that fatal push, to imagine anything beyond the immediate tasks of the day seemed pointless.

After a while, Callaghan said, 'I'm sorry, I'm nervous, I get snappy.'

'No problem, you're fine.'

They were sitting at the kitchen table, Callaghan eating the omelette, Novak with a ham sandwich.

'Maybe now Walter's dead, maybe that's the end of whatever that was about. And once I get the Frank Tucker thing — '

Novak said, 'I rang Tucker's place this morning. Like getting an audience with the Pope. I left a message with one of his toadies, they're to ring back.'

Danny said, 'Thanks. That's good.'

'It'll get sorted.'

Danny nodded. 'One way or the other.'

★ ★ ★

Novak's wife arrived as Callaghan was washing up.

Jane was in her mid-fifties and a couple of inches taller than her husband. Blonde and slim, a briefcase in one hand, a cigarette in the other. Before marriage and raising a family, she'd worked with the probation service, advising ex-prisoners. Now she worked part-time for a citizens' advice centre. She put down the briefcase and said, 'He been poisoning you?'

Callaghan grinned. 'It was lovely, an omelette.'

'I can do you one,' Novak said.

'Ate at the canteen.' Jane turned to Novak. 'Did you ask him?'

'Ask him what?'

'Christmas?'

'Oh, yeah.' Novak turned to Callaghan. 'You're coming for Christmas dinner, okay?'

Jane adopted a withering tone. 'You're full of the social graces.' To Callaghan she said, 'We do a low-key Christmas. Jeanie's coming home from London, Caroline and her boys are coming up from the country. Gordon Ramsay here will do his usual turkey dinner, I do the veg, and I'll be highly offended if you don't turn up.'

Novak's tone was mock outrage. 'Gordon Gobshite? Not fit to wipe Delia Smith's wooden spoon.'

Callaghan smiled. Jane said, 'No kidding, you've got to come. Your first Christmas on the outside — you shouldn't spend it alone.'

He hadn't thought as far ahead as Christmas. It was — what? — two weeks, maybe less, something like that. 'Thanks, both of you — but let's see how things go, okay?'

Jane said, 'That's a yes, then.'

★   ★   ★

The clatter of the police helicopter woke Danny Callaghan. First time in a couple of weeks. Before that it was every night for a week. That was the pattern, on and off, since he came to live at the Hive. The local community groups kicked up a fuss, the police denied that they used helicopters to patrol working-class areas, things went on as before.

Callaghan glanced at the clock. Just past midnight.

The *kotcha-ta kotcha-ta* of the engine wasn't just loud, it sounded like something was loose inside and at any moment the whole thing might break apart and come down from the sky like a falling truck. Standing at the window, Callaghan looked up to where the helicopter was hovering, red light steady at the tail and a brighter white light flashing somewhere underneath. It would stay for a while, maybe five minutes, low enough to shake the windows and get the dogs barking, long enough to wake all but the heaviest sleepers, then it would piss off to some other estate.

Callaghan's father had had a thing about helicopters. When he was a kid, helicopters were rare in Ireland — wondrous machines that attracted great excitement on the rare occasions they made an appearance. 'Even now,' he'd told Callaghan, 'any time I hear a helicopter I automatically look up, like it's some exotic sight. Must have been like that for people who grew up when cars were a novelty — they heard a car, they rushed to the window.'

When his father died, Callaghan got two days' compassionate parole. Finding himself wrapped up in the rituals of the funeral, it was a strangely unemotional time. His father had never wavered in his love, but had never been able to conceal his shame at his son's crime. He'd visited the prison, but infrequently, his unease obvious. A week or two after the funeral, back in prison, reading a newspaper, Callaghan saw a piece about how helicopters had become the new definers of super-wealth. Newly prosperous Ireland had acquired more private helicopters than any other country. He made a mental note to mention that to his father, and seconds later he was bent over, the newspaper crumpled, tears streaming down his cheeks.

A searchlight came on near the cockpit of the police helicopter, moving erratically for a moment, then it found its target, the group of kids drinking around the fire on the green in front of the Hive. Danny saw a couple of the kids raise their cans in a toast to the pilot, another kid gave the helicopter the finger. One kid put down his can and stood up, arms stretched out, and began to dance, a cross between Travolta and a drunken sailor. Danny recognised Oliver. The dance in the spotlight continued for a minute, then Oliver gave the helicopter a cheery wave and sat down. The kids ignored the clattering noise and after a while the spotlight went out and the helicopter moved away.

Day Five

Chapter 18

When Danny Callaghan's black Hyundai came to a stop, Karl Prowse was thirty feet behind. He was driving slowly enough to be able to immediately and smoothly park his Toledo without any sudden swerves. Karl watched the interfering bastard get out of the car and walk into the driveway of a large detached house.

'You come back here, you'll get your pimply arse kicked.'

We'll see who gets his arse kicked, smart bastard.

The call from Lar Mackendrick had ruined a potentially good Saturday evening with an old girlfriend. Lar's surveillance people were all tied up — could Karl handle the smart bastard for a couple of hours?

Karl watched as Callaghan pressed the bell and a woman with short dark hair opened the door and greeted him with a hug. She ushered him in.

Callaghan's ride?

Probably not. Family-sized house. Probably a couple lived here. Maybe her old man's away. Or she's divorced and she got the house.

There were two cars in the wide driveway, a Nissan Patrol and a Saab. His and hers, probably. Or it could be the woman had a selection of cars, so she could accessorise according to the occasion. This part of Blackrock, when it came to building your image, no expense was spared, on your house, your clothes or your cars.

Woman like that — a bit out of Callaghan's league, though.

The way Lar Mackendrick told it, the smart bastard was a bit rough for this neighbourhood. 'Daniel Callaghan, age 32, seven months out of prison, served eight years of a twelve-year sentence for manslaughter — he killed a cousin of Frank Tucker's.' A man like Lar Mackendrick, the kind of money he paid, had handy access to anyone's Social Welfare records and phone records, and his solicitor had a choice of garda contacts who'd take a backhander to fill the blanks in anyone's history. He looked up at Karl, from the typed sheet of paper.

'This Callaghan bollocks, he could be a loose end or he could be an asset, depending on how we handle things.'

That was the way Lar worked — consider all the possibilities. All Karl Prowse wanted to do was show the smart bastard the business end of a Glock. Give him time to shit himself before Karl squeezed the trigger. Lar Mackendrick, he knew how to play all the angles.

'Mother died when he was a kid, father was a baker — died while Callaghan was in prison. One brother, something in engineering, lives in Belfast. Callaghan's a cabinet maker — or used to be. Married Hannah O'Connor, no children.

Divorced while he was in prison. Juvenile record — petty shit. A few years with nothing on his sheet, then he hammers Frank Tucker's cousin into the grave.'

No time for personal grudges, was what Lar Mackendrick said when Karl suggested they take no chances with the smart bastard. 'We have a job to do. Personal feelings, they come later.'

About ten minutes after Callaghan went into the Blackrock house, an e-series Mercedes parked across the road and a couple got out — an overweight man and a woman to match. He in a long black overcoat, she in something shorter and furry, with a matching hat. When they rang the bell the same short-haired woman greeted them with hugs.

The windscreen was beginning to fog, so Prowse switched on the engine and left it on long enough to allow him to demist the glass.

After a while a taxi stopped and a blonde got out. This time, a heavy man wearing a rugby shirt opened the front door. After he'd hugged the blonde they went inside.

So, the tart in the black dress, she's not Callaghan's ride, she's spreading for the prat in the rugby shirt. The blonde, maybe she's Callaghan's ride.

Karl Prowse waited another half-hour and nobody else came visiting. He left the Toledo and when he came back two minutes later he had the street address and number of the house, plus the licence-plate numbers of the Nissan, the Saab and the visitors' Mercedes. He called Lar Mackendrick and gave him the info. Lar repeated each number as he wrote it down.

'Dinner party,' he said.

'May as well leave them to it, then,' Karl said.

'You have time to nip off, get something to eat. We've nothing to get a handle on the blonde woman. Better follow her home.'

'Are you sure that's — '

Lar Mackendrick's tone was amiable. 'I know you need your beauty sleep, but it's best to leave nothing to chance.'

Just what I need.

Maybe, what — two, three hours — maybe more — scratching my balls in a cold car, waiting for nothing to happen.

* * *

Hannah smiled and said, 'Come and help me in the kitchen.' Danny Callaghan said okay and they left the other four chatting in the living room. The kitchen was brushed steel and matt-black surfaces. Hannah took down half a dozen dinner plates, then raised the lid on a saucepan, had a quick glance inside and stirred the contents. When she turned to Danny she was smiling and she said, 'I'm *not!*'

He stared in silence.

'Honestly, I'm *not* matchmaking.'

'A bore and his wife, plus you and Leon. Then what's-her-name and me.'

'Her name is Alex and you can stop worrying. Her only ambitions involve law, money and property. Besides, if she's partial to the occasional shag, what's your problem?'

144

'It feels odd — my ex-wife pimping for me.'

'Danny.'

Callaghan closed his eyes and tilted his head back.

'I'm sorry.'

Her voice softened. 'Take it easy. We eat, we drink, we chat — nothing depends on it. A pleasant evening goes by. Okay, it's not the glamorous life you're used to, but — ' She took his hand. 'Hey, come on, you're entitled to live a little.'

'I'm sorry.'

'And stop saying you're sorry.'

She held him for a moment in a hug. As Callaghan stepped back from the embrace he nodded towards the living room and said, in a mock whisper, 'Tough going in there, isn't it?'

'Ah, Malcolm's a little pet.'

'He's a bore.'

Malcolm Croke was a former adviser to ministers in four separate governments, over a period of a couple of decades. He was a man once trim and he now carried his excess weight uncomfortably. Telling his stories of ministerial vanity and backstage backstabbing, he obviously enjoyed his own performance.

'He may be tedious, but Malcolm's one of the pillars.'

'He must be retired.'

'Formally — but he's been snapped up by the boards of one major bank and three mid-sized companies, including Leon's.'

'Hotshot?'

'Malcolm knows things, he knows people.

People hire Malcolm because they know that when you have Malcolm on your side you're halfway towards closing whatever deal you're after.'

Callaghan paused a moment, then he said, 'What does he know about me?'

Hannah laughed. 'Good God, you don't think Malcolm has the least interest in anyone below the rank of managing director?'

Callaghan remembered Croke's weak smile and distant nod when Hannah introduced them.

'He's not suddenly going to ask me to give him the low-down on life behind bars?'

'Can you imagine Malcolm asking anyone else to take centre stage?'

'And Alex?'

'Alex is my friend, we've known each other for years, and she knows my background, so she knows yours. She's a lawyer — she takes people as she finds them.'

Callaghan nodded.

Hannah said, 'No time for chat — I've guests to feed.' She lifted a pan off the stove and shook it, took the lid off and began to transfer the rice into a large serving bowl.

'You've picked up some domestic skills.'

'Who's got time for cooking, these days? The Butler's Pantry — they cook the stuff, you heat it up — twenty minutes later you're taking bows.'

★ ★ ★

Alex volunteered to pour the coffee. Callaghan offered to help. They were at the sideboard at the end of the dining room. Around the dining table, Hannah was relaxing, Leon and Malcolm Croke's wife were chuckling dutifully at another of Croke's anecdotes — this one about a hair-wrenching fight between a minister's wife and his girlfriend.

Alex said, 'It's six months since I last met Malcolm, and the stories are the same, word for word.'

'Hannah says he's a big shot.'

Alex nodded. 'Big shot, Irish style. The bottom line on Malcolm is that he's got a little black book of private phone numbers, and for a price he'll make a call to a helpful politician or a senior civil servant. I've seen him work his magic for a couple of my clients and they say he's worth every cent.'

'You do mostly corporate work?'

'It's where the money is.'

Back at the table, Hannah's husband was busy squeezing a word in. Leon was wearing his green Ireland rugby shirt, somewhat tight on his beefy frame. 'And, if it was up to that sort, this country would still be all about moral victories and the politics of envy.'

'Precisely,' Malcolm Croke said. He grunted thanks to Alex as she handed him a coffee. 'Whether acknowledged or not, exclusion has always been an indispensable element of democracy. The Greeks and the Romans understood that — these days, they'd be hauled up before a commission for political correctness. But it was squabbles about widening the democratic base that weakened them.' He tentatively sipped at his coffee, then left it to cool on a side table. 'These days, political democracy is subject to the electoral whims of every brain-dead gobshite, which is what cripples us. How did Yeats put it? 'The bitter faces, the vinegar-heavy sponge' — that man knew his Ireland.'

'No more than yourself, Malcolm,' Leon said.

'Politicians looking over their shoulders at the rabble — that's what makes it hard to take the kind of tough decisions that a recession demands.' Croke folded his arms, then unfolded them, as though he wasn't comfortable having them resting on his belly. 'Political democracy — the begrudgers are welcome to it, it's economic power that matters. Always has done, always will.' He raised one hand, like a magician flourishing a wand. 'As long as that remains unsoiled by the grubby fingers of the hoi polloi — ' And he smiled.

Danny Callaghan looked across at Hannah, who was gazing at Malcolm Croke like he was her favourite uncle.

★　★　★

When he took a break from watching the house, Karl Prowse found a café ten minutes' drive away that did a nice curry and chips. On his way back to the car he stopped at a Centra shop. Used to be that, most of these shops, the owners worked the place all day. In the evenings, their sons and daughters did a couple of hours for pocket money, and they didn't bother hiding their resentment. Carefully arranged petulant expressions let you know that this wasn't the kind of work they were born to do.

Spoiled brats. The way Karl Prowse saw it, the one good thing about the waves of immigrants over the past few years was that you didn't get so many stroppy Irish bastards behind the counter. Not that the stroppy Asian bastards were much of an improvement — though they probably cost less than the pocket money the sons and daughters were paid. The tall Chink behind the counter in the Centra scanned Karl's twenty Silk Cut and the can of Coke, his face blank, like in his head he was dreaming of a rice sandwich. Didn't even say thanks, just took the money and gave the change and looked over Karl's shoulder at the next customer, like Karl didn't exist.

Fuck you, too, Charlie Chan.

Karl parked down the street from the house he was watching. Nothing seemed to have changed. The Merc still there, the two cars in the driveway, Danny Callaghan's black Hyundai. Karl lit up a Silk Cut and lowered the window an inch.

Day Six

Chapter 19

Danny Callaghan was woken by the sound of the shower. When Alex came out of the bathroom she was wearing a pair of denim jeans and a bra. She pulled on a light brown roll-neck sweater and gave him a smile.

'Morning.'

'You going somewhere?'

'Work — it's almost ten o'clock.'

'It's Sunday morning.'

She grinned. 'Business doesn't take a day off. I've got a couple of clients who have a big meeting coming up tomorrow and they need to be prepped.'

'Sundays — you don't lie in, have a long breakfast, listen to the radio, read the Sunday papers?'

She sat on the edge of the bed. 'I don't read newspapers, unless they're writing about my clients. I don't listen to the radio, too much chatter. And I don't have a television, it rots the brain.'

'How do you know what's happening in the world?'

'What affects me, I know about. The rest — why do I need to know about wars and famines and elections and celebrity nonentities?'

The apartment was an upmarket version of Danny Callaghan's own place. Slightly bigger, with a better finish. More ornate skirting boards and architraves, a better quality of light fittings. The furnishings all had the feel of money. The difference in locations meant that Alex's place was likely four times the price, but the two flats offered the same functional qualities — a place to keep clothes and belongings, a place to eat, a place to park your body at night.

Sipping coffee as the dinner party shuffled to an end, Hannah had said, 'You'll give Alex a lift, won't you — she lives down by the docks?'

Alex made a perfunctory protest, saying she'd have no problem getting a taxi. Callaghan said it was no trouble, he was heading across the river anyway, it was practically on his way.

Alex lived on the fifth floor of an apartment block fronting onto the Liffey, across and down the river from the financial centre. When Callaghan stopped the car she gave him a smile, then she leaned across him and opened his door. Callaghan waited a moment, then he switched off the engine.

When they were still half-clothed, Alex pulled away, opened a bedside drawer and took out a small box made of dark wood. She opened the lid and took out a spoon, a credit card and a short yellow plastic straw. She took a small packet of white powder from the box and used the spoon to sprinkle some onto the top of the bedside table. She used the credit card to chop the coke into lines, and the straw to snort it. When she offered him the straw Callaghan smiled and shook his head. She put everything back into the wooden box before shedding the rest of her clothes and getting back onto the bed. A minute later, she fetched a condom from the same drawer.

The sex was urgent and, on her part, loud, and afterwards Callaghan lay quietly while she did something gentle with the hair above his left ear.

After a minute, she said, 'You've got a terrific relationship with Hannah.'

Callaghan gave a non-committal tilt of the head.

'I think you've still got a thing for her.'

Callaghan said, 'It's not like that. We're good friends.'

'Not even a teensy-weensy crush?'

'We're friends.'

'She left you, right? When you were in prison?'

'No, we — ' Callaghan felt uneasy talking about Hannah. 'It's more complicated.'

'How so?'

Callaghan felt he was being cross-examined. He said, 'It's all a long time ago.'

At the time he'd killed Big Brendan Tucker, the marriage was uneasy. Perhaps things would have been okay if they'd kept their home and work lives separate, but Hannah — her own print shop in its infancy — was increasingly involved in Callaghan's cabinet-making business. She sought out and won contracts for apartment fit-outs and multiple installations on new housing estates. Callaghan took on a staff of three to make units, and a separate staff to fit them. The business was thriving and it wasn't what Danny Callaghan wanted to do. Increasingly, he felt like he was one part of an unfamiliar mechanism.

'I make things,' he explained to Hannah. 'I fit them. I make a good living at it, and I like all of that. The other thing I like is that all over this city there's stuff that I made, handsome stuff, stuff that people use every day. It's not curing cancer, but it's what I want to do. And what's happening now — I spend less time, and soon it'll be no time, doing what I want to do.'

Hannah didn't understand how anyone could be so illogical. 'Nothing stands still — expand or contract — without a business plan you'll end up no more than an employee.'

'So? That's a good thing to be, if you're doing what you want to do. Anyway, the way it's going, I *am* turning into an employee — yours.'

She thought at first that it was resentment against her having a significant say in his work. It took a while — and long after the divorce — before they realised there was no right or wrong involved, just a different way of seeing things.

When Callaghan was arrested all the bickering stopped and Hannah was at his side throughout the trial. A year into his sentence Novak came on a visit, with a message from Hannah. A week later she came into the prison and they agreed to begin divorce proceedings. Two years before he was released, Hannah told him about Leon.

Alex said, 'Do you think she still cares for you?'

Callaghan said, 'We'll always be friends.'

Reluctant to be drawn further into the conversation, he closed his eyes and after a while he heard Alex's deep breathing.

Now she took a brown leather overcoat from a closet and put it on. She leaned over the bed and kissed him. 'Make yourself that long, leisurely breakfast, okay? Pull the door to after you.'

He watched her go, doubting he'd ever see her again. Then, his mind clear and calm, he turned over and fell asleep.

★   ★   ★

After he'd had a shower, Callaghan made coffee and looked out across the river. The morning was sunny and cloudless, up to the left the glass office buildings were at their best against the blue sky. To the right, the docks, the multicoloured rows of containers, the cranes and the ships waiting for service.

There was a small bookshelf on the wall in front of the Apple Mac in the corner. Callaghan scanned the titles — legal textbooks and reports. The magazines stacked neatly on the floor beside the leather armchair were all *Vogue*, *Elle* or *Marie Claire*.

Feeling hungry, he checked the fridge and found one egg, a head of iceberg lettuce and three containers of Cully & Sully soup. He decided to walk up to the city centre to eat.

He washed the mug and the spoon and put them away and cleaned out the cafetière.

Nothing out of place in the tidy apartment. He had a vague memory of tossing his suede jacket onto a chair last night. He went to the bedroom and found the jacket hanging in a closet.

Standing there, jacket in hand, it was the LK he noticed first, the small silver initials against the black leather of the briefcase on the floor of the closet. He threw his jacket on the bed and picked up the briefcase.

The same. No mistake.

He'd seen it two months ago, when he'd had lunch with Hannah.

'What do you think of it? They customise.'

She'd been to the gift shop across the street from her print shop, to get Leon a birthday present.

Callaghan had thought it was a bit tacky. The LK was attached to a short, wide strap, near the clasp. Callaghan had said, 'He'll love it.'

Now, although coincidence was unlikely, he opened the briefcase and thumbed through a couple of folders. There were several envelopes tucked into a pocket. He took out three of them. They were all addressed to Leon Kavanagh. *No coincidence.* On impulse, he put the briefcase on the floor and tore the envelopes and their contents in two, then dropped them back into the briefcase.

He knew immediately it was a silly thing to do and he didn't care.

Leon's grinning face.

'Fancy meeting you here.'

It was in the Mint Bar, downstairs in the Westin Hotel in Westmoreland Street, five or six weeks earlier. The pub in Temple Bar in which Callaghan had been drinking had become too crowded, so he moved on to the Mint. Not much better. Fewer people, but louder. The bar's hard surfaces, the bare walls and the stone floor, amplified the sound. Callaghan had already ordered his Jameson when he spotted Leon at a table on the far side of the bar. Leon was with a woman, big eyes, very thin, with streaked hair. Their heads were close and their smiles intimate. Just then, Leon looked up and saw Callaghan, who immediately took his drink to a table.

'Didn't think this was your kind of place.'

Leon was standing beside the table, looking down at Callaghan. Big grin on his face. It was the first time Callaghan had met Leon without Hannah.

Leon said, 'You come here a lot?'

Callaghan felt like he'd been caught doing something wrong. He had no idea why he should feel guilty, while Leon behaved as though there was nothing to worry about.

'You're not keeping an eye on me, I hope?'

His voice was light, his smile wide, but Callaghan felt like everything was going into a skid.

He knows.

Half a dozen times since he'd got out of prison, Callaghan had gone to Hannah's street, always in the evening or late at night, and parked his car near her house. Just sat there for perhaps an hour, sometimes a lot longer. Then he'd go home. It first happened a few weeks after he got out of prison. Callaghan woke in the middle of the night and lay there, trying to measure what it was he felt. He sat silently on the edge of the bed, elbows on his knees, eyes closed, palms each side of his head. Thoughts surfacing, then popping like bubbles. No sound in the Hive, no sounds from outside. It was as though the whole world had shut up shop and moved away while he slept. The emptiness was a massive physical presence inside his chest.

He'd been to Hannah's house in the days after he got out, and now he dressed, went down to his car and drove to her street. After a while, the emptiness wasn't there.

Looking up at Leon, thinking *He knows*, Callaghan felt as if the adults had discovered his dirty little secret. Then Leon was bending down. 'This — ' and he jerked his head towards the skinny woman on the other side of the room' — is exactly what it seems like, okay?' He winked.

Leon had more than a few drinks in him. Callaghan's panic subsided. If Leon knew about Callaghan's nocturnal visits he'd be blunt about it. He was letting Callaghan know what was expected.

Callaghan said, 'None of my business.'

Leon's smile was larger. 'That's right.'

Callaghan said nothing.

Leon said, 'Nice to see you again.' Then he left.

When Callaghan told Novak about the night-time visits to Hannah's street, Novak said, 'You'll never get her back.'

Callaghan said, 'I don't want her back' and it was only when he said it aloud that he realised it was true. He had no yearning to rebuild anything

157

with Hannah. Their marriage had run its course, ended for good reasons. The visits to her street had to do with something else. Maybe it was about feeling the emptiness dissolve, feeling reattached to the world around him. Whatever it was, he knew he wasn't looking to rebuild bridges — it was more like an animal seeking warmth.

When he finished his whiskey, Callaghan left the Mint. As he passed Leon and the skinny woman Leon raised his glass and smiled. Callaghan walked out of the bar, up the stairs and quickened his pace as he hurried across the hotel lobby and out into the air.

Now, in Alex's flat, Callaghan looked again at Leon's briefcase.

None of my business.

Whatever about Leon's relationship with the skinny woman, screwing around with Hannah's friend was scummy.

But none of my business.

Callaghan left Leon's briefcase on the floor of the bedroom, the closet door open. He pulled on his jacket and went down to his car.

★　★　★

Callaghan was getting out of his car near the Hive when his phone rang. It was Novak.

'Yeah?'

'I got a call just now from Frank Tucker and he says yes, okay, he'll meet you.'

Callaghan locked the car door and stood looking out across the green in front of the Hive.

In the distance he could see smoke rising from the embers of the fire the kids had made the previous night, to heat up their drinking party.

'Good, thanks.'

'Tomorrow afternoon.'

'Where?'

'The Venetian House.'

'Best to get it over with.'

'You okay?'

Callaghan was walking towards the Hive. This Frank Tucker thing, he didn't need to think about it any more. One way or another, it would be sorted.

'Fine, everything's fine. But I've got a couple of jobs lined up for tomorrow.'

'Don't worry. I can get another driver to fill in.'

'Thanks.'

'I'll take you there.'

'No need.'

'I'll take you there.'

Day Seven

Chapter 20

Danny Callaghan and Novak drove to the Venetian House in silence. Off the M50 at the Lucan junction and down the N4 to the West End Park Road and out past the Cullybawn housing estate. They pulled into the almost empty car park. Novak turned off the engine.

'You ready for this?'

'As I'll ever be.'

'No law says we can't drive away from here — let it go.'

Danny Callaghan shook his head. 'It's one thing or the other — and I need to know.'

He sat there, looking across the car park at the pub. After a while, Novak said, 'That's some pile.'

Wedged between three vast west Dublin housing estates, the Venetian House was just a few years old but it strained to look like it had been there since the nineteenth century. Mock leaded windows and decorative beams gave it a vaguely Tudor look, mixed with a vaguely Italian style. The pub was an assemblage of units of various shapes and sizes, combining space and intimacy. It was a local institution, the centre of birthday, wedding and First Communion celebrations, gala lunches and post-funeral commiserations. It provided mid-range enter-tainers at weekends and a consistent level of drinking all week. The Venetian House attracted custom from the nearby estates and from more distant areas that didn't have similar facilities. It had a kitchen that could cater a soup-and-sandwich lunch or an evening banquet.

A far cry from Novak's own pub, a neighbourhood convenience used only by locals. He looked across the car park and said, 'A gold mine.'

Danny Callaghan said, 'You reckon it's true — that Frank Tucker owns it?'

'Could be — probably gossip. My guess is he just likes the place. It's his neighbourhood.'

If you wanted to meet Frank Tucker, you made an arrangement to come to the Venetian House. He ate there most days, had all his parties there, and had daily meetings in a side room, along with his lieutenants and their soldiers.

'See that window, looks like stained glass?'

Novak was pointing to a wide window covering the width of an extension that jutted out into the car park. The image was of a singing gondolier, one arm held aloft, the other holding his trademark pole as he guided a pair of lovers beneath a bridge.

'Tacky, isn't it?' Callaghan said.

'Whether or not he owns the place, rumour is that Tucker bought that window — because he wanted something fancy in his home from home.'

'Nice to have it to splash around.' Callaghan

took a long, deep breath. 'Time to go in.'

'I'll be waiting.'

Callaghan smiled. 'Keep the engine running — and if you hear a bang — '

'Nothing like that's going to happen. Seriously. If Frank Tucker wants you dead, it won't be done here. In Frank's business, you don't piss on your own doorstep.'

★   ★   ★

Just inside the front door of the Venetian House, a bulky man stopped chewing gum long enough to ask, 'You're Callaghan, right?'

Danny Callaghan nodded.

'The jacks.'

Inside the inner door the pub was doing light business. Lunch was finished, here and there a customer lingered over the remnants of a meal or nursed a drink. The place was well staffed, the bartenders and waiters, male and female, wearing black trousers, white shirts and red waistcoats.

Callaghan followed the man to the gents toilet. There the man told Callaghan to take off his suede jacket and hold his arms out from his sides. He ran what looked like an electronic table-tennis paddle along Callaghan's body — over his arms and legs, between his legs, down his back and across his chest. He then lifted up the front of Callaghan's T-shirt and checked for wires.

Satisfied, he led Danny Callaghan through the pub to a side room. It was more of a large nook,

162

the kind of place a family might hire for a small birthday party. Most of one wall was taken up by the leaded window with the image of the gondolier. Pub tables and chairs in the centre, with deep sofa-type seating at the back. There, sitting near the window in a chunky wooden chair that could pass for a throne, leaning back, one knee crossed over the other, sat Frank Tucker.

That day in court, all those years back, Frank Tucker had been 19, his dark hair curly and full, his chubby but handsome face spoiled by acne. He was wearing dark blue Nike bottoms and a grey hoodie top.

Dead man, Callaghan — blood for blood.

Today, Frank Tucker was 27, hair cropped to a thin dark layer. He'd lost weight, his face now angular and tight, his frame obviously muscular beneath his well-cut dark grey suit and his open-collared blue shirt.

'Take a seat.'

Callaghan sat down and the man who'd searched him sat somewhere behind him. An Asian waiter appeared and Tucker said, 'What'll you have?'

'I'm okay,' Danny said.

Frank Tucker made a gesture and the waiter left.

He looked at Callaghan, his face blank, for a moment. Then he said, 'You've got something you want to say?' His voice was relaxed.

'I thought we ought to talk.'

'Did you, now?'

No sign of tension, no evidence of hate or

163

loathing, just mild interest. Tucker seemed relaxed, even amused. He made a hand gesture. 'Now's your chance. Don't be shy.'

'It's been eight years.'

'That long? How time flies.' He smiled. 'Or, in your case, maybe it dragged a bit.'

'I'm sorry. What I did to your cousin — I wish it had never happened.'

Tucker tilted his head. He nodded and said, 'There's a lot to be sorry about.'

'What you said, that day in the court — '

Dead man, Callaghan — blood for blood.

Tucker said, 'Bad times, when that happened. For everyone. Brendan's dad — my uncle — he drank a lot back then, drinks a lot more now. Used to be a man with a future. Brendan's ma — she's been in Swansea the past seven years, living with some young bloke.' He shrugged. 'I'm not saying that's all on account of what you did to Brendan. I'm just saying, when that happened, it was like something came unplugged in that family.'

'I never meant for any of it to happen.'

'You did what you did.'

'Have you had someone watching me?'

Tucker made an amused grunt. 'That's what this is about?'

'Some people in a blue van?'

'Fella — I haven't given you a thought in eight years. Your friend — Novak — when he called, said he was speaking on behalf of Danny Callaghan, I thought Danny *who?* Then he said it was about my cousin Brendan, and the penny dropped. When he told me you were out — eight

164

years, he said — all I thought was, Jesus, eight years, is it that long?'

'You threatened me. That day in court.'

'Did I?'

'You said you'd kill me.'

Tucker seemed surprised. 'If I did — we were all upset, relieved it was over, pissed-off. The blood was up.'

'You sounded like you meant it.'

'Probably I did, at the time.'

Tucker looked beyond Danny Callaghan, as though looking into the past. 'Brendan and me, he was, what — about fifteen years older. He saw himself as a sort of uncle, I suppose. He was my cousin and I loved him, but what Brendan did best was throw shapes. He got a swanky car, swanky clothes, jewellery, bodyguards. You could quote any line from *Scarface* and he'd do the whole scene for you.' Tucker's tone changed. 'Too tall to be Pacino, though. Too fat, and too dumb. Brendan talked to the crime hacks from the Sunday papers, made himself out to be a big player. But everyone knew Brendan would eventually fuck up. He did a bit of boxing early on, wasn't much good at it but he knew how to push people around. Hardly a week went by he didn't beat the shit out of someone. No way to build a business. Attracts the wrong kind of attention. And sooner or later — '

Tucker made a face.

Danny Callaghan said, 'All those years — in prison, I was warned, his family would get someone to do the job. Then, when I got out — '

'If I wanted to swat you, you wouldn't see it

165

coming. Why would I do that? Why would I bother? Have the cops crawling all over me? Like I say, I'm a busy man these days, I've got a business to run — didn't even know you were out. If I knew, it wouldn't have meant a thing.'

Callaghan felt uncertainty mixed with relief.

Is this real, or is it bullshit?

'What about the rest of the family?'

'Brendan's dad, like I say — the only way he's going to hurt anyone is some night he's driving home from the pub and he runs the car over some poor loser. Brendan's kid brothers — those two, I wouldn't worry. Dumber than Brendan ever was. Besides, they wouldn't lift a finger without asking me, and they haven't.'

Callaghan felt a sudden rush of anxiety — it had been stupid coming here. Just stirred things up.

'Blood for blood, you said.'

Again, Tucker was amused. 'Very Italian — I must have been watching *The Godfather* around that time. If you'd beaten the rap — probably I'd have swatted you. Me or one of Brendan's brothers — because watching you walk away, that would have put it up to us. Going to jail, that saved your life. The time you spent in there, eight years — you got what, twelve? — that was about right for what you did.'

Tucker was at ease, he wasn't trying too hard. He didn't give a shit what Callaghan believed. He was just saying the way it was.

Callaghan said, 'I appreciate you telling me this — what I mean is — '

Tucker said, 'I think that's that, then.'

Callaghan was about to get up. *Let it be.*

Then, knowing it would be unlikely he'd ever speak to Tucker again, he said, 'One thing — I'm not dragging all this back up again, but there's something I want you to know. About that night, with Brendan.'

Tucker didn't seem at all curious.

'You were wrong. I know you said what you thought was true, in court. And Brendan's dad, too. But you were wrong. It doesn't matter any more, but I want you to know that. The golf club I hit him with, it wasn't mine. I didn't bring it to his house. It was Brendan's. He came at me, I took it off him, he — '

Tucker nodded. 'I gave it to him. Birthday present — he taught me the game. Bloody awful golfer, I was. Never took to it.'

Danny Callaghan stared.

'It was part of the image he was working on — golf. Bought me membership in his local golf club — insisted on teaching me. His birthday, the one before he died, I gave him a club. The one you killed him with.'

Callaghan was breathing hard.

'Brendan was a prick — okay, we know that — but he was my cousin.' Tucker leaned forward. 'You killed him. Why it happened, that doesn't matter. As far as we were concerned, there was no way you weren't going to spend a long time in the smelly hotel. Eight years — I think that's about the right tab for killing my cousin.'

Danny Callaghan stood up. He turned and walked out of the nook, the bodyguard leading the way. The bodyguard held the front door open. 'Mind how you go,' he said.

★   ★   ★

'Everything okay?'

Getting into the car, Danny Callaghan just nodded. He didn't trust himself to speak. Novak looked across and said, 'Take your time — we'll talk later.'

As the car started up, Danny Callaghan stared at the leaded windows with the coloured glass. Somewhere behind that glass the bastard was sitting, his mind already on something more important than eight years wasted.

'That *fucker*!'

'Take it easy', Novak said.

'Eight fucking *years*.'

'Tell me about it when we're clear of this place, okay?'

Chapter 21

It was dark by the time they got back to Glencara. Half a mile from the Blue Parrot, Novak pulled his Audi into the car park of St Aidan's church and switched off the engine.

'Okay, tell me.'

'The golf club I killed Big Brendan Tucker with was the odd one out. It didn't match any other club in his bag.'

'I know all about that.'

'That *fucker*!'

168

Across the road from the church, an end house on a street of small council houses was ablaze with coloured lights. Santa sat atop the roof — his reindeer were on the side of the house and also lined along the front gutter. The legs of an upside-down Santa stuck up from the chimney. Another lit-up Santa tirelessly climbed up and down a short ladder. A blow-up snowman swayed between a blow-up Santa and an under-dressed Angel of the Lord. Christmas stars of assorted colours blinked from all sides. There wasn't a surface left undecorated. Before Callaghan went to prison, Christmas lights were an indoor thing, draped on the Christmas tree, with maybe a few lights around the front window. Now, on estates all over Dublin, the competition to see who could publicly hang the most bulbs per square foot was relentless. This house had to be the champion.

'Talk to me,' Novak said.

Callaghan told him that Frank Tucker seemed to have genuinely forgotten about his threat. He considered Danny Callaghan dealt with long ago.

'And you're pissed off why?'

'It wasn't manly fisticuffs, the judge said. What made the difference was whether I brought that golf club.'

He told Novak what Tucker had said about the club.

'*Eight years*, he said, *just about the right tab for killing my cousin.*'

'It's done now.'

169

'Eight years. And those years — if I hadn't been sitting in that shithouse — my whole *life* might — *fuck* it!'

Callaghan's eyes were closed, two fingers pinching the bridge of his nose.

'Let it go,' Novak said. 'It's all done now — the good of it and the bad, the right and the wrong — all set in stone, no way of changing any of it.'

'I deserved it.'

'What's done is done.'

Callaghan was calm now. 'That night, I hit him — he came at me with the knife and I saw the golf club in the corner and I went for it and I hit him once and that should have been enough.'

'Look — '

Callaghan held a hand up. His voice was low, he spoke quickly. 'I've never told anyone this — not the lawyers, not Hannah. After I hit him with the club, it just felt right. Big bad Brendan, the heavies at his beck and call, he could stomp on anyone, as the mood took him. No fear at all, just contempt. So I hit him again with the club. Because I wanted to.'

'Danny — '

'He'd already dropped the knife — no *need* to hit him again, but I did. Because it *felt* right.' Callaghan paused, then he said, 'Maybe because it felt *good*. I hit him again and he screamed, and I knew right away I'd done damage, and I threw the club down and I walked away.'

Callaghan's head was low, he was looking straight down at his feet.

'Danny, let it go. Chance and impulse, that's

what it's mostly about — people act on instinct, do what they think is best at the time. Let it go.'

They sat in silence for a while, then Callaghan sat up straight, his head back against the headrest. 'Frank Tucker's changed. Used to be a small-time thug, now he's Mr Cool.'

'They all want to be Al Capone, those guys, or Don Corleone or Tony Soprano. I've met that sort, down through the years — through Jane's job. She dealt with a lot of today's hard men back when they were teenagers. She still goes to the occasional funeral when one of them's found toes-up in an alley. And they're all nice guys, they love their grannies and they're mad about their kids. Get in their way, they'll nail you to the floor and then complain you spoiled their evening.'

Across the road, in front of the Christmas house, a couple of kids had linked arms and were twirling in a circle, singing about Rudolph's nose. Their parents, all woolly hats and scarves, smiled and stamped their feet against the cold.

Callaghan sat there, his head back, and Novak sat beside him for about twenty minutes, by which time the dancing kids had gone and been replaced by new waves of sightseers come to visit the glowing house. Finally, Novak said, 'You ready?'

Callaghan nodded.

It took just a few minutes to drive to the Blue Parrot, where Callaghan had left his car.

'You going home to mope all evening?'

Callaghan smiled. 'No, I've got to do some

grocery shopping. Then I'll go home and mope.'

'Drop down later for a drink.'

'Maybe.'

'I need the business.'

Callaghan held out his hand. 'Thanks again.'

Novak shook his hand. 'No problem.'

'All those years, I should have told you how it happened, what I did.'

'None of us is going straight to heaven.'

He watched until Danny Callaghan had driven away.

★   ★   ★

His name was Stephen. It was cold inside the car, he was wearing just his jeans and a T-shirt and a thin Hugo Boss jacket, but he was sweating.

Get it right.

He liked this part of it. The anticipation was almost as —

But right now there was something —

Could be important, might be nothing —

He couldn't remember.

A thought, sliding, like it was a picture falling through his head, and it wouldn't stay still long enough for him to —

Gone —

And then there was another one, sliding down behind it, and he tried to get hold of that — *shit, gone.*

Zippo said, 'You ready?'

Stephen said, 'Just a minute.'

Sweat trickling down the side of his face, sweat

on the back of his neck.

'Come on, let's get it over.' Zippo was a nervous type, never seemed to enjoy his work.

Fuck him. Get the feeling right.

When there's a job on, you need a few lines of blow — it clears all the shit away so the inside of your head is clean, everything's got a sharp edge to it —

Sometimes, though, it was like this. Things sliding, things —

Stephen shook his head violently, took a long breath and used the back of his hand to wipe the sweat from his cheek.

He reached down to the floor of the car and picked up the big black automatic. In his hand it was massive and it weighed nothing. Smooth, hard.

Yes.

He was out of the car and walking, Zippo ten paces behind, watching his back.

Left the car unlocked.

Minute from now, don't want to be fumbling with keys.

That'd be fun — come back, car's gone.

He made a small hooting noise.

The sweat on his forehead was icy cold.

He could feel a single drop of warm sweat running down his back.

Everything clear, everything sharp.

Clear sky.

Stephen could see the craters on the moon.

Everything around him.

Sharp, every edge.

Smooth, every surface.

Nothing sliding now, nothing falling inside his head.

His pace regular, in time with the beat he could feel in every part of his body.

Me and him.

It was like there was no one else in the world, just Stephen and his target.

Almost there.

Nothing else on the Earth. No buildings, no mountains, no seas, no other people. Nothing. Not even Zippo. Just a big, smooth ball turning in space. Two little dots — Stephen and the loser he was about to kill, the distance between them closing down.

Him and me —

Clear as that, sharp as that. Two people on a big, smooth ball in space. One living, one dying.

The big gun was a feather in his hand.

Two in the chest, one in the head.

This machine, this big fucker — you put two from that in an elephant's chest and down it goes.

Then one in the head, for keeps.

Two in the chest, one in the head.

Mozambique Triple Tap.

Closer, steady stride. Any second now, his victim would turn and see him coming.

Big boys' rules.

★ ★ ★

'Arogancki bestie.'

The first time he'd heard the words was the afternoon all those years ago when his father came home early from work and announced that he'd been fired.

Novak slipped into his leather swivel chair, behind the oak desk in the back office of the Blue Parrot. Another hour before business got heavy. About the time he usually poured himself a coffee and came back here for a break. Stay away from caffeine, his doctor told him. Novak figured an evening without the respite of his ten-minute break and his mug of coffee would be far more damaging than anything the caffeine could do.

'*Arogancki bestie.*'

That time, towards the end of the 1950s, Novak had been approaching his teens, his father had been in Ireland for a dozen years and only when he was angry would he lapse into Polish. There had been problems at the furniture store where he worked. One of the four dispatch workers had been let go and the other three would have to work extra hours without overtime. Bad times, few jobs, waves of emigrants leaving for England. Of the three remaining workers, only Novak's father made a token protest about the buckshee overtime. Then he joined the others in doing as he was told.

Two weeks later, his boss called him in, told him to fuck off.

'What have I done?'

The boss's face was blank. No anger, no gloating. He was doing what he had the power to do. There was a price to extract for the momentary rebellion and now it was safe to use his strength.

'I don't have to explain myself to you. Get out.'

At home that afternoon Novak's father spent an hour in the front garden, on his knees, using a shears to trim the grass, the repetitive labour helping the anger seep away. Sitting at the kitchen table, he poured Novak a glass of Taylor-Keith. 'Arogancki bestie.' His tone was mild. 'That's how I think of such people — arrogant beasts. The strength of the beast and the arrogance of the man. People with position, people with guns, people with the power of the state behind them, people who wield power over others — in business, in war, in the home, wherever. They feel the strength of the beast, they taste the arrogance of the man, and the sickness takes them. All my life I've seen it, everywhere I've been.'

Novak's father had been 22 and a merchant sailor, his ship docked at Liverpool, when the Germans invaded Poland from one side and the Russians went in from the other. He didn't return home for over fifty years. After fighting with Sikorski's army in France, he escaped to England and was reorganised into a Polish rifle division under Allied command. 'Butchery on a grand scale, all sides, all the time. In those years, the arogancki bestie struggled to own the very world we stand on.'

Badly wounded, he sat out the last year of the war, then he married an Irish nurse and they came to Ireland. He didn't visit Poland until 1995, two years before he died. Most of his immediate family were among the country's five million casualties. There was a dispute about which side, the Germans or the Russians, exterminated which members of his family.

'The Cardinal Sins you learned in school — lust and gluttony, greed — just human weakness. But the real sins, they come when you surrender to the power of the beast.'

Shortly after he took over his pub, Novak opened up one morning and two men in cheap suits came in and told him they were there to help. 'Bad neighbourhood — lots of tough bastards.' The taller one made little effort to hide his sneer. 'The kind of people who'd set fire to a pub just to warm their hands on the flames, you know what I mean?'

He leaned across the counter, big smile on his face. 'Know what I mean?' he said again. His shoulders were broad, his hands big, and when he put his elbows on the counter and leaned towards Novak he casually coiled his fingers into fists.

'How much?' Novak said.

'Two hundred a week,' the smaller man said, and Novak hit the bigger one in the face with a beer glass. They both started running — Novak was slimmer then, fitter, and he caught the bigger one before he'd gone fifty yards. He went through his pockets and found a name and address on a doctor's prescription.

'Anything happens, I know where you live.'

Nothing happened. Fifteen years had passed and Novak wondered if he'd have the nerve now to fight back. These days, the arrogant beasts had guns, and they were usually high

177

on something or other.

After his meeting with Frank Tucker, it seemed like Danny Callaghan had nothing to worry about from that quarter. But something was stirring and Callaghan had been drawn into it. The arrogant beasts that slaughtered Walter Bennett, whoever they were, were still roaming. Since the shooting, Novak had hidden an extra three hammers at strategic points around the pub. He wondered if he should have something more lethal within reach. He pictured himself those years back, angered as he had been by the two thugs, this time with a gun in his hand. No, he decided. There were enough arrogant beasts around.

★ ★ ★

Danny Callaghan parked in his usual spot across from the Hive and took two bags of groceries from the boot. He'd read for a while. Eat, then maybe go down to Novak's place, finish the day off with a couple of drinks.

To his right, from the corner of his eye, someone moving fast. He turned and saw Oliver's grandfather, running. Away from the Hive, out onto the green, his step irregular and ungainly on the uneven ground. In the middle of the green, lit only by sparse light from distant lamp-posts, half a dozen people gathered. Before Oliver's grandfather reached them he gave a harsh, despairing cry that echoed across the green. A woman moved towards him, attempting to hold him back, but he brushed past her. After a few more steps he bent over, then went down on his knees, a young man reaching out to help him.

Danny Callaghan stood there, staring out across the green, until he heard a siren in the distance. Then he went upstairs to his flat.

Day Eight

Chapter 22

Of the forty or so police officers in the room at Garda HQ in the Phoenix Park there were half a dozen uniforms, the rest were plainclothes detectives. All but three of those attending what had been labelled the 'special incidents conference' were men. Tables had been arranged in a rectangular shape around the periphery of the room, with the police officers facing one another.

Detective Sergeant Bob Tidey nodded to a colleague across the room, a detective sergeant with whom he'd worked a couple of years back. Some of the faces were familiar, most were strangers. At the top of the room, instantly recognisable to everyone present, Assistant Commissioner Colin O'Keefe was getting to his feet. To O'Keefe's right, three chief superintendents. To his left, a young woman garda taking notes.

'Sit down everyone, let's not take all day.'

Bob Tidey found one of the last empty chairs. Those left standing clustered near the door.

O'Keefe sat down, tapped the table with the butt end of his pen and waited for the incidental noises of shifting chairs and tailing-off conversations to end. Then he said, 'As you know, this special incidents conference was scheduled in advance of what appears to be the latest gangland killing. The function of the conference was to pull together the members involved in the various threads of recent gangland investigations. We'll have a report on this latest murder presently.'

Each detective had been given a blue cardboard folder on entering the room. Bob Tidey opened his and found that it contained several sheets of A4 paper, blank except for the Garda Siochana letterhead at the top of each page.

That's helpful. He closed the folder.

Assistant Commissioner O'Keefe continued. 'This morning, the aim is to familiarise ourselves with the totality of the various cases under investigation — if anything rings a bell, any linkages, any patterns, speak up. The minutes from this conference will be circulated later today — discuss it with your fellow officers back at the station. If any two pieces of information look like they might fit together, if you need further detail — there'll be a sheet going around. I want names and stations from you all, along with mobile numbers and email addresses. Don't be shy, keep in touch with one another — that's what these meetings are about — ask questions, share information.'

O'Keefe leaned forward and ticked off a line on a sheet of paper in front of him.

'Let's go over the details of the current incidents. For the benefit of any member who doesn't know you, begin with your name, rank and station.'

Member.

After twenty-six years in the force, Detective Sergeant Bob Tidey still found the use of the word silly. Over the years, the in-house term *member* had derived from *Member of the Garda Siochana.* New recruits, back in Templemore, not yet used to referring to one another as *members,* used to joke about members rising in the morning or members waving from trains. They perpetually promised to introduce members to their girlfriends. Even now Tidey never heard the word in a police context without thinking of his colleagues as pricks — which, in the case of some of them, was fair enough.

'Conor?'

A detective inspector from Finglas nodded to Assistant Commissioner O'Keefe and began outlining the details of the four gangland killings, much of which was already known to most of those in the room. 'Murders one, two and three came out of a business deal that went sour — the Colleys and the Molloy gangs, all locals. We're expecting another one or two before they call it quits, but hopefully it won't spread beyond that. Victim number four was an idiot who pulled out of a plan to shake down a racehorse owner — and then went ahead and did the job on his own. His former partners caught up with him.'

Assistant Commissioner O'Keefe said, 'As we thought, it looks like it's just a localised spasm — two minor sets of headbangers.'

The Finglas detective said, 'It's simmering. There've been several beatings, a number of death threats, three people have gone out of circulation — we assume they're lying low, probably outside the country.'

Colin O'Keefe said, 'Given that there's a dozen or so heavyweight gangs in the city, a lot of their people permanently coked-up, occasional bloodshed is to be expected. The lesser incidents — they don't make as big a media splash, but they may be a symptom of problems to come.'

A sergeant from Coolock gave details of an incident in which four shots had been fired into the living room of a house. 'The woman of the house came close to being clipped — says she knows no reason why the house might have been targeted. Her husband works for a bookie, so it could be some kind of extortion racket, though he says not. There's another family, same name, two roads away, the older son isn't long out of Mountjoy, two years on a drug charge. It might be that he stepped on someone's toes and they shot at the wrong house.'

An inspector from Clondalkin gave details of the beating of a young man, four nights back. 'He's one of Tommy Farr's enforcers — what we hear is Tommy's semi-retired, living in Spain for the past few weeks. And now that this kid hasn't got Tommy to hide behind he ended up being stomped on by some people who figure they owe him a thumping.'

'My heart bleeds for him', Assistant Commissioner O'Keefe said. 'The Glencara killing a few nights back, Walter Bennett — who's got that?'

To Bob Tidey's left, a garda said, 'Me, sir,' and identified himself as Detective Sergeant Michael

Wyndham. He rattled off the known facts. 'I got word yesterday, sir, from Gravesend Street station, a member there tells me he recruited Bennett as a confidential informant some weeks ago. Might be related to that. Bennett had a record — burglary, car theft and the like — nothing you'd expect to get him killed. We're still exploring the possibility of a gang connection. The manner of the killing — it was particularly vicious — suggests a personal motive.'

O'Keefe nodded his thanks. 'As we see, although the media is drooling at the thought of all-out gang war, these killings seem isolated. All of them can be explained in terms of local feuds. However, in this kind of situation the media has great fun roasting the Minister for Justice. And over the past few days the Minister has — ' O'Keefe paused ' — expressed his concern. As a result, the Garda Commissioner will be announcing the setting up of Operation Sledge Hammer — '

O'Keefe smiled as a low-key chuckle rippled around the table.

' — To which the Minister, as part of his War on Crime, has pledged his full support. Increased overtime has been authorised. Rapid-response units have already stepped up activities within the areas of the city where the most serious of these offences have occurred.'

O'Keefe looked down at his clipboard. 'Now, this latest killing, at the Hive last evening. That has all the hallmarks — Bob?'

Detective Sergeant Bob Tidey looked up. 'I

184

should be out there now, supervising the searches, not — '

O'Keefe didn't look up when he spoke. 'Details, Bob.'

Tidey nodded. 'Oliver Snead, aged — '

'Name, Bob, and station. For members who don't know you.'

Tidey held back a moment, as though he was waiting for his blood pressure to stabilise. 'Detective Sergeant Bob Tidey, Cavendish Avenue. This kid's named Oliver Snead, aged 19, both parents are dead, he lived with his grandfather. He had no record. He was shot dead last night, on the green in front of the Hive. End of story.'

O'Keefe stared. 'And that's it?'

Bob Tidey said, 'More or less. We know why, we don't know who, and I doubt if we'll catch them.'

O'Keefe kept his voice steady. 'Perhaps you'd share what details you have with us, Bob?'

'He owed them money. He couldn't pay. They shot him.'

'Witnesses?'

'Several.'

'And?'

'Deaf, dumb and blind.'

'Forensics?'

'They used a gun.'

O'Keefe made a face. 'Bob, please.'

'Large-calibre automatic. We already found two of the shells, I expect the gun went straight to the bottom of the Liffey. Two shots in the chest, third one in the head.'

185

'Any known connection with any of the other incidents?'

'Here's what we know. Three months ago, a patrol pulled over a car on Oscar Traynor Road. About ten in the evening — no particular reason, except there were two young fellas inside. The passenger did a runner, the driver was arrested. There was an amount of heroin in the pocket of the passenger door — the driver said he knew nothing about it, claimed he didn't know the passenger's name, said he was just a fella he gave a lift to. Lying, of course.'

'How much heroin?'

'Couple of grand, street value. The passenger was Oliver Snead. Seems young Oliver was a user, ran up a bill with his suppliers. They offered him a way to work it off, making heroin deliveries to retailers around the Coolock area.' Tidey glanced up. 'We got all this from the kid's grandfather. I know him — James Snead.'

O'Keefe's double nod said get on with it.

'When Oliver lost the heroin package he was told he had a month to come up with three grand. When that didn't work they put the arm on the grandfather — the most he could put together was fifteen hundred. They took it, and last night they killed the boy.'

'Who are the witnesses?'

'Some of the kid's mates were there — apparently they had a regular cider party — and we talked to them. The gunmen weren't masked. But no one's saying anything.'

'The grandfather?'

'He says if we find the man who threatened

him he'll identify him, and give evidence.'

'If he'd had the guts to come to us in the first place — ' O'Keefe shook his head. 'The message we need to get out to these people — and this applies in most of the cases we're dealing with this morning — is that we can't do this alone, we need them to stand up to the thugs. And we'll back them all the way if they do that.'

Bob Tidey leaned forward towards the Assistant Commissioner. 'We're among friends here, sir — no media, no need to throw shapes. These people — '

'If the grandfather had come to us — '

' — We might have pulled in the bastard who threatened him and after a couple of days Oliver and James Snead would have been dead. Standing up to the thugs — it's a hard line to sell. Because these people live with the thugs. The thugs know where they work, where they shop, where they drink and where their kids go to school. And if I lived in that fear factory I wouldn't talk to us either.'

'Bob — '

'This shit has been building up for thirty years and we left them to stew in it. We patrol some areas of this city like we're dealing with Fallujah. People get murdered there — for a long time we could live with that. The way a lot of people see it, the ghettoes aren't a problem, they're a solution — containable units to isolate the people who don't matter.'

O'Keefe said, 'That's not the way it is today.'

'Really? If things are different now it's because the financial-centre crowd and the models and the lawyers and the journalists are powdering their noses. And the gangs that supply their jollies are swaggering around on the stylish side of town and the Minister is worried.' He paused to lower his voice. 'He wants us to go into the estates and break up the gangs, and we want people like Oliver Snead's grandfather to stand up to the thugs and do the job we never did.'

In the silence that followed, Assistant Commissioner O'Keefe stared at the detective sergeant. In the fifteen years since he'd worked with Bob Tidey, as a fledgling detective, O'Keefe had taken the high road to senior office. All that time, Tidey had continued rummaging in the city's wastelands, where the villains called the shots and the bodies were found.

O'Keefe said, 'All very fine, Bob. But we are where we are — however we got here — and what we need to be is constructive, and I don't see how this helps.'

Tidey took a long breath. His voice was quiet. 'It doesn't help — it's just the way it is. And what we're doing this morning, it has nothing to do with the way it is for these people. It's about the way it is for us. Our image problem. It's about the Minister and the Commissioner, and it's about looking like we're on top of things.'

One of the chief superintendents to O'Keefe's right leaned forward. 'Detective Sergeant Tidey, the lack of moral fibre among these people is one thing — but when experienced police officers pander to spineless behaviour we're lowering ourselves to their level. This — ' and the point of his rigid index finger tapped the table in front of him ' — is about taking responsibility.'

Bob Tidey nodded. Then he sat up straight and folded his arms.

His tone was conversational. 'Would you like a sausage to go with that waffle?'

The chief superintendent stared, as though mentally photographing Tidey.

Colin O'Keefe raised a warning hand. 'Bob — '

Tidey said, 'No offence, sir, but I've got an active investigation. So, if it's all right?' He stood up.

Colin O'Keefe nodded.

Chapter 23

Way out on the green, eight uniformed policemen were down on all fours, in a line, inching forward, doing a fingertip search of the grass around the murder scene. Danny Callaghan stood at the window of his third-floor flat, cup of coffee in hand. The cops were wrapped in bulky pants and thick winter jackets, but that still had to be miserable work on a misty December morning. An hour back he'd watched a hearse make its way onto the green area. They were preparing to remove Oliver's body.

'It's wrong, it's not fair,' was all Oliver's grandfather said when Callaghan went up to the fifth floor last night and knocked on his door. A couple of neighbours were inside, women, sitting silently with the grandfather. One of them nodded at Callaghan, the other whispered that there was a pot of fresh tea. Callaghan shook his head.

He bent down in front of the grandfather. 'I'm sorry for your trouble,' he said. It was limp, but sometimes the routine phrases said it best.

The grandfather nodded, as though he valued the words.

'He was a good kid,' Callaghan said.

'It isn't fair.'

Callaghan didn't stay long.

Now, down in front of the Hive, a couple of uniformed gardai hurried across the green as an unmarked black Volvo came to a halt. A tall uniformed officer climbed out of the back seat and went to meet them.

★ ★ ★

Detective Sergeant Bob Tidey turned in time to see Assistant Commissioner Colin O'Keefe arrive.

Tidey sighed. 'Wonderful. That's all we need.' He waited while O'Keefe, accompanied by the two uniforms who'd gone to greet him, made his way across the green.

'Sir.'

'Bob.'

O'Keefe's expression suggested that he was mending fences. 'In case you're worried, I'm not here to add pressure. I just wanted to take a look at the scene, if that's okay.'

'I'm not worried.'

O'Keefe took Tidey by the elbow and moved

190

him some distance away from the others. 'Are you okay, Bob?'

'I'm fine.'

'That's not the impression — '

'Okay, I'm not fine. I'm tired.'

'It gets to us all, from time to time.'

'I'm tired of this crap, yeah, but I'm more tired of the ignorant bullshit. For Christ's sake — *moral fibre* — you've got idiots who want me to pressure Oliver's friends to make themselves the next target — Jesus, Colin, where do you get these gobshites from?'

'He's a good administrator, one of the best.'

Tidey gave a dismissive grunt. 'This kind of thing, it's not like some evil spirit descended on the city. We sow, we reap. Chicago in the 1920s, London in the 1960s, Moscow in the 1990s — when things change, and people have money that they didn't use to have, they find new ways to spend it. Other people find new ways to take it. Supply and demand, market forces.'

O'Keefe said, 'Not that it matters, but I agree with most of what you said this morning. About the Minister and the Commissioner and about being seen to do something.' His voice softened. 'But that's the real world, too, every bit as real as this shit, and it has to be handled.'

Tidey was quiet for a moment. Then he said, 'A generation ago, it was booze and grass for the relaxing classes, and heroin in the ghettoes. The smack killed a lot of kids — overdosing, dirty needles and HIV — but that was okay. We left them to it. Then the middle classes got a major taste for cocaine, which means there're market opportunities for any kid fucked-up enough to risk a bullet in the head.'

'The Minister — '

'Ghetto entrepreneurs. Look around you, Colin — we're not the island of saints and scholars any more, we're the nation of entrepreneurs. Everyone wants to be an entrepreneur, including the psychos who run the drug business. They understand the importance of market share. They can't use the courts to enforce their mergers and acquisitions, so they use guns.' Bob Tidey kept his voice low and even. 'I've known James Snead, Oliver's grandfather, for a long time.'

'Did he have a record?'

Tidey shook his head. 'James Snead was a brickie — from back in the bad old days, when brickies had to spend half their time looking for work in England, because there was damn-all happening here. He was a union man, and by the time the construction boom came along he was on a couple of blacklists, so he didn't do so well, but that was okay — he had a family and he got enough work to get by. His wife died young, he raised his daughter himself. She got pregnant, she had Oliver, and when the kid was eight months old she and her boyfriend overdosed on heroin in their flat in Ballymun.'

O'Keefe said, 'That's hard.'

Bob Tidey was looking up towards the Hive. 'James Snead came visiting next day. He heard Oliver crying, so he broke in, found the bodies, found Oliver sitting in his own shit in a playpen, six feet away from his dead mammy. That's how

James came to raise Oliver.'

O'Keefe nodded. 'Some parts of this city, back in the eighties and nineties, there were a lot of grandparents raising kids.'

'When Oliver got in trouble, James Snead gave the thugs all he could raise and a promise of the rest. It ought to have worked. Maybe some tosspot wanted to send a message to everyone who owed him money. Or maybe he was just feeling under the weather and he wanted to cheer himself up. These days, killing some poor fucker's sometimes just a way of marking your territory. We've managed to create a lot of young thugs who know nothing about life except how to take it.'

O'Keefe said, 'You know this kind of thing is taken seriously these days, Bob. And that's why a coordinated response, at the highest level, is what I've been — '

Bob Tidey smiled. 'Operation Sledge Hammer, is it? The Minister and the Commissioner must have done some late-night brainstorming to come up with that one. Everything sounds more efficient if you give it a military title. These people can't do a shit without announcing that they're launching Operation Bowel Movement.'

Tidey bent and picked up a shard of glass hidden in the grass at his feet. He walked about ten feet to a litter bin beside a bench and dropped it in. When he returned, O'Keefe said, 'We do PR because we have to — there are needs that have to be met. That doesn't mean we're not also trying to get on top of this mess.'

Tidey looked at the Assistant Commissioner.

'I'm sorry, Colin, you didn't make things the way they are. All those years ago, when James Snead rang 999, I was in uniform, I was first on the scene. I went up to the flat and I saw the bodies, the shitty playpen. And I found James Snead next door, in a neighbour's flat, with Oliver in his lap. He was shushing the baby, telling him everything would be okay. And last night I went to James Snead's flat, to tell him Oliver was dead. And, all down these years, I don't know what I could have done differently — or what you could have done differently, or what the fucking Minister could have done — so that it wouldn't work out this way.'

★ ★ ★

Danny Callaghan finished his coffee. His first job this afternoon was to collect a package from the Mater Hospital and deliver it to an address on the south side. Later, he had to drive some business type from Clonskeagh to Wicklow town, wait for a couple of hours and then drive him back in the early evening. He dumped the half-eaten cheese sandwich he'd made, washed his cup, plate, knife and spoon and put them away. He checked again the notes he'd made on the day's jobs, put on his brown suede jacket and inspected himself in the mirror.

On his way to the car, he could see a gaggle of cops, uniformed and plain-clothes, heads together, near the white tent out on the green. Despite the light rain, the line of cops was still inching across the killing ground. Approaching the black Hyundai, Callaghan thumbed the remote and the central locking clicked open. Inside the car it was cold. When he started the engine he used the wipers to clear the rain from the windscreen. The front passenger door opened and a young man in a Nike top and sweatpants got into the car, sat down and held a gun in his lap, the muzzle turned towards Callaghan.

He won't shoot.

Not with the police just fifty yards away.

'This distance, they won't even hear the shot,' the man said.

For an instant, Danny Callaghan could see himself slumped against the wheel, bleeding, while the man got out of the car and walked away.

'He told me everything was cool,' Callaghan said.

The man said, 'Who?'

'Frank Tucker.'

'That right?'

'He said — '

'Drive,' the man said. 'We're not going far.'

Chapter 24

On the way out of the estate they drove past a parked police car, the driver chatting on his mobile.

'Take a left here.'

'You ought to ring him. Me and Frank Tucker, everything's okay.'

'Shut up and drive.'

Pointless.

This wouldn't happen unless Frank Tucker gave the go-ahead.

Mistake, going to see him.

All it did was remind him of a loose end he had to cut off.

The young man gave directions and several minutes later they were driving under a railway bridge, then a sharp left and into a cul-de-sac.

'Here.'

When Callaghan pulled in to the kerb behind a light grey Toledo the young man said, 'Kill the engine.'

The driver's door opened and fear jerked Callaghan's head around. For a moment he couldn't place the face of the man who stood there, a small pistol down by his side.

'Last time we met,' the man said, 'what you told me was if you ever saw me again I'd get my pimply arse kicked. That still the case?'

★   ★   ★

The houses in the cul-de-sac were mostly boarded up. The street was worn and dirty, as if it had been carelessly used for a long time, then abandoned. 'Get out, get into the back of the car in front.' Karl Prowse stood back as Callaghan got out of the car. His partner got out the far side and climbed into the driving seat of the Toledo.

Karl said, 'Give me an excuse and we can end it right here.' He followed Callaghan into the back of the Toledo.

He used a plastic strip to tie Callaghan's hands and put a black hood over his head. He patted him down, found his mobile and switched it off.

'Why don't we see how far down you can crouch?' For encouragement, he used the butt of his gun to hit the smart bastard on the side of the head, just above the ear.

As the car moved forward, Karl told Robbie, 'We're in no hurry — rules of the road all the way.'

★ ★ ★

When they took off the hood Danny Callaghan found that he was standing inside some kind of warehouse. It was Karl who took off the hood. The other guy, standing off to one side, had put away his gun. There was a man in his early sixties standing in front of Callaghan. Short grey hair and a face with as many creases as a crumpled paper bag.

'Bit cold in here. Sorry about that, but I needed somewhere quiet for a chat.' His hands were in the pockets of his bright red anorak. 'My name is Lar Mackendrick.'

There were empty steel shelves running along both walls, steel pillars at intervals down each side. The floor was bare and dirty. A couple of rickety chairs and a dirty table. In one corner, a makeshift canteen — a sink, a counter with a dusty camping cooker.

'Why am I here?'

Mackendrick gestured. 'Look around you — a

bit of a dump, this place. It's a has-been industrial estate, mostly closed down. The kind of place where no one would hear you scream.' He smiled. 'But you don't want to find that out the hard way.'

Callaghan stared at the man's lined face. Mackendrick spoke of violence in the calm tones of someone musing over the choices on a menu.

Mackendrick said, 'Talk to me about Frank Tucker.'

'What about him?'

The young man who had the gun said, 'He told me Frank Tucker said everything's cool.'

Mackendrick said, 'Is that right?'

'What's this got to do with Tucker?'

'You went to see Tucker recently. Are you working for him?'

'I killed a cousin of his, a long time ago. Went to jail for it.'

'I know that.'

'I just got out a few months back. I went to see him, to clear the air. He told me he doesn't hold a grudge.'

Mackendrick smiled. 'Frank's a forgiving kind of guy.' He looked down at the floor, kicked idly at a pebble. 'Tell me why you interfered when my good friends here went about their business with Walter Bennett?'

The plastic binder around Callaghan's hands seemed suddenly to tighten.

'These two, they came into a pub, waving guns — people having a drink. I did what I did, it was instinct.'

'We had business with Walter, you interfered.'

'This hurts.' Callaghan held up his hands. 'Could you at least loosen it?'

Mackendrick said, 'I'll be honest with you — the way it is, someone sticks his nose in, screws up something important — normally you'd have been stiffed by now. And Karl here would've been delighted to oblige.'

Karl Prowse's voice was harsh. 'Not such a big guy now.'

Mackendrick said, 'You've already met Karl Prowse. This other young chap — Robbie Nugent. Last time you met he was carrying a shotgun. These lads were just doing a simple job — you fucked it up. Maybe we're entitled to some kind of compensation.'

Callaghan wondered if he should say he was sorry, make some gesture of submissiveness.

A bad move.

There'd been a lot of this type in prison. You grovel, it brings out the contempt, they enjoy seeing you hurt and they want more of it.

Perhaps he ought to put up more of a front? His hands bound, that wouldn't be very convincing.

Mackendrick said, 'Your ex-wife's name is Hannah. You're still close with her. Her new husband's name is Leon.' He was ticking points off on his fingers. 'Your girlfriend's name is Alexandra Kane. We know all about where these people live, where they work.'

Callaghan stared at him.

'Your girlfriend, for instance, has an apartment down by the waterfront, fifth floor. She — '

'She's not my — '

' — took you home Saturday night. Your ex-wife — '

'What's this about?'

'What I want you to understand is this — at any time, I lift a finger and someone close to you is stiffed. One or two of them, or three. And you too. We do who we can immediately, and when everything calms down we wipe up whoever's left.'

'This is — '

Mackendrick put a finger to his lips. 'Pay attention. Your ex will get preferential treatment. First on the list.'

'*For Christ sake!*'

'It's not just Karl here you've to worry about — there's a whole army of people I can tap into. One word and she's in the boot of a car, and the last thing she'll do before she dies is curse your name.'

'This is crazy — '

'What I want you to say is — *yes.*'

'To what?'

'To everything. Anything. Whatever I want from you. Before we go any further, I want you to say yes.'

'You can't just — '

'Oh, I can.' Mackendrick came closer. His left hand held Callaghan's chin. His touch was gentle. He moved his face to within inches of Callaghan's. 'Think of ten years from now. Coming up to Christmas. You're what — what age are you now?'

'I'm thirty-two.'

There were tiny hairs at the corners of

Mackendrick's mouth, where he'd shaved carelessly. The skin on the bridge of his nose was dry and rough.

'Imagine you're forty-two. Can you do that? Fifty-two. Sixty-two. Ten more years. Another ten. Imagine you're eighty-two. Imagine the next fifty years. All the Christmases. All the meals you'll eat and the booze you'll drink, the places you'll go, the things you'll see. Imagine the women you'll ride. The children — you don't have children, right? — imagine the children you'll have, the grandchildren.' He snapped his fingers close to Callaghan's face.

'Gone. Snuffed out. I click my fingers and it disappears. Never happens.'

He snapped his fingers again.

'Bit of a waste, right? I've nothing to gain from killing you. What I need to do is show you how important it is to please me. You please me, I don't click my fingers. I don't send Karl to kick in your ex-wife's ribcage before he cuts her throat. Your girlfriend gets home from work and she finds Robbie lying on her bed, waiting to show her what he can do with a knife — no need for that to happen.'

'What do you want me to do?'

'Say yes.'

Callaghan said, 'Yes.'

Lar Mackendrick nodded. 'Walter let us down. We needed Walter for some routine jobs, nothing too heavy. Then we found out Walter was a bit of a mouth. I had to click my fingers. You got in the way, but that's been put right. What we need done, you're well able for it, a man with your record. Do it, and you and your ex-missus and your friends, you stay healthy. And I bung a couple of grand in your pocket.'

'I don't want money.'

Mackendrick smiled. 'That's up to you.'

'What do you want me to do?'

'Nothing too difficult. Driving, mainly.'

'That's all?'

'Mainly.'

'Just tell me.'

'The reason Walter died, he had a mouth. What I'm about to tell you — it could make you die, if you get talkative. Maybe your ex-wife, your girlfriend too, whoever we can reach in a hurry.'

'I don't gossip.'

'I have a project that needs someone who can get me a car when I need it. No questions asked. And do some driving. And since Walter's out of the picture, you're elected as my little helper.'

'If I get caught doing anything illegal — I've got four more years in jail hanging over me.'

'Then you'll have to make sure you don't get caught.' Mackendrick raised his eyebrows, tilted his head, inviting a response.

Callaghan said, 'I'll do it.'

★   ★   ★

When they took him from the warehouse, Callaghan had a panicky moment. The urge to run surged through him and walking the ten or so feet to the car his eyes jerked this way and that, in search of a way out. A couple of hundred yards away someone was loading boxes into the boot of a car. A guy in yellow overalls. No other sign of life on an industrial estate that seemed forsaken. Everything looked like it was closed — a tyre importer, a warehouse with *Peterson Desks* stencilled in white on the dark green door, a barred window below a shabby plastic sign that said *McCall's Interiors*. Mackendrick was right — it was the kind of place where screams wouldn't bring anyone running.

In the car, Callaghan bent to allow Karl to pull the hood over his head. At first he sought to remember the twists and turns of the car, but within minutes he'd lost track.

The last thing Mackendrick said before they left the warehouse was, 'We know everything the police know. We know everything about your life — there's no stroke you can pull that we won't know about. We're replacing Walter, and we can replace you just as easily.'

'I've agreed to do what you want.'

'The first thing I want you to do is nick a car. You've done it before.'

'That was when I was a kid.'

'Walter was good at that kind of thing. If I left it to these two, they'd smash the car window, then wreck the wiring trying to get the fucking thing started. I expect you to do a professional job. New plates, the whole thing shipshape.'

'What kind of car?'

'First time out — something roomy, newish, with a bit of power. I want you to do that tomorrow afternoon and I want you to bring it to the shopping centre at Dunmanlow. The car park. I'll give you the details before you go.'

'What's this for?'

'You heard me say *no questions asked*, right?'

'And that's all you want?'

'That's the kind of thing I want from you — I'll be in touch from time to time.'

'Tools, the reg plates — I'll need money.'

'No problem.'

When Karl pulled off the hood they were driving through Phibsboro. He used a knife to cut the plastic tie. Callaghan rubbed his wrists.

'This'll do,' Karl said, and Robbie slowed down, pulled in and stopped with two wheels on the pavement.

'I'm not near home,' Callaghan said.

'This isn't a fucking taxi. Get out.' He handed Callaghan his mobile.

Standing on the pavement, watching the car drive away, Callaghan powered up his phone. There were texts from Novak, all demanding that Danny call him.

'Christ sake, where've you been?'

'I'm sorry, something happened.'

'The Mater had a conniption — I had to pull someone off another job to make that delivery. Then you had — '

'I'm sorry.'

'Jesus, Danny.'

'I'll explain later.'

'You okay? What happened?'

'I'll explain later.' Callaghan ended the call.

Day Nine

Chapter 25

The street was empty, a long, straight valley of middle-class houses, with pavements decorated with trees. Lots of greenery in the front gardens to protect the residents' privacy. That kind of street, once you went into the driveway you were close to invisible. It was late afternoon, already getting dark.

This looks like a possible.

Neat garden. Everything in its place.

There was a maroon Toyota 4×4 in the driveway. The burglar alarm high on the wall above the door was a cheapie, strictly ring-a-ding, without remote monitoring. If the house was empty, Danny Callaghan had a possible target.

He'd thought of telling Novak about Mackendrick, but he didn't want to drag his friend into this. He had the card the police had given him — Detective Sergeant Michael Wyndham — but Wyndham's instincts first and last would be to make an arrest. Besides, Lar Mackendrick probably wasn't bluffing — '*We know everything the police know.*' The consequences of crossing him would be deadly for Callaghan, and perhaps for Hannah, maybe for Leon and for Alex.

Best to do what Mackendrick asked — steal a

car for him. If it ended there, Callaghan could swallow it.

If all that was needed was wheels, the simplest thing would be to take a car from a quiet street — and there were a few ways of doing that. If the demand was for a new model, which might have the latest immobilising gadgets, the most reliable option was to get hold of the keys.

Sometimes you could tell a lot just by the way a house looked — which lights were on, the way the curtains or the blinds were arranged. The best way to check if anyone was home was to ring the doorbell.

Walking up the driveway, Callaghan resisted the urge to glance around. Best to make like Mr Innocent, calling at the house on business. It was people with something to hide who checked out their surroundings. Callaghan involuntarily tapped his jacket's left pocket, although he knew the set of bump keys was there.

'It's all about the basic skills,' Jacob Nash used to say. 'Once you've got the basic skills and the tools — open a lock, climb a wall, find a weak point — you'll never go hungry.'

Nash got out of Mountjoy four years before Callaghan, after doing almost two years for a series of breaking and entering jobs. A few hours after receiving his orders from Lar Mackendrick, Callaghan drove out to Nash's house in Skerries with enough money to buy what he needed. He found Nash up a ladder at the side of the house, fixing a leaky gutter.

Nash came down from the ladder. 'What do you need?'

'Slim jim, jiggler set, bump keys and a shim — and I need some plates.'

'You're going into business, then?'

'Just keeping my hand in.'

The house with the Toyota 4×4 was the fourth one that Callaghan had tried in this area in the last forty minutes. At each of the other promising targets he rang the bell and a woman answered. Callaghan said he was from the cable television company and when the woman said there must be a mistake he asked if this wasn't the Riordan household.

No.

Oh, sorry — I'd better check they've given me the right address.

Fourth time lucky.

He pressed the bell and waited.

After a minute he pressed again and after another minute passed Callaghan took out a keyring with half a dozen bump keys on it. He chose one, much like an ordinary front-door key except that the teeth were filed into a series of five regularly spaced triangles. When he inserted it in the lock, Callaghan used a thumb to apply minimum sideways pressure to the key. He took a small block of wood from an inside pocket and hit the key with it, like a hammer hitting a nail. The force should have caused the triangular teeth to jerk forward, jolting the pins out of place, the sideways pressure of his thumb forcing the cylinder to turn.

The lock stayed locked.

It was the timing that mattered, twisting the key — not too soon, not too late — in the fraction of a second after the whack of the bump key's teeth bounced the pins upward. The trick was to get it turning before the pins fell back into place. Too soon or too late, nothing happened. He did it three more times and got the same result. The fifth time, the key turned, the lock opened and Callaghan stepped inside and shut the door behind him.

He had probably twenty seconds before the alarm went off. He glanced around — saw a key box on the wall, black with a colourful butterfly picture on the front. He opened it. Three keys, none of them a car key.

There was a hall table with a lace runner and some pieces of paper held down by a glass paperweight with a 3-D image of the World Trade Center. At the far side of the table, a shallow dark blue bowl with hair clips, safety pins, a small roll of Sellotape and a car key.

Just as he took the key the alarm went off.

No panic.

No problem.

Not yet.

Mostly, neighbours assumed that a ringing alarm meant a false alarm. Only when the noise had had time to become a nuisance did they look out of their windows to see if there was something wrong. Lots of time to start the engine, back out and be gone.

Callaghan forced himself to stay well within the speed limit for the ten minutes it took him to drive to the Dunmanlow shopping centre. He stopped in the corner of the car park furthest from the shopping-centre entrance. The false number plates were in a deep inside pocket of his overcoat and it took him just a couple of minutes to swap them for the originals.

He walked away from the Toyota, towards the O'Brien's sandwich bar that looked out onto the car park. He bought a coffee and sat near the window. He'd been there ten minutes when Karl Prowse and his sidekick came in and sat down across from him.

'Maroon Toyota, four by four,' Callaghan said. He passed over the keys.

Karl said, 'Well done, Junior.'

Callaghan didn't reply. He stood up and left the cafe.

★ ★ ★

'We've waited long enough,' Robbie said. They'd been sitting by the window of the sandwich bar for almost an hour and Karl too was impatient. But he didn't want Robbie making decisions, so he said, 'Another few minutes, just to be sure.'

Not a hint of any cop activity around the shopping centre. The car park was filling up. A van had parked beside the Toyota, blocking their view, but the driver went into the shopping centre and was back out within minutes and drove away.

After a while, Karl said, 'Let's go.' He gave the keys to Robbie and outside the sandwich bar they split up. Karl went to his Toledo and sat behind the wheel, Robbie left the car park and crossed the road to a nearby estate. He came back twenty minutes later and sat in the car.

'How much?' Karl said.

'Fifty euro each. Two of them. Half now, half later.'

After a few minutes, two boys, late teens, both wearing Reebok clothes, crossed the road and headed across the car park. Robbie said, 'That's them.' Karl started the engine.

When the kids started up the Toyota they took the long way towards the car park entrance, then around the roundabout and towards the main road. Ten minutes later Karl was driving behind them up the Malahide Road, then across towards Swords. He stayed a couple of cars behind the Toyota, alert for any sign that the 4×4 was being followed. Nothing suspicious. At the Swords Pavilions shopping centre they followed the Toyota past the open car park, into the indoor parking garage and up to the third floor. After sitting there for five minutes, Robbie said, 'Looks like that's okay.'

There was still a possibility that Callaghan had ratted them out and the cops were waiting for the Toyota to leave the car park, but Karl was hopeful. After a while the Toyota moved again and this time they followed it to the Airside retail estate. After parking for ten minutes there, Karl said, 'Waste of money, giving them the second fifty.'

Robbie said, 'A deal's a deal.' He got out and walked to the Toyota. After he paid the money, the kids drove away.

When Robbie got back to the Toledo, Karl was tapping out a number.

Lar Mackendrick put down the phone. Now that Callaghan had passed the test, he should be a reliable source for wheels in the days to come. The Walter blip was sorted.

He went back to his fireside chair and sat down. He'd left *The Art of War* open and face down on the arm of the chair. He picked it up, closed it and studied the dark leather cover.

Worth the wait.

Without the book, he knew, he'd have gone at this whole thing bull-headed, gun in hand. And he'd have gone down in flames.

He stood up and went into the kitchen. He watched May place a slice of lemon on a salmon fillet, wrap the foil around it and slip it into the oven. In the two years since Lar'd had his health scare, May had been a star. She'd cooked whatever Lar's nutritionist decreed, abandoned all her old heavy sauces, and steamed or baked where once she'd fried. If it hadn't been for Lar's determination and May's care, he'd no doubt that he'd be dead by now.

'We're back on track. Like Walter never happened.'

May said, 'You're ready?'

He told her that Callaghan had passed the test, didn't rat them out.

May took him in her arms and held him, her warm face next to his. She whispered, 'Time to show the fuckers what we're made of.'

Day Ten

Chapter 26

In the 24 hours since he'd stolen the maroon Toyota, Danny Callaghan had spent most of the time at home. He turned off his mobile and kept the radio on, tuned to 98FM, and let the mindless music crowd out thought.

It was getting on for early evening and he was hungry. Lunch had been coffee and a slice of cheese between two pieces of brown bread. He put on his jacket and on his way down the stairs he switched on his phone and found he had eight voicemails. He'd reached the ground floor when the phone rang. He waited a moment, looking at Novak's name on the screen, then he answered.

Novak sounded pissed off. 'I've been calling you.'

'Sorry, my phone was off.'

'All day?'

'Sorry.'

'You didn't get my messages?'

'Novak — '

'You said you'd explain later, Danny. It's later.'

'I said I'm sorry, it was — '

'You're my best driver, the most reliable — for seven months — then suddenly you disappear and leave two customers hanging. Reliability, Danny, that's what this business depends on.'

'Look — '

'What's wrong? What's happened?'

'Nothing, I just got held up.'

Novak's tone was deliberately cold. 'Fuck you, Danny. Talk to me.'

Callaghan said nothing.

Novak said, 'There's something wrong.'

'I have to deal with this myself.'

'Deal with what?'

'*Please.*'

'Has this anything to do with Frank Tucker?'

'No, nothing like that.'

'Don't shut me out. If you need help — '

'Please.'

Novak was silent. Then, 'Ring me when you can,' and he ended the call.

★   ★   ★

Callaghan was halfway to the shopping centre when Hannah rang.

'What the fuck do you think you're doing?'

Callaghan said, 'I — ' and Hannah steamrollered over him.

'You're fucking with my *life*!'

'Hannah — ' Callaghan stopped walking, stood there in the street. He leaned over, pressed the phone closer to his ear, trying to block out the sound of traffic.

'Leon told me — so I know now, and there's nothing you can use against him.'

'Hannah — '

'Don't deny it.'

Callaghan said nothing. He wasn't sure if he

213

had anything to deny.

'I know about Leon and Alex, he told me last night. You found his briefcase at her place and you made that obvious — I don't know what you thought you were going to do with that information, but it's all in the open now and there's nothing to it.'

The strain in her voice was something he'd never heard before.

'Alex told Leon you'd found his stuff at her place. And he told me — and there's nothing to it. He told me you've been watching the house, he told me you threatened to make up shit about him and now you think you've got this to hold over — '

'Hannah, this isn't — '

'What Leon and I have — whatever he's done — I just want you to know that you can't — '

'Hannah, please — '

'Don't contact me again.' She ended the call.

Callaghan stood near the edge of the pavement, his back to the noisy traffic. He wasn't sure what he felt. He'd lost something, and he wasn't sure yet how much it mattered to him.

★ ★ ★

The third call came when Callaghan was in the coffee shop at the shopping centre, ordering a sandwich. He recognised Lar Mackendrick's voice.

'Danny?'

'Yeah.'

'You free?'

'Just getting something to eat.'

'I want to show you something. Now.'

'I need to change, have a shower, it won't take — '

'You're fine as you are.'

★   ★   ★

Half an hour later, driving a green Isuzu, Lar Mackendrick picked up Danny Callaghan near Mountjoy Square. They crossed the river and headed out through the southern suburbs.

'Where are we going?' Callaghan said.

'The mountains.'

'Why?'

'Something to show you.'

'What?'

'You'll see.'

After a while, Mackendrick said, 'Over the next couple of days, I want you to do something for me. It was Walter's job, now it's yours. I want six cars.'

'Over a couple of days?'

'No problem to you. You nick them, stick on false plates. Karl and Robbie will collect them from you, put them away safely. We'll need a lot of transport. Nothing too flash, but everything in good nick.' He tucked something into Callaghan's top pocket. 'A few hundred there, for the plates — and make sure they've had a fill-up.'

They drove past Rathfarnham and eventually Callaghan saw a signpost for Glencullen. Mackendrick turned onto a twisting bushy lane, the view restricted. He stayed silent, concentrating on driving. Ten minutes down the lane they took a left and began climbing on an even narrower, more twisting rough road. In the mirror, Callaghan caught glimpses of the lights of Dublin, far behind.

'We're here.'

When they stopped, Mackendrick cut the ignition and turned to Callaghan.

'You afraid?'

Callaghan didn't reply.

'You're okay — if I'd wanted to hurt you I'd have sent a couple of lads to take you up here. I want you to see something.'

Mackendrick got out of the Isuzu. There were fields sloping down to the left, woods to the right. One tall, thin tree, a spruce, had keeled over, its fall broken by another tree equal in size. Together, they looked something like an elongated X.

'Over here.'

Callaghan followed Mackendrick towards the woods. The air was icy. Closer to the trees Callaghan could see beams of light shining several yards inside the woods.

'Someone expecting us?' Callaghan whispered.

Mackendrick, his breathing heavy, just grunted. He switched on a small flashlight.

When they got to a small clearing, Callaghan saw that the beams of light came from the headlights of a Toledo, driven in from the far side and parked at an angle from the clear space. Karl Prowse was standing several feet away. He was holding a pistol. There was an older man standing in a long shallow hole. He was wearing a hat and coat and had a spade in his hand and he'd just stopped digging. He watched the arrival of Mackendrick and Callaghan. Despite the cold, his face was sweaty. There was a streak of blood on one cheek. His body had the stooped posture of a man tired and frightened.

Lar Mackendrick turned to Danny. 'This is Declan Roeper. As you can see, Declan's been digging a grave.'

Mackendrick took a couple of steps to where Karl was standing. He bent down and picked up a second spade. When he threw the spade, Callaghan instinctively reached up and caught it.

'Help him,' Mackendrick said.

Part Three
In the Beginning

Three Weeks Earlier

Chapter 27

When the thugs came the shop owner was on a ladder, hanging a string of plastic Santa Clauses over the chocolate display. Almost a whole month to Christmas, but there was no point putting it off any longer. Some shops had begun putting up their Christmas decorations before Halloween. Bloody nonsense, but if you didn't do it people put you down as a Scrooge, and that wasn't good for business.

The far end of the string was hooked above the stationery shelves, and the trick was to leave enough slack so there was some distance between the Santas, so they weren't all bunched up in the middle. The ladder rocked as the shop owner stretched to connect the other end of the string to a hook. It wasn't easy, doing this with one arm in a sling.

When he saw the two men coming through the front doorway the shopkeeper's face went red. The older one was in his late thirties, the other was barely out of his teens.

'Get out!'

'No need for that, Mr Finnegan,' the older man said.

The shopkeeper let go of the string and the Santa Clauses fluttered away from him, dangling down over the notepads and pencils.

'Just get the *hell* — '

'Mr Mackendrick wants to see you.'

'Fuck off.'

'He wants to apologise.'

'*Out.*'

The expression on the face of the older thug was regretful. Matty was his name, Matty something.

'Mr Mackendrick feels terrible about this.'

'It's okay, it's over now.'

'It wasn't supposed to happen.'

'I didn't go to the police.'

'He knows that. He's very grateful.'

'He can fuck off.'

'It was a mistake — it was just supposed to be a verbal warning.'

The younger thug leaned towards the shopkeeper and said, 'Let's go.'

'*No!*'

Matty said, 'Mr Finnegan, all Lar wants to do is tell you himself how sorry he is. I'm asking you, please — we'll drive you there, door to door. Have a chat with Lar, then Todd here drives you back to the shop, door to door.' The thug reached into an inside pocket. He took out an envelope, opened it and counted six fifties onto the counter. 'So you're not out of pocket, having to leave the shop for an hour or so.'

This could be —

Or —

In the end, the shopkeeper thought, it wasn't as though he had a choice.

The younger thug drove. Matty sat alongside

the shopkeeper in the back of the car. They didn't speak.

It was the second time in two weeks that Matty and his young friend had come to see the shopkeeper. The way Matty put it when he came first was, 'The Mackendrick family's been good to you — Lar just wants a little favour.'

'I don't do that kind of thing any more.'

Two days after that, two other men came and the shopkeeper found himself lying on the floor, his face bloody, two teeth broken, watching his hand being shoved into the drinks fridge, feeling the chill of the Coca-Cola bottles, and screaming when the door of the fridge slammed against his arm.

Past Clare Hall now, out along Grange Road, through Sutton Cross, up Carrickbrack Road and past the summit of the Howth peninsula. Over to the left there were some small private estates and council houses, but around here it was all about levels of wealth. There was a time when you just needed to be well off to live here — now the very seriously rich were all over the place. It was far from this that the Mackendricks had been raised.

They were living off Ballybough Road, in the inner city, when the shopkeeper got to know Jo-Jo Mackendrick. Back then, few in the area cared that Jo-Jo was on the rob. There was wariness of his mother Pearl, and resentment from those who got caught up in her money-lending operation and ended up paying crushing interest for years. But Jo-Jo was a neighbourhood star. He was like a local

223

development agency, slipping loans and grants to people who needed a dig-out. It wasn't charity, and Jo-Jo expected to be paid back, but if things didn't work out — and if he was sure he wasn't being taken for a ride — he sometimes scrubbed the debt. If it worked out, as the shopkeeper's first tiny shop did, Jo-Jo might or might not accept repayment. He might take a partnership in the business, as Jo-Jo had with the shopkeeper's place, or he might merely ask for a favour.

The arrival of the Criminal Assets Bureau put a crimp in everyone's business. Show the CAB how you got your assets, or get hauled into court and maybe lose them. Lots of hard cases, after years of graft, had seen the proceeds taken away. Everyone had to look for ways to shift excess money offshore, just like the smart businessmen had been doing for decades. Spain, the Netherlands, even into Eastern Europe. The Mackendricks had long ago forged the legitimate links that allowed them to launder most of their income.

Everyone benefitted — Jo-Jo and Lar, and the people doing the laundering. The shopkeeper, Finnegan, had moved on and up, and now had two medium-sized shops in different parts of the city. Jo-Jo was dead and the connection with the Mackendrick family was long ago, until Lar needed an outlet to run some money through and Matty and Todd came calling, and the other two thugs came to break the shopkeeper's arm.

Pulling into the driveway of Lar Mackendrick's house in Howth, Matty said, 'The view

— it'd take your breath away.'

Getting out of the car, despite his fear, the shopkeeper looked back down towards the sea. Matty was right. Even on a cloudy day. Take your breath away.

★   ★   ★

The winter wasn't too bad — which was a blessing, after the lousy summer when it seemed like most days of the week God woke with a smirk on his face and sent the angels to line up and take turns pissing down on Dublin.

Now it was late November and there were a few days of unseasonal weather. No sun but warm enough not to have to heat the large sun room overlooking the harbour. Lar sat with his feet up, a pitcher of iced orange juice on the table. He watched Matty and Todd approach, one each side of the shopkeeper. Lar got to his feet as they came through the doorway.

'Mr Finnegan — what can I say?'

The shopkeeper indicated the cast on his arm. 'There was no call for that.'

'None at all. Not my instructions — but it's my responsibility and I'm sorry.'

'Those bastards enjoyed it.'

'They went beyond their orders. Say the word and they suffer — same as you.'

'No, please.' Finnegan said it quickly. Last thing he wanted, his tormentors nursing broken arms and a grudge.

'Sit down — please.' Lar indicated one of the half-dozen teak chairs. He poured a glass of

225

orange juice and left it on the tiled table beside Finnegan, then he did the same for himself and sat down. Matty and Todd stood several yards away.

'I want to make sure we're okay, me and you.'

'I didn't tell the police.'

'I know — that was good of you.'

'I said it was a couple of shoplifters, said I got into a fight with them.'

'Good.'

'They believed me.'

'We're good then, me and you?'

Finnegan didn't want to agree, he didn't want to disagree.

'We need to talk — the thing you wanted — '

'Ever been out to the island?' Lar gestured towards Ireland's Eye, a couple of kilometres offshore.

Finnegan shook his head.

'I was sitting here, thinking. When we were kids, Jo-Jo and me used to come out to Howth from the city, every chance we got — halfway down the pier they still have motorboats that'll take you out to the island for a few hours. Haven't been out there in years. Terrific place — thousands of seagulls, puffins, gannets, plover. I used to know about all that shit. A Martello tower out there on the left tip of the island. In the middle there's the ruins of a church, hundreds of years old. Way up on top, near the cliffs, the earth is so springy it's like a mattress. That's what we called it when we were kids — mattress grass. We used to hold our arms out like this — ' he stretched his arms out to the

226

sides, at shoulder height ' — throw ourselves backwards, bounce on the mattress grass — it was magic.'

'I've never been out.'

'When you look back, its like we went out there time and again, every summer. But it couldn't have been more than a couple of times a year, for two or three years.' Lar was staring out at the island. 'Jo-Jo loved it. Pearl would take us out there in the morning, we'd take the last boat home. Dad never came out there.' His gaze was fixed on the island. On the other side of the table, Finnegan had to strain to hear Lar's words.

'One time, Jo-Jo found an injured seagull, something wrong with one of its wings, it was fucked. He wouldn't leave it. We stayed out there all night — missed the last boat. He wouldn't leave it to die alone. Late in the evening it died. We spent the night out there, the two of us with Pearl in between, arms around us, trying to keep us warm.'

The shopkeeper said, 'He was a good man, Jo-Jo was.'

Lar said, 'Can't believe it's three years gone by — they shot him like a fucking dog.' He put a hand to his face, the fingers stroking one cheek. 'My poor mother.'

'I'm sorry, it must bring it all back. The two of them.'

Lar nodded. 'I shouldn't be bothering you with this, Mr Finnegan — I wanted to talk to you about your troubles. What do you think now, after all that's happened?'

'I've suffered enough.'

'More than enough. No one should have to go through that shit, just because you take a stand on your principles. I admire that. Sticking up for what you believe in.'

Lar's admiration seemed genuine.

'But that doesn't solve my problem. What I do, some of it can't be run past the Revenue people. And the CAB — those bastards drag people into court, they get a wimpy judge and they call every last stick of furniture a criminal asset. I need legitimate businesses that I can run some money through, make it come out clean at the other end. I need to switch things around from time to time — they're forever poking their noses in. You did stuff like that for Jo-Jo. Give and take, that was how it worked. Now, I need a favour.'

'Please, Lar, I thought — '

'You'll do well enough out of it.'

'What I did for Jo-Jo, that was paying a debt. I don't do that kind of thing any more. That's all done now.'

'Not really.'

'And *this*.' The shopkeeper indicated his broken arm. 'Like I say, I've suffered more than enough.'

'Mr Finnegan, I'll be blunt. It's not like I want you to do something and you say no, then you get your arm broken and that's the end of it. That seems to be the way you see things. As though it's a fair exchange. You turn me down, so you get hurt and it's all over. But that's not the way things are.' Lar stood up and took his time moving closer to the shopkeeper.

'I want something — I get it. That's the way it works. We're not equals. I say what happens.' He leaned down, his face close enough so he could smell the fear from Finnegan. 'I don't have to make an effort.' He pursed his lips, made like he was blowing out a candle. 'Like *that*, you're gone. Ten minutes later, I've forgotten your name. You're not even a dead body, you're just a missing person and your family doesn't even have a grave to put flowers on.'

Finnegan flinched as Lar laid a hand on his shoulder. 'You're entitled to bitch about it — I admire that, really I do. Then you do as you're told.'

The shopkeeper said nothing, just sat there, Lar looking down at him. After a moment, he averted his gaze, looking past Lar, out towards Ireland's Eye.

* * *

Lar watched as Finnegan got into the car. Todd slid in behind the wheel.

'Look at him,' Lar said to Matty, and he raised one hand and gave the shopkeeper a small wave. When Finnegan waved back, Matty laughed.

'The little lamb,' Lar said, and closed the door.

He made coffee for Matty and they sat in the sun room.

'What about the Macy brothers?' Matty said.

'Gobshites.'

'I haven't paid them yet.'

'Pay them off — tell them goodbye.'

They'd used the Macy brothers for the odd soft job. The way they handled the shopkeeper thing meant they wouldn't be hired again — breaking the stupid bastard's arm when all the job needed was a mild slapping.

'How's it shaping up?'

'Nicely,' Matty said.

For three months Lar had been coaxing along a potential job. He hadn't done an art robbery before, but this promised to be too easy to pass up.

One of the super-rich had bought an old house in Meath, not far over the line from Dublin. Big family place with two additional wings blended in with great care to match the period style of the house. The buyer knocked it down and built a house to his own design, three times as big. After four years' work it was almost finished. Lar's contact in the auctioneering business told him that the owner had assigned one of his people to source a handful of appropriate artworks to decorate the walls. The budget was almost four million.

After up-to-date reports from his contact, Lar Mackendrick concluded there would be a few hours when the house was vulnerable — the paintings assembled for installation, the security not yet fully in place.

'Four people or five?'

Matty was in charge of putting together the team, from the couple of dozen regulars who worked for Lar.

'Five, to be on the safe side.' Matty listed the people he wanted and Lar okayed it. Over the previous four years, Matty Butler had become Lar Mackendrick's most trusted associate, the hands-on manager. 'Right-hand man, eyes and ears,' Lar told him one time. Matty had done most of the work on this art robbery. He'd chosen the safe house for storage, and he'd twice been to Brussels to talk to a potential buyer. Although Lar hadn't promised anything, it was understood between them that when the art job was over Matty was in line for a cut not just of the proceeds of that robbery but of the outfit's overall income.

On the way to the door, Lar said, 'I'd ask you to stay for something to eat, but me and May are heading into town soon for a bite. You heading straight home?'

'Yeah, but I've got to see Todd later. He's buying a car — wants me to kick the tyres.'

'What kind of car?'

'Three-year-old Avensis.'

'A dealer or private?'

'He's a mechanic, runs a little repair place.'

'Those are the fellas that can get you a bargain.'

Lar watched Matty turn his car in the driveway, easing down the slope towards the gateway, and returned Matty's nod.

They would never meet again.

Chapter 28

It started that evening, about eight o'clock, while Lar and May were eating at Le Caprice. It was a place that May was fond of — experienced waitresses who knew about food, helpful, no attitude problems. Lar liked it because they told him exactly how the dish was served, and left out anything that was outside his diet. Tonight, his chicken — served as requested, without sauce — was tender, May's fish was tasty, and the pianist at the top of the room was playing 'Stardust'. It was the kind of quiet evening that Lar most enjoyed.

Five miles away, in a Coolock housing estate, Matty Butler and Todd Reynolds were walking down a back lane, behind Weir Road. On each side the eight-foot-high walls marked the boundaries of back gardens. Todd was talking about how the last time he bought a car he got taken by a chancer. 'Fucking thing fell apart after a couple of months.' Coming out of the lane, they turned into a wide yard lit by an orange light atop a lamp-post. Across the yard a man in overalls and a heavy anorak was replacing a battery in a Fiat. Behind him, the half-open doors of a ramshackle building, halfway between a barn and a shed. The man waved to Todd.

Todd nodded towards Matty. 'Mate of mine — want him to have a look.'

'The car's inside.' The man in overalls gestured for the two to go ahead.

When Matty Butler saw the dimly lit inside of the building he knew it was too late. No car in there, most of the floor and one wall lined with white plastic. The man in overalls was behind them. 'Cool it, lads, take it easy.' Matty glanced back and saw the automatic pistol. On the far side of the garage, a door opened and another man came in holding a gun.

The one behind Matty pushed him over to the left, towards a side wall. When Matty turned around Todd was standing beside the two men. Todd shrugged his shoulders and he said, 'Sorry, Matty.'

★ ★ ★

An hour later, as he was walking up Grafton Street, arm in arm with May, Lar Mackendrick's phone rang and when he answered he heard Matty say, 'Boss — ' Then the call ended.

★ ★ ★

The package arrived at Lar's home almost twenty-four hours later.

May was visiting a friend, Lar was watching an old James Stewart movie on TCM. Every time he rang Matty's number that day he got taken directly to the message service. After the fourth call he stopped leaving messages. Couldn't raise Todd, either. He made several calls to people who worked for his outfit, but no one had seen Matty.

He told the three best of them to come to the house. Two were sitting outside, in a car. The third sat at the window of a bedroom with a good view over the back garden. All of them were armed.

When the taxi arrived, shortly before eight o'clock, the two men out front stopped the taxi driver on his way to the front door, envelope in hand. He said he'd picked up a fare in Sutton and the guy had given him the envelope to deliver, and paid him over the odds, in advance.

When Lar tore the envelope open he saw Bruce Willis, gun in hand, looking at him from the cover of a DVD case. It was the original *Die Hard* movie, the first of the series. The DVD inside was a Sony disc with no label. Lar went into the living room alone and sat down in front of his 42-inch LCD to watch.

He put the disc on pause as he heard the front door open and May come in. He went to meet her.

'I left the car at Edel's,' she said. She mimed taking a drink. 'Took a taxi.'

'You had something to eat?'

She nodded. 'I'm having an early night.'

She spent the next ten minutes pottering around and Lar had to hold back from saying something that would speed her up. He had no idea what was on the disc, but he didn't want to take the chance that May would walk in in the middle of it. He waited until he heard their bedroom door close before he went back to the television.

The screen was dark at first. He could see the outline of two people sitting on chairs, against a pale background. He thought the one on the right was Matty. Then the lights went on, bright lights — and it *was* Matty, squinting a little at the sudden glare. He and Todd were tied to chairs, wide straps around their arms and across their chests. Todd's upper body was shivering,

234

his nostrils flared. There was blood on his forehead. Matty was still, his eyes glancing this way and that, weighing things up. His right ear was bloody, the lobe an odd shape.

From the right of the screen, behind the two men, a third one emerged, wearing overalls and a balaclava mask. He was holding a black automatic with a long slim silencer that gave it an unbalanced look.

'Hello, Lar.'

He stood behind and between Matty and Todd.

'If there was another way — ' He shrugged. 'Anything less than this it wouldn't work.'

Lar knew the voice.

'The old way, we'd be swatting one another's people from one end of the week to the other. This way, I hope you accept there's no point.'

No mistaking that voice.

Three months trying to come to an agreement with Frank Tucker, four meetings, all nice and friendly. Frank's idea. He's strong in the west of the city, Lar's strength is on the northside. *Put us together*, Frank says, *and we can start something totally new in this city.* The idea came out of a successful sales trial of crystal meth. Frank's product, distributed on the northside through Lar's outfit. *We make this permanent,* Frank argued, *by and by, we work up the market — there's no limit.*

Frank didn't seem either surprised or upset when Lar got cold feet. *Agree to disagree,* he said. *Maybe next time. No harm done.*

'Used to be, every street had its corner shop,'

Frank Tucker is saying now on the screen. 'Now it's a handful of supermarket chains run everything. It's the way it works.'

He comes around the two seated men, still facing the camera, with his back to Matty and Todd.

No doubt about it. The voice, the stance — Frank Tucker.

'A lot of the Flash Harry types, they're in it for the coke and the swagger — they've no sense of building something for the long run. You and Jo-Jo, you were the first to set things up so you could account for the money you were spending. You bought property, you got into businesses — you were smart. I take my hat off to you.'

Tucker does a little bow.

'*Please,*' Todd says.

Frank Tucker turns to him. 'Be quiet.'

'Why me? Please, I did what you told me to — '

Tucker turns back to the camera. 'We'll meet, Lar, we'll work something out — you know from this that I mean business.'

Todd's voice is limp, repetitive. '*Please* — '

Matty, his voice a mixture of anger and contempt, turns to Todd and says, 'Shut — the *fuck* — *up!*'

Frank Tucker says, 'I agree.' He leans towards the camera. 'Sorry about this, Lar.'

He turns, moves to one side, raising the automatic. Todd wrenches his head sideways, screaming a long 'Nooooo!' — the cry interrupted by the bullet that hits him in the mouth. Silence, then his mouth is gushing blood,

236

he's gulping — making pleading sounds. The masked man shoots him in the forehead and Todd's head jerks back and remains still, his chin pointing towards the ceiling.

Matty is white-faced, breathing heavily.

Watching the DVD, Lar Mackendrick focuses on Matty's eyes. Hard, angry — behind it all, Matty's still thinking, assessing.

Frank Tucker says something to someone off-screen. There's a laugh. A second man appears, moving from behind the camera, wearing denim jeans and a rough plaid shirt. He's not masked but he keeps his face turned away. He bends and looks at Todd's face, then he uses a couple of fingers to take some blood from Todd's wound and smears it on Matty's face.

'Sick fuck,' Matty says. The second man spits in Matty's face and walks off to one side, out of camera range.

Matty is looking towards Frank Tucker. His voice is low, trying for calm. 'You've made your point. It can stop here.'

'You're a very good man, Matty. Lar relies on you a lot.'

'There has to be a way.'

'Don't think so, Matty.'

The masked man reaches into a pocket and takes out a mobile. He taps several keys, then he holds it to his ear and when he's sure its ringing he says, 'You want to talk to Lar?'

Matty says nothing.

After a moment, the masked man holds the phone close to Matty's mouth and nods and Matty says, 'Boss — ' and the masked man ends the call. He turns and walks forward until he fills the screen, blocking out Matty. He holds up the phone and says, 'You remember that call, Lar?'

He turns back to Matty, goes around behind him, points the gun at the back of his head. Every muscle in Matty's face is straining, his mouth emits a harsh, rising, wordless sound that becomes louder the longer it lasts.

Lar Mackendrick forces himself to continue watching, even as the unseen gun belches and Matty's face erupts. In the silence that follows Lar continues to stare at the screen, at Matty's head slumped forward, his shirt-front bloody.

Frank Tucker moves towards the camera until he fills the screen again. 'We'll be in touch,' he says, and the screen goes black.

Chapter 29

Twenty minutes later, Tommy Farr rang.

'I know about Matty, and we need to talk.'

'Did you have anything to do with — '

'Don't be a fucking sap, Lar.'

Despite the arrival of a lot of competition from the young and the aggressive, Tommy Farr had until recently run a number of profitable enterprises in the Dolphin's Barn and Rialto areas. Although never close to the Mackendrick brothers, the two outfits didn't directly compete and the relationship was cordial and respectful. On one occasion, Lar arranged for the kneecapping of a young tearaway from Cabra who was troubling Tommy. Tommy promised to return the favour but the necessity had never arisen. Last thing Lar heard, a couple of months back, was that Tommy had cashed in his winnings and retired to Spain. A bit young for that, but Tommy had put a lot of his money into property and got out of it before the collapse.

'Where?' Lar said.

'You name it.'

'There's safety in numbers. The lobby of the Shelbourne.'

Lar had a tool shed in the back garden, an old pitched-roof type, raised on a breeze-block base. Halfway along the bottom of one side of the shed a section of weatherboard could be lifted, revealing a shallow space from which Lar withdrew a heavy plastic Ziploc bag. He checked the semi-automatic Walther P22 inside and inserted the clip that came with it. It was the only firearm at his home. Twice, when Lar's house had been raided by the police, the Walther had lain undiscovered under the shed.

He had no reason to mistrust Tommy Farr, and the Shelbourne Hotel was an unlikely location for a hit, but he wasn't going anywhere without firepower.

Lar went upstairs and found May asleep, a book open on the pillow, the bedside light still on. He turned down a corner of the page of the book, put it away and switched off the light. Then he leaned down and kissed her.

'Love you,' he whispered.

Her voice was faint. 'Night.'

Lar had his hand inside the deep square pocket of his black overcoat, holding the Walther, as he entered the Shelbourne. The hotel lobby was noisy with late-night shoppers, many of them already carrying big bags with tasteful Christmas motifs from Grafton Street stores. Drink-powered chatter and occasional whoops leaked from the nearby Horseshoe bar. A woman in fur and jeans laughed loudly as she squeezed out from the crush in the other bar on the left of the lobby.

Tommy Farr was standing off to one side of the lobby. He was a couple of years younger than Lar, but his lined and pale face made him look older. The Spanish sun hadn't done him a lot of good.

They went into the large, busy Lord Mayor's Lounge and found three tanned blondes getting up from around a table, yakking and taking their time about gathering their belongings and leaving. Two couples hovered nearby, drinks in hand. Lar and Tommy pushed past them and took two of the seats across the table from each other.

'Charmed, I'm sure,' one of the blondes said. Tommy told her to fuck off. The two couples who had expected to sit down exchanged uneasy glances, then moved away. Tommy took off his overcoat and threw it on the third seat.

Lar, his face close to Tommy's, said, 'First thing, Frank Tucker is a dead man — no matter what else goes down, there's no way that doesn't happen.'

Tommy Farr said, 'It's what I said, too — but that's not the way it is, Lar.'

Lar's voice was harsh. 'Tell me how it is.'

'Frank brought me home from Spain for this. He didn't tell me what was happening, just told me to be here.'

'You his messenger boy?'

'I'm retired. Tucker wants you to do the same.'

'He can — '

'Hear me out.'

'I'm going to kill him — whatever else, that I'll do.'

'Can I help you, gentlemen?'

Tommy Farr ordered two coffees.

The waiter's voice was wrapped in sweetness. 'I wonder, sir, if I could ask you to remove your coat from the seat, and perhaps if one of you could change seats — we're rather busy and we could arrange the seats so — '

Tommy made eye contact with the waiter. 'Haven't you got those coffees yet?'

★　★　★

The way it happened with Tommy Farr, he got a taxi driver knocking on his door one night, handing over an envelope with a DVD inside.

'My nephew, my youngest sister's youngest kid — '

Tommy looked down at the carpet. 'The newspapers said it was some bastard he'd had a row with, over a job they did — I never said anything different. That's what my sister believes.'

Lar said, 'I was at the funeral — I believed it, everyone did.'

Tommy met Lar's gaze. 'Soft lad, he was,

hardly involved in anything. Tied to a chair.' Tommy's face was stiff, his nonstop blinking the only clue to the emotion inside. 'Standing behind him, wearing a mask — Frank Tucker. All business. Sorry about this, Tommy, he says, nothing personal — we do it this way or it doesn't work.'

Lar leaned forward, his voice low and tight. 'You let him get away with *that*?'

'It's not that simple.'

'How come he's still breathing?'

Tommy shook his head. 'There isn't a day goes by, and not an hour in the day, when I don't see that kid looking out from that screen, pale as a sheet, tears running down his cheeks, asking me to do something — *Help me, Uncle Tommy, please.*' Tommy Farr lowered his head for a moment.

'He shot him in the back — twice. Later on, he said he did it that way because he didn't want to make it worse by letting the kid see what was coming. And he didn't do the head, he didn't touch the face — the fucker told me this, like it was a sign of his fucking humanity — he didn't touch the face because he wanted the kid's mother to be able to — *fuck!*'

'Tommy — '

Farr's head was bent, the fingers of one hand holding his forehead. He pressed the tips of two of his fingernails hard into his temple.

Mackendrick had to lean even closer to hear Tommy's whisper above the hotel hubbub. 'Jesus, Lar, I've thought it through a million times, what I'd do to the fucker if I could. But I had to make a choice.'

'We'll do it together, Tommy — you and me, we can raise a fucking army, cut the bastard to pieces.'

'Lar — I made my choice. That's why he has me here tonight — to tell you about your choice.'

'My choice — he gets an automatic in his mouth and I look right in his eyes when I squeeze the trigger.'

Tommy looked around. The lounge was getting even more crowded. 'This place is getting on my wick. Let's go for a walk.'

Lar Mackendrick looked at him. Tommy was tired, beaten. A crowded hotel was some protection — Tommy might be under orders to bring Lar outside, where there were fewer potential witnesses.

Screw it.

Lar too was tired of the noise and the crowds and their pre-Christmas cheer. If Frank Tucker or one of his people wanted to get up close and personal — what the fuck.

★   ★   ★

Tommy said, 'My choice — walk away from it all. Leave the operation to Frank Tucker — the coke trade, the protection, everything else. Or have a war I couldn't win.'

'You could take him — I could take him — together — '

They were on the footpath across the road from the Shelbourne, beside Stephen's Green, walking towards Grafton Street. Inside the railings of the park, out of sight, some young drunks were whooping and cackling. Tommy Farr stopped and turned to Lar Mackendrick. 'First thing that happens — if I didn't do what he said — my kid sister would get a DVD in the post. She gets to watch her son pleading for his life before that fucker wastes him. And whenever it's convenient for Tucker he takes another of her kids.'

'We can crush him.'

'I have three sisters, they've got six kids between them — five now. I've got three daughters. And I can't protect them all, all the time, for ever.'

'*He*'s got family.'

Tommy said, 'And what? He does one of mine, I do two of his — then, how many does he do and where does *that* end?'

'He's not invulnerable.'

'He'd got to some of my people — he showed me that. Any step I might take, he'd know about it from the off.'

'That shouldn't — '

'He knows what he's doing, Lar. You and me, I'm pushing sixty, you're a bit older. We've got things to lose — people to lose. And we've got enough put by that we can afford to walk away. Jesus, Lar, look around you. Jo-Jo, God rest him, he's gone. Martin Cahill's dead, Gilligan's in jail — and a whole lot more got tapped in the head. Bet you've had the same thoughts?'

'*I* decide when I walk away, not some jumped-up prick from Cullybawn.'

'That's what I said, at first. But that's pride

— and when you weigh that against what you've got to lose . . . it's not worth it. Tucker's another generation, Lar. It's like fighting time — there's no point. It moves, we don't.'

They started walking again. The taxi rank was busy. Across the road, near the top of Grafton Street, four teenage girls were doing some kind of pop dance routine, their movements choreographed, their voices loud, half a dozen friends cheering them on.

Lar said, 'What does he want me to do — just hand over the keys to everything and get on the next plane to Spain?'

'He wants to talk. Tomorrow. He's got it arranged.'

'Where?'

'He wants me to call you, first thing in the morning. To make the arrangements. He says you should stay home.'

'And that's it?'

They were close to the gates of Stephen's Green. Across the road a giant Christmas tree dominated the junction. All down Grafton Street the night was radiant with sparkling chandelier-like lights strung across the street. Tommy Farr looked at the display for a few moments.

'He sends me a couple of grand a week — severance pay, he called it.'

'Nice of him.'

'He'll probably offer you the same.'

'No one tells me I'm finished.'

Tommy said, 'If I can ever tear his throat out, without risking my family, I'll do it — in the meantime I do what I'm told. He's more ruthless than we ever were, Lar, and there's a time to fight and a time to walk away. And this is a time to say *fuck it* and do the sensible thing.'

★   ★   ★

At home, Lar checked that May was still sleeping, then he went downstairs and watched the DVD again. When it was done he broke it into a dozen pieces. He put on his overcoat again and left the house. He walked down the hill to Howth village, then he crossed to the east pier. A handful of teenagers were making a racket close to the water. Lar walked down the pier, the broken DVD in one pocket, his hand clutching the Walther in the other.

Tomorrow Matty's wife and Todd's parents would be pestering him. He decided he'd play it like he was mystified, and say truthfully that he hadn't seen either of them in a couple of days. And that he hadn't a clue where they were. Matty had some businesses of his own in Spain, and Lar could wonder aloud if he might perhaps have gone there in a hurry to sort out a problem.

A hundred yards down the pier, he stopped and looked back at the village. Pushing one o'clock in the morning, everything quiet except for the distant squawks of the teenagers. Lights along the waterfront, fishing boats lined along the west pier, pleasure craft dotting the harbour, the whole thing overseen by the three-quarter moon in an almost clear sky. A few yards from where he stood, the stone stairway led down to the water. It was where he and Jo-Jo used to take the boat across to Ireland's Eye.

It might have been a fishing village over on the west coast, rather than a haven for the Dublin gentry.

The peace was stained by the sound of a car accelerating along Harbour Road, a low sports model passing out a family car. Lar stood in the cold, looking at the village. Pretty and familiar and all in his past, all the things that made his life comfortable, if that mad fucker had his way. He went close to the edge of the pier and dropped the pieces of the DVD into the water.

Chapter 30

In the end he did as Frank Tucker instructed, through Tommy Farr. 'Choose a hotel, book a room, anywhere in the city centre,' Tommy said. 'You pick the place, you tell no one until you get there — that way you know there'll be no surprises waiting. Have your people check it out, then call me — I'll tell him you're ready. He's got it worked out so it's safe for everyone.'

Lar Mackendrick chose Buswell's Hotel. It was central, busy, close to the Dail. The police and the army had permanent posts in Leinster House, protecting the politicians, so the area had slightly more security than most. As instructed, he booked two rooms on the same floor, under a phoney name.

Lar got there at ten in the morning. After he called Tommy Farr to say where he was, he waited half an hour until a young man arrived in the lobby and introduced himself to Lar's people. They took him into the toilets and patted him down, then brought him up to the second floor. The young man was a civilian, a technician with a laptop. He put the laptop on a table, logged on, then crouched down by the skirting board and ran a phone cable up to the computer. He spent a minute tapping keys, then he gestured for Lar to pay attention.

'That's the camera, that little round thing over the screen. There's the mike — speak normally, the sound levels are set, there should be no problem.' The picture on the screen was of a room like this one, probably a hotel room.

'Where's that?'

'I've no idea — another hotel, I'd guess.'

'How do I know this thing isn't wired to blow up in my face?'

'I bought it yesterday, in Dixon's. No one's messed with it.'

Lar said, 'You wait across the hall, with my people, just in case. If anything goes wrong, your family will always wonder what happened to you.'

The technician nodded. He seemed unconcerned. He made a call on his mobile, then left the room and a few seconds later Frank Tucker appeared on the screen. He was wearing a dark blue suit, with a pale cream shirt and a dark blue tie. He sat down and said, 'You're looking well, Lar — all things considered.'

'You cunt.'

'Doing it this way means no cops had a chance to tap anything, bug anything. We can speak freely — no one has to wonder if anyone's got a gun in his sock.' Tucker put regret in his voice. 'First off, I'm sorry about Matty.'

Lar said nothing.

Tucker said, 'Any other way of opening negotiations, it wouldn't have worked.'

'I'm going to do you myself, cunt.'

Tucker stared out of the screen, his expression patient and sympathetic. 'I know how you feel, Lar. You need time to think this through, to see what the choices are. You spoke to Tommy, so you know what I'm aiming at.'

Lar said, 'From what I gather, you reckon we need a new high king and you're the man for the job.'

Tucker turned his hands palms up. 'Self-protection, really. It makes sense. The setup we have now, it's a mess. Any number of gangs, some of them nothing but coked-up kiddies who'll swat you if you look crooked at them. They kill one another because someone insulted someone else's uncle — a waste of energy. Then, there's a handful of smart guys like you and Tommy Farr.'

'So, you take us out of the game?'

'Like I say, Lar, it's a mess. It's all based on neighbourhoods and families, people who grew up together. Everyone's got their own little market, their own suppliers, their own distribution. All that shit, it's a recipe for small wars and endless feuds.'

'There's room for everyone.'

'The boom years, we all got rich, even the coked-up kids. So much money around — the rugby crowd and the business crowd, the celebrity set, they all need a little toot to keep them at their peak. This isn't a cottage industry any more — someone's going to consolidate the market and the losers go to the wall.'

'And you've got yourself down for Mr Big.'

'Leave it too late, someone sees me as a soft, juicy target.'

'That's how you see me?'

'You made your money a long time ago, Lar, same as Tommy Farr. Most of us, me included — we're too scared to spend real money. We've got the CAB looking over our shoulders, so we live in poxy little houses in the old neighbourhoods. Your money's been well laundered for years, before all that crap started. You're settled, comfortable. What they call you, in business terms, Lar — you're low-hanging fruit.'

'Mr fucking Big.'

'I've got troubles of my own, Lar. There's some mad bastards out in Clondalkin — they've got me in their sights. I've got one of them in my pocket, so I know what they're thinking. It's just a matter of time. They reckon they're the dog's bollocks — all they have to do is point a finger and go *boom* and they're in the big time. Soon as you and I reach an agreement, I've got plans for that shower.'

'I'm a detail, then, before you get onto the main agenda.'

'Consolidation, Lar. I've got Tommy Farr's operation in the bag, I come to an arrangement with you and I'm bigger than Manchester United. The Clondalkin crowd are a couple of leagues too small — when they see that, they back off and hope I don't swat them.'

'So, I just walk away — with what?' Lar's head was down, his gaze unfocused, staring at the keyboard of the laptop.

'No one goes away empty-handed. Same deal I offered Tommy Farr. You can sell most of your property, or rent it out if the market's too depressed — you leave the businesses to me. Then, two grand a week — call it a pension.'

Lar Mackendrick looked up, teeth bared.

'Cunt.'

'No offence taken, Lar. I know it hurts.'

'Piece of shit. You strut around this fucking town, Mr Big — you piece of *shit* — but you won't see me coming.'

'There was a time, Lar, when that would have been true. It was your brother who built up the tight outfit, it was Jo-Jo who made it work, set up the money laundering and the property shelters. You're different, Lar. You have employees, casual labour. Apart from Matty — most of them you don't know their names. There isn't one of them would risk a cut finger for you, let alone a bullet in the head.'

Tucker leaned forward towards the camera. 'I could swat you tonight, Lar. I reached into your outfit and I took Todd, and he set up Matty. You don't know who else I've got. And that makes every one of them suspect, and that means there isn't one of them you can count on.'

'*Piece of shit!*'

'You've got a week to get back to me.'

Lar pointed at Tucker's image on the screen.

251

'You think you can just — '

Tucker reached forward and tapped three keys on his laptop and the screen went blank.

' — tell me — you *fucking* — '

Lar stopped. He stared at the screen, aware of the sound of his own loud breathing. He stood up, grabbed the laptop by the screen and threw it against the wall.

Chapter 31

May knew something was going on, but when she tried to get Lar to talk about it he waved her away and found something that urgently needed doing.

On the second day of his sour mood, he lost his temper with her. She was cooking dinner and Lar was sitting at the kitchen table, with the *Evening Herald* spread in front of him. He'd been staring at the same page for ten minutes.

'What's wrong, love?'

'Nothing.'

'Please, let's — '

'Just stop — leave it alone.'

Her tone was soft. 'Whatever's going on — '

'*Christ sake!*'

The fear beneath the stubbornness was unmistakable. Lar left the house and when he came home two hours later May could smell the drink off him.

'Tell me.'

He told her.

She said, 'Well — '

Lar said, 'He's right — the little fuck is right. There's nothing more to say — it's over.'

Frank Tucker had the balls and the organisation he needed to cut out Tommy Farr, and he knew how to dismantle Lar Mackendrick.

'I can go after him — I go after him, I'm dead. And it won't take a war to do it — he's already got his moves mapped out. He'll already have some of my people in his pocket — there isn't anyone I can trust.'

Lar's gaze was focused a couple of feet in front of him, somewhere in mid-air. 'If I do what he says, I get to fuck off out of the country. And if I stand up to him, I get to lie beside Jo-Jo in Sutton cemetery.'

'You've got money, you've got people.'

Lar's outfit had an inner circle of half a dozen, revolving around Matty Butler. Beyond those were the dozen or so in the wider team, and then the freelancers who signed up for particular jobs. Tucker would know every one of them.

'For years, it was Jo-Jo ran everything. Without Matty, I'm — ' He gestured with both hands held wide. 'And that little bastard knew that was where to hit me.'

'You're giving in?'

'What else can I do?'

★   ★   ★

Lar changed his mind next evening. He didn't use the phrase *blaze of glory* but that was what it sounded like to May.

'Whatever happens — if I can hold my nerve I

253

think I can take that little bastard.'

She asked what he had in mind, but there was no plan. Just a surly reaction against Frank Tucker's demands.

'I won't piss off and vegetate. I won't count the days. I won't watch the Christmases clicking by until I stroke out.'

It was the end of a long day, in which one draining hour of depression followed another. It was as if Lar had weighed the consequences of resignation against those of rebellion and he'd made a choice.

May was in bed, Lar was standing by the bedroom window, looking at the lights of Howth village below and the darkness beyond.

'People come to me, they offer me deals, they ask me to come into things with them, they tell me what they're planning, like they want me to give them the nod. I need all that.'

Lar turned to May. 'It isn't just the money. There's things that wouldn't happen without my say-so. I make a difference.'

He turned back to the window. The sea had never been darker, the sky had never been more clear. The lights in the houses scattered around the hills below had never seemed more like jewels set on black velvet.

⋆　⋆　⋆

Maybe he was right. Maybe that was the best way. Lying in the darkness, May Mackendrick pondered the choices. Rebellion and perhaps a quick retribution from Frank Tucker and his

254

scumbags. Or years of festering resentment, vegetating in some foreign resort.

Maybe Lar was right.

Go for it, damn the risk.

The odds were with Frank Tucker, but it was better than counting down the days.

Lying there, listening to Lar's breathing, May considered her own prospects. There was money safely put away, she was three years younger than Lar and she could see a very different life waiting.

She would miss him.

★   ★   ★

At breakfast, Lar was silent. May couldn't tell if he'd changed his mind again.

After she'd put milk on his porridge and poured his tea, she stood behind Lar and one hand gently stroked his hair. She said, 'What would Jo-Jo do?'

'Jo-Jo wouldn't run.'

'But how would he fight, what would he do?'

If there was one image that outweighed all others in Lar's memories of his brother, it was Jo-Jo in an armchair or sitting at a table, a book open in front of him. Jo-Jo was the bright one, Jo-Jo used his head.

A year after Jo-Jo and his mother Pearl were murdered, Lar finally got around to clearing out their things. He shared some mementoes with family members and gave the rest to a charity shop. One drunken evening, playing one of Jo-Jo's Marty Robbins CDs, he went through

Jo-Jo's books and chose about a dozen of them to keep on a small shelf in his living room. The John Grisham novel that Jo-Jo had been reading just before he was murdered, the three old Alistair MacLean paperbacks he'd had since his teens, James Plunkett's *Strumpet City*, which Jo-Jo had read and reread back in the 1970s and had urged all his friends to read. There were a few books on Irish history and a tattered guide to hillwalking in Wicklow. *Strumpet City* reminded Lar of the stories of old Dublin that his grandfather used to tell. He liked the Grisham book but he thought the MacLean stories were old-fashioned. He didn't open the history books. Then there was the little book he now took down from the living-room shelf.

The Art of War by Sun Tzu.

The book had impressed Jo-Jo so much that he claimed Sun Tzu was almost a partner in the various businesses the family dominated in their area of northside Dublin — protection, cigarette smuggling, armed robbery, bootleg CDs and DVDs, the financing of drug deals.

'Without his advice, I'd have been dead years ago.'

The Mackendricks had family links with two outfits in the Finglas area, both of which Jo-Jo had guided through several rough confrontations with rivals. Freelance operators kicked in a cut from the robberies and drug distribution they carried out in the Ballycarrig and Glencara estates to the south and west of

Finglas. Dealing with such people required nerve and decisiveness and Jo-Jo claimed he never made a big decision without consulting the little book.

'No better pair for a bumpy ride,' he used to laugh, 'than the Chinaman and meself.'

What would Jo-Jo do? First, he'd consult his Chinaman.

When Lar began reading the book he decided that a lot of it was pointless. Which wasn't surprising, given that this Sun Tzu was born five hundred years before Christ. Take the bit about how dust rising high was a sign of chariots advancing. And how low, widespread dust was a sign of infantry on the move. And it wasn't just that the book was out of date, some of it was just shite.

The clever combatant imposes his will on the enemy, but does not allow the enemy's will to be imposed on him.

More than a bit obvious.

To lift an autumn hair is no sign of great strength; to see the sun and moon is no sign of sharp sight; to hear the noise of thunder is no sign of a quick ear.

Lar got that bit. It's no big deal, doing stuff that's easy. That's what it meant — but, why not just *say* that? The Chinaman seemed to enjoy making things unclear. Like it wasn't enough to give advice, he had to make you work for it.

257

Lar used a green highlighter to underline a passage that clicked with him.

All warfare is based on deception. Hence, when able to attack, we must seem unable. When using our forces, we must seem inactive. When we are near, we must make the enemy believe we are far away. When far away, we must make him believe we are near.

For the first time since Jo-Jo's death Lar felt like he was making some kind of contact with his brother. This stuff was beginning to make sense. It wasn't like a DIY manual that might tell you how to work on a car engine. It was a way of looking at the world, a way of bringing out things you didn't know you knew, putting all that shit into words.

What would Jo-Jo do?

Jo-Jo would take his time, give himself some room. He'd assess his forces and he'd find the best way to cut the throat of any fucker who tried to walk all over his life. That's what Jo-Jo would do.

Lar used the green highlighter again.

Hold out baits to entice the enemy. Feign disorder, and crush him.

That was more like it. Advice plain and simple, no fucking about.

Chapter 32

Declan Roeper was twenty minutes late. He was glad to see that Lar Mackendrick looked impatient.

Mackendrick was sitting in a shelter on the Clontarf seafront, hands in the pocket of his heavy overcoat, facing out towards Dublin Bay. He'd lost a lot of weight a few years back, but he'd put a little of it back on. There was a noticeable double chin beneath his ill-tempered face.

As he reached Mackendrick, Roeper didn't slow down, his stride long, his back straight. 'Let's walk,' he said, and he smiled as he heard Mackendrick scramble to his feet and hurry to catch up.

'You're late.'

'How can I help?'

It had been a couple of decades since Declan Roeper had done any field training, slogging about in the Donegal mountains with a pack on his back, but he was still fighting fit. He increased his pace and listened as Mackendrick came alongside. No hint of puffing. Lar was in fair enough shape for his age.

'I need weaponry.'

'You think I'm some kind of arms supermarket? *Aisle six, handguns and Armalites. Aisle seven, hand grenades, Semtex and C4.*'

'Name your price.'

Roeper laughed. 'Haven't you heard? The IRA decommissioned, the rest of us went out of business. It's all peace and brotherly love these days. Instead of shooting the Brits we snog them to death.'

'Five clean pistols, no markings, no history. With silencers and ammo to match. And explosives — something big enough to take down a house.'

Roeper stopped walking.

'Jesus, Lar, which country are you planning to invade?'

'Will you do it?'

'Your kind of people — you've never played with anything bigger than a few pipe bombs or hand grenades. What makes you think — '

'Cash, up front.'

'Suppose I had access to that kind of stuff — why would I let a gangster get hold of it?'

'I'm paying above the odds.'

'That stuff's not for playing with. Besides, there'll come a time when the complacency is gone, when there's a new IRA and serious people need serious material.'

'In the meantime, serious people need serious money.'

Roeper began walking again, more slowly this time.

Mackendrick said, 'I need the material two weeks from today.'

★ ★ ★

Using clean mobile phones — prepaid, off the shelf, untraceable, untappable — Lar Mackendrick conducted negotiations with Frank Tucker over a day and a half, before they reached agreement.

'We need to get the mechanics of this thing

260

right,' Lar said. 'I can't just walk away. I need a couple of weeks.'

'You can't string things out, Lar.'

'Three weeks — maybe four. I've got people to talk to, things to — look, this is a complicated business. If I just walk away, a lot of people get screwed. People I owe money to, people I've made promises to — then there are people who owe *me* money, they need time. I've got to get things in order.'

'There's no point dragging things out — nothing's going to change.'

'That's not what this is about. We're agreed, deal done — I just need some time.'

And Lar gave him the sweetener.

A petrol-smuggling operation, back and forth across the border, using a farm in the area where Monaghan pokes up between Fermanagh and Armagh. Although the farmer had twice been arrested and questioned, there were no charges and no one knew of Lar's involvement. Not the police on either side of the border, not the smuggling outfit in the north, and only one of the Monaghan people.

'I could have kept that quiet, held on to it. Instead, I'm giving it to you. I've thought this through and I don't like it but it's the sensible thing to do. I hate your fucking guts, but I've got to do business with you — and this is a goodwill offering. Take it, and let me wrap this up with a bit of dignity.'

He sacrifices something, that the enemy may snatch at it. By holding out baits, he

261

*keeps him on the march. Then, with a body
of picked men, he lies in wait for him.*

Frank Tucker didn't get back to Lar until the
following day. 'Okay, three weeks.'

'A month — tops.'

'Fuck that.'

'Probably I won't need the full month, but I'm
in London all next week — my wife had the trip
planned and I'm not cancelling — and it'll take
me two or three weeks to wrap this up at the
other end and that takes us into Christmas.
What's the difference?'

There was an amused twist to Frank Tucker's
voice. 'Okay, Lar. But not a single day into the
new year.'

'And that two grand a week?'

'Agreed.'

'I want three.'

Frank Tucker laughed. 'Don't push it, Lar.'

They settled on two and a half.

⋆　⋆　⋆

Walking back towards Fairview, Declan Roeper
and Lar Mackendrick crossed the road and
found a quiet corner of The Yacht. After the
barman had brought their coffees Roeper said,
'Lar, you're the enemy.'

Lar Mackendrick made a dismissive noise.
Roeper leaned closer and said, 'We've done a bit
of business, strictly small-time. But you're
talking now about serious firepower. I'm in the
patriot game. And, bottom line — you're part of

262

what's wrong with this country.'

Lar Mackendrick smiled. 'Come on, Declan. Everyone's got an angle. Half this city was built on crooked land deals and politicians selling bent planning permission. How much of the building trade operates off the books? How many of the big family businesses were built on bribery, extortion and tax evasion? All those big-time tax frauds the banks organised — you see any bankers in jail? The difference is I steal thousands, they steal millions.'

Roeper looked like a man who'd been walking up an endless hill — worn out, but reluctant to write off all the time and effort, barely hanging on to the belief that he'll ever see the summit. 'This country used to be something special — it had a spirit. Now it looks and sounds like anywhere else. The kind of money that used to buy a house, they started paying that much for a car. The kind of money that used to buy a car, they started paying that much for designer handbags. Even when the economy goes into the tank, all they can think of is getting back to the good old days of infinite squander. Offer them sacrifice — they think it's the height of patriotism to recycle their champagne bottles.'

'When's it ever been any different?'

'We've got a whole new gentry. Fake tans and fake tits. Sleazy parties and bowls of happy powder to impress their friends. And you and your like are happy to kill each other for the privilege of serving their needs.'

'And what's your dream? Blow the whole thing up?'

'Don't be simplistic.'

'Thirty years you spent blowing things up, shooting people dead in front of their wives and their kids — and you're lecturing *me* on the spirit of the fucking nation?'

Roeper took a sip of his coffee, leaned forward and held Mackendrick's gaze.

'I've got people who sacrificed everything. People who could have had good jobs, a good living — they're getting old now and they've nothing to show for it.'

'Which is why we ought to do business. You need the money now.'

'It's not all about money. I need to know what you need the explosives for.'

'Can't tell you.'

'This stuff doesn't grow on trees. It cost a lot to import, back in the day — and it costs a lot to store securely, until everyone gets over the lovey-dovey shit and we need it again. It would cost even more to replace.'

'Name your price.'

'I need to know what it'll be used for.'

Mackendrick hesitated. Then he said, 'A diversion. I've got a job coming up in the centre of the city — I need a big distraction. Something so big that it throws a shadow over the city for an hour or two. And while the cops are dealing with that, they won't have time to notice what's happening in the backstreets.'

Declan Roeper's smile was bitter. 'Everything's turned on its head, these days. My old comrades are playing footsie with the Brits, and it's the ordinary decent criminals who're giving the establishment nightmares.'

'You approve?'

'No.' Roeper's smile was gone now. 'But a whole lot of smug people are going to have their assumptions shattered. That I like.'

'How much is this going to cost me?' Lar Mackendrick said.

Chapter 33

Lar and May Mackendrick flew to London for a couple of days and stayed at the Kensington Jury's. On the first afternoon, Lar linked up with a friend down from Formby, in Liverpool. In the bar of a hotel on the Strand, the friend introduced Mackendrick to two former officers from the Metropolitan Police who now operated an unlicensed private inquiry agency. Mackendrick laid down fifteen thousand sterling in cash and passed over a list of sixteen names and addresses — Frank Tucker's inner circle. He specified the depth of surveillance required, covering routine movements over a couple of weekend mornings. No locals to be employed on the surveillance.

'Tucker gets a whisper of this, the balloon goes up.'

After some discussion he was told that level of work meant that the previously quoted price of fifteen grand was a serious underestimate. The job would require an extra ten thousand. Mackendrick agreed. The additional money would be delivered by courier next day.

While May headed for Harrods on the second afternoon, Mackendrick kept an appointment at O'Neill's Pub on Euston Road.

'Call me Michael,' Dolly Finn said. 'My papers say Michael Sheehan.'

Without someone as hard as Dolly Finn it wasn't a plan that Lar had, it was a reckless gamble.

'You settled down here yet?'

Dolly was tucking into the all-day breakfast. Lar had a mineral water. In the background, Bono was warbling about it being a beautiful day.

'Very much so.'

'Going home for good is still out of the question?'

'It doesn't bother me.'

In recruiting foot soldiers for the job of taking down Frank Tucker, Lar Mackendrick was flying blind. There wasn't anyone inside his outfit who mightn't have been squared away by Frank Tucker. Approach the wrong person and Lar would be dead by nightfall. Matty had known who the up-and-comers were in the city. Lar's knowledge was limited.

Almost a year had passed since Lar had told Karl Prowse to fuck off when the young smartass called and offered him a piece of a jewellery robbery. Karl said all he needed was someone to help sell the stuff. Lar had hung up. A month later, Karl Prowse made the papers when a murder charge was dropped. Karl was pulled in after a Chinese student was mugged in St Anne's Park and died two days later. On the day the case

266

opened, the prosecution disclosed that the two witnesses who had identified Karl as the assailant were refusing to verify the information they'd given in statements to gardai. The judge ordered them onto the witness stand and threatened them with strict penalties and they all swore they couldn't remember anything about the crime.

Prowse had been stupid to ring Lar out of the blue, offering stolen jewellery. But the killing charge said he could handle himself. The fact that he could arrange to frighten witnesses into silence suggested that he wasn't as thick as he might seem. He should be good enough for the kind of work required. Crucially, he was off the radar as far as Frank Tucker was concerned. Karl brought his friend Robbie Nugent into the game.

The third recruit was Walter Bennett, a low-profile moocher who stole cars and whatever else he could sell. Nicking cars without wrecking them, and supplying credible plates, were the kind of skills that didn't come off the peg along with muscle like Karl and Robbie.

Forced to recruit from outside his usual circles, with just three untried foot soldiers, Lar needed someone with hard experience, and no one came harder than Dolly Finn.

'I owe you,' Dolly Finn said.

'Jo-Jo and me, we owed you a lot more,' Lar said.

'I did what I thought was right.'

Dolly Finn had been an independent operator in Dublin, mostly doing hold-ups. It had been several years back that he'd been approached to do a hit on Jo-Jo Mackendrick. Dolly informed Jo-Jo, the would-be assassins were dealt with and Jo-Jo gave Dolly sixty grand and his eternal gratitude. After a kidnap job went wrong Dolly had had to leave Dublin. He spent a year in Nottingham and when that didn't work out he headed down to London. Some months later, adrift and unconnected, he risked a visit back to Dublin, where he approached Lar for help. Lar gave him money and a recommendation to a London outfit with which he'd done business. Since then, Dolly had thrived. He insisted on repaying the money that Lar had given him.

'Who are we talking about?'

Lar gave Dolly Finn the background on Frank Tucker.

'Gang war — I don't do gang wars.'

'Neither do I.' Lar told him the plan.

There were several business types in the pub, and a well-dressed woman who kept checking her watch. Over near the door a white-haired man was talking loudly, angrily, to a woman half his age. Lar thought he heard him say something about a drum solo. Though there was no one within earshot and they were talking in soft tones, Dolly looked around before he said, 'You got the IRA to sell you that stuff?'

'No, the Provos have gone hippie these days. A spin-off, people I've dealt with before. Declan Roeper?'

Dolly shook his head. 'Never heard of him. Is he in on this?'

'No chance — first-class wanker. I gave him some shit about using the stuff to cause a distraction so we could pull off a job.' Lar leaned closer. 'What I need the stuff for is to take out a very specific building at a very specific time.'

Dolly raised an eyebrow. 'A bomb in Dublin — the way things are these days, it won't just be the gardai checking that one out. You'll have everyone from the MI6 to the FBI sniffing around.'

'I've made provision. They'll round up the usual suspects — but one likely lad will be missing, presumed to have fled the jurisdiction.'

'This Roeper fella?'

'Big-headed bollocks. Couple of years ago, he and his people wasted a couple of drug dealers in Dundalk. The cops know it was him. When Frank Tucker's hotshots get taken out and Roeper's gone missing, he'll fit the bill — the police will put it down to another Republican clean-up job.'

'You want me to do him?'

'No — that'll be done by the time you come over. I need you for three jobs, same day. One day's work — then you come back here, that's the end of it.'

'All in one day?'

'All going well.'

'Ambitious.'

'Has to be. If we drag things out, give them a chance to hit back — they'll slaughter us. Has to be quick, clean. We waste Tucker and a handful of his top people — take the head off the snake and it's a goner. Frank himself, I'd love to do him personally, but it's not practical.'

'Long as he goes, it doesn't matter.'

Lar nodded. 'You're in, then?'

'Like I say, I owe you.'

'If this works, Dolly — anything you want.'

'Call me Michael,' Dolly Finn said.

★   ★   ★

Lar met May at the hotel and they took a taxi to Covent Garden, then they strolled until they found a restaurant that May thought looked nice.

They sometimes had their individual schedules that parted them for a day or two, but mostly in their long marriage they'd spent hardly any time apart. They maintained this evening ritual, at home or in a restaurant, sitting across a dining table, looking back on the day. Over the years, it was like Lar and May had seeped into each other. They'd become not Lar and May but Lar-and-May, a single unit made of two equal parts.

After dinner, they walked up towards Leicester Square and strolled a while, enjoying the buzz. They continued on down to Piccadilly Circus, arm in arm, then they got a taxi back to the hotel in Kensington. May went up to the room, and Lar sat for a while in the hotel bar. He was on his second vodka when he remembered the bar served spirits only in doubles. There was a time when that wouldn't have mattered, but those days were gone. He'd had a glass of wine with the meal, and now more vodka than he intended. He left half the second glass on the table and went up to the room. After they'd made love, Lar and May lay in the dark, talking quietly about the Tucker problem. Before they fell asleep they'd agreed on a definite date on which to make it go away.

Chapter 34

The policeman was middle-aged, with a flash suit, bad teeth and a hunger for money.

'What did it say?' Lar Mackendrick asked.

'I couldn't very well take notes, could I?'

'You saw it or you didn't.'

'Just a glimpse.'

'Couldn't you get a copy?'

'Look — it wasn't like that. I was leaving a report on the Chief Super's desk — I bent down, had a look, just curiosity. Then I heard someone coming — it was the station sergeant coming in with some filing. I went about my business.'

'The gist — what was the gist of it?'

'It was an authorisation sheet. For what, I don't know. Disposal of charges, non-standard expenses or whatever. That's what they're used for.'

'And?'

'That's it — I saw Detective Garda Templeton-Smith's name, and Walter Bennett — I know he's done stuff for a lot of people, so I thought I ought to put the word around about the little fucker.'

You thought it might be worth something.

With a week to go before the opening of hostilities against Frank Tucker, this was more of a nuisance than a disaster. Walter, as a driver and provider of cars, knew bugger-all about the plan. But he was in a garda's pocket and he could yap at any time. The project would have to be put on hold until the problem was fixed.

There's always an upside.

Karl Prowse and Robbie Nugent needed a blooding. They'd need strong nerves in the days to come, so a little taster would do no harm. Taking care of Walter would settle their nerves. The wise leader takes advantage of a change of circumstances.

Water shapes its course according to the nature of the ground over which it flows; the soldier works out his victory in relation to the foe whom he is facing.

The way it worked out, the smartass who poked his nose in and kept Walter Bennett alive for a few days turned out to be useful. Danny Callaghan was younger than Walter, bigger and tougher, with a killing on his record. Lar liked him for the job — and the fact that the person he had killed was a cousin of Frank Tucker made Lar like him even more. He was easy to get a grip on. His ex-wife, and the bitch he was screwing — all Lar had to do was threaten to shred them and Callaghan was putty.

It went well after that. Karl and Robbie successfully did the job on Walter, second time round. Danny Callaghan passed his test. If he'd chickened out and gone to the police the stolen

4×4, and the two kids in it, would have been lifted.

Then there was one last job before it was time to move against Tucker. And that job would be useful for nailing the new boy down even more firmly.

'Danny?'

'Yeah.'

'You free?'

'Just getting something to eat.'

'I want to show you something. Now.'

'I need to change, have a shower, it won't take — '

'You're fine as you are.'

Part Four
At the End

Chapter 35

'This is Declan Roeper. As you can see, Declan's been digging a grave.'

When Lar Mackendrick threw the spade, Danny Callaghan instinctively reached up and caught it.

'Help him,' Mackendrick said.

'What's this about?'

'It's about you doing as you're told.'

Callaghan stood there holding the spade. There was a small smile on Karl Prowse's face, as though he was hoping that Callaghan would do something silly.

After a moment, Callaghan stepped down into the grave. Roeper nodded to Callaghan, almost a companionable gesture.

'Keep at it,' Karl Prowse said. 'We don't have all night.'

The grave was less than a foot deep. It was cold up here. Even so, Roeper — in a three-quarter-length waxed coat and leather homburg hat — was overdressed for the task. He resumed digging, very slowly. Callaghan hefted the shovel and began work.

It took about twenty minutes before the grave was almost two feet deep. Roeper's breath was loud, his face was sweaty. He'd taken off the coat, though he still wore the leather homburg. He was bent forward, each shovelful an effort.

'Enough,' Lar Mackendrick said. He motioned to Callaghan to get out of the grave. Callaghan put the spade aside and stepped up from the hole. He could feel the beat of his heart echoing in his throat. Roeper continued digging.

Mackendrick said, 'Declan.'

Roeper turned and looked from Callaghan to Mackendrick. He dropped the spade. His movement jerky and unsteady, he stepped up out of the grave. 'Lar — ' he said.

'No point.'

Roeper stared, then he made a noise in his throat and spat into the grave.

'Give me time for a prayer.'

Mackendrick shrugged. He pointed at the grave. 'Get in.'

Roeper grunted as he stepped back down into the grave. He turned and made the sign of the cross. His puffs of breath, visible in the cold air, were small and each quickly followed the one before. He took off his leather hat and dropped it at his feet, then took a pair of rosary beads from a pocket and held them, his hands loosely clasped, as he silently mouthed the words of a prayer. When he finished he made the sign of the cross again, kissed the rosary beads and wrapped them around his left hand.

Lar nodded to Karl Prowse.

Prowse lifted his automatic pistol, released the safety and pulled back the slide. Then he took his time walking around the grave. He stood next to Mackendrick.

Roeper looked at Mackendrick for a moment, then turned away to look instead towards the trees. He straightened up, as if his spine had unwound and the exhaustion had left his body. He raised his head, thrust his chin forward and put his arms down by his sides. Staring out into the darkness, seeing whatever he saw out there, an old soldier standing to attention.

It lasted two or three seconds, then Karl Prowse shot him twice in the chest and Roeper fell straight back and rolled onto his side.

From several feet away, Robbie came forward and fired another bullet into the limp body. Prowse looked at him in irritation, as if his friend had nicked a piece of food from his plate without asking.

Lar Mackendrick said, 'Cover him up.' Callaghan looked up from the body and saw that Mackendrick was speaking to him.

'I'm not — '

'Cover him up.'

Slowly, Callaghan stepped into the grave. He reached down and turned Roeper onto his back. He stood a moment, looking down at the body, no puffs of breath now visible around the face. Callaghan straightened out the legs and put the arms down by the sides.

Lar Mackendrick said, 'You're not arranging flowers — get the fuck on with it.'

Callaghan got out of the grave, threw Roeper's coat and hat alongside the body and picked up the spade that Roeper had used. He threw a spadeful of earth onto the body, then another.

'I'll wait in the car,' Mackendrick said. He

turned to Karl Prowse and Robbie. 'Get a good night's sleep. We'll have a war council tomorrow, and the fun starts the day after.'

Mackendrick walked away. Robbie lit a cigarette, Karl Prowse moved off and sat in his Toledo. Danny Callaghan kept shovelling earth.

After a few minutes Roeper was covered from the legs up, along with most of his torso and arms. Callaghan flinched as a clump of soil landed on Roeper's left cheek. He stared at the body.

He doesn't feel it.

Just a piece of meat now, getting colder by the second.

He threw another shovelful of dirt onto the body and saw Roeper blink.

Callaghan paused, holding up a spadeful of earth.

Just a shadow.

He threw the earth onto Roeper's legs. He aimed the next few spadefuls away from Roeper's face.

Oh, Jesus, please. Please, Jesus.

Callaghan wasn't sure if he was praying for Roeper to be alive or dead.

If Roeper was breathing it was too slow and shallow to show on the cold air. The blink had to have been a trick of the shadows.

Has to be.

Roeper blinked again.

Fuck.

Oh, shit.

Christ.

To draw attention to the fact that Roeper was

alive would bring Karl and Robbie, who would gleefully empty their guns. To continue burying him would kill him just as surely.

Callaghan put down the spade, got into the shallow grave and felt around in the dirt until he found Roeper's leather hat.

'What you doing?'

Callaghan turned to Robbie. 'It's freaking me out — throwing dirt on his face. I need to cover his eyes.' Robbie turned away, stamping his feet. 'Get a move on,' he said, 'it's fucking cold.'

Callaghan bent over Roeper. He looked down into his eyes, saw recognition and gave the man a slight nod. Roeper blinked again. Then Callaghan put the leather hat on Roeper's face, the crown across his mouth and nose, the brim covering his eyes. He stepped out of the grave and resumed shovelling clay.

When all but the space around Roeper's head was filling up, Callaghan eased a shovelful onto Roeper's hat, letting the earth slide gently off the spade. The grave was about two feet deep. Between Roeper's face and the surface there were about twelve or fifteen inches of earth, with several inches of that taken up by the leather hat. If the hat held its shape it might provide a pocket of air around Roeper's mouth. Callaghan filled in around Roeper's head, then eased more soil onto the hat until it too was covered.

It took maybe five more minutes to fill the grave and disperse the leftover earth. Karl Prowse returned from sitting in his car and began stamping on the grave. Callaghan stepped forward and stamped on the clay above each side of Roeper's head, trying to leave the soil above his face loose and untrodden. He didn't know who Roeper was or what he did. He didn't care what these people did to one another. But his mind was inflamed with the image of the man lying under several inches of earth, injured, frightened, eking out a tiny measure of air.

Karl and Robbie collected undergrowth and debris and scattered it across and around the grave.

Karl said, 'That'll do.'

* * *

'Done?' Lar Mackendrick said.

Danny Callaghan nodded. As the Isuzu pulled away across the bumpy ground towards the road, Callaghan tried to remain casual as he desperately looked for landmarks to identify the site.

If he could get back here before the air ran out for Roeper.

If he could find the grave.

Day Eleven

Chapter 36

Dolly Finn was awake, lying on a lumpy bed in a B & B in Gardiner Street, Billy Bauer's gentle 'Night Cruise' playing in his iPod. The light was off, the small room lit only by the street lamp outside. The silenced .38 automatic he'd received from Lar Mackendrick was underneath the mattress.

Arriving early on the flight from London, he'd spent the afternoon walking around the city centre. In the old days in Dublin he'd felt a revulsion against moving beyond the tight boundaries within which he lived his daily life. Forced to flee the city, and finding himself surprisingly happy in the vast fields of play that were London, he was surprised to realise that he felt no more than a vague affection for the old place.

Standing in the centre of O'Connell Street, he tried to remember what it had looked like before the renovation. The street seemed wider now. They'd cut down the hundred-year-old trees, narrowed the roadway on both sides of the street and laid wide new pavements. O'Connell Street used to feel like it had somehow just evolved into what it was. Now everything looked like it came out of a catalogue. It was as though a class of

283

architecture students had won a competition and the prize allowed them to implement all their pet ideas on the capital city's main street.

Upriver from O'Connell Bridge, on the north side of the Liffey, Dolly found an Italian place, ordered chicken in a mushroom sauce, and had a single beer. Then he took a taxi to a pub in Finglas, where he met Karl Prowse and got a lift to a warehouse on the Carrigmore industrial estate. Lar Mackendrick and his two new recruits were waiting.

The war council had been short enough. Mackendrick distributed guns and silencers and off-the-shelf mobiles, then he went over the plan, so each would know what the others had to do. Dolly Finn wasn't too concerned about anyone else's work — he had three killing jobs, and it all sounded very doable. Karl Prowse was playing Mr Cool, trying to impress the new guy. The kid, Robbie Nugent, seemed moody, perhaps nervous.

'There's a driver, too — Danny Callaghan. I had a meet with him earlier — no need for him to be here.'

To Dolly Finn, the hired help weren't too impressive, but it was a straightforward job as long as no one lost their nerve. His work done, his Michael Sheehan bank account replenished, Dolly would be back in London by tomorrow night.

The street outside the B & B had been noisy earlier, but it was quiet now. Dolly felt sleep lapping at his mind, so he killed the iPod, slid off the headphones and turned his face towards the wall.

Danny Callaghan looked at the clock again, the *12.18* glowing in the darkness, on the table beside his bed. He'd tried reading, but his mind was skimming from one thought to another, unable to settle, unable to absorb. It was more than twenty-four hours since the shooting of Declan Roeper in the Dublin mountains.

Beside the clock there was a folded piece of paper.

'That's Karl's address in Santry, okay?' Tonight's meeting with Lar Mackendrick, five hours back, had taken place in an upstairs room at Kimmet's Ale House, in Wakeham Street.

'Needn't keep you long, Danny,' Lar Mackendrick said.

'What do I do?'

Mackendrick spoke above the noise from the traditional band downstairs — guitars, fiddles, a *bodhrán* and a lot of *didley-eye-de-da*. He and Callaghan were in a second-floor room with a weak bulb. They were alone — the bar at the end of the room was closed.

'All you need to know is that this whole thing depends on everyone doing their job. Take one piece away, it doesn't work. And your piece is this. Nine-thirty in the morning, you pick up a white Ford van from Karl Prowse's garage — at that address. Karl's wife is expecting you. Take it to Cullybawn, park in the grounds of St Ursula's church. Make sure you bring your mobile along — soon as you get there you ring me. The number's on the other side of that piece of

285

paper.' Lar smiled. 'When this is over, Danny — if you want regular work, you're a good team player.'

'I don't think so.'

'To each his own. We don't need to be friends, but there's one reason you want to hope that this works out okay.' Lar's voice lowered. 'I've made arrangements. Anything goes wrong, say I take a fall, your ex-wife's going to do a lot of screaming before she dies. I've got people lined up — '

'My ex-wife's got nothing to do — '

'She's handy. Your girlfriend, too.'

'She's not my girlfriend. She — '

'Whatever. Here's how it is.' He held out one hand, palm up. 'You'll do what you're told. Exactly the way I want it done, and afterwards you and yours get left alone.' He held up the other hand. 'You stab me in the back, and you get to mourn what you've done to — what's her name — Hannah, lovely name. And the girlfriend, whatever her name is — my people have the details and, believe me, they'll enjoy their work.'

'I'll do what you say.'

'They'll die hard. And you won't get to mourn for long.'

'Okay, okay.'

'Just so you know.'

★ ★ ★

Lying in the dark now, staring at the ceiling, trying not to see Declan Roeper's eyes.

After the shooting of Roeper, the evening

before last, Lar Mackendrick and Danny Callaghan began the drive down from the Dublin mountains. After a few minutes, Callaghan said, 'I'm not feeling well.'

'You'll be okay,' Lar Mackendrick said.

Somewhere near the Old Bawn Road, Callaghan demanded that Mackendrick stop the car. 'Look, you go ahead home, okay? I need — I'm going to be sick.'

'I'll wait.'

Feeling the seconds race past, his mind full of the image of the leather hat sagging above Roeper's face, Callaghan tried to keep the urgency out of his voice.

'No, I think I'm going to throw up. I need a walk, to clear my head — and I'll get a taxi home. I need to calm down.'

'It's no — '

'Please — I'll be okay.'

Mackendrick said, 'Suit yourself.'

After Mackendrick drove away, Callaghan found a quiet street and smashed the driver's window of a car. With no tools and no time for subtlety, he ripped the wires from under the steering column and hot-wired the engine. It took him fifteen minutes to find the two spruce trees forming an X shape, and another couple of minutes to find the clearing, his breathing noisy as he stumbled through the woods.

He'd brought along three CD cases he'd found in the car and he used one to dig at the earth and when the case broke he used a second to gouge a hole above where he reckoned

Roeper's face to be. That got him down far enough to use his fingers to tear at the earth. When he got to Declan Roeper's hat and pulled it away the eyes stared straight up, nothing there.

Danny Callaghan sat cross-legged on the grave, the fingers of one hand clutching tightly at his hair, his head back, his eyes closed, his teeth bared, his breathing harsh in his throat.

His hand slid slowly down his face until it held his mouth, and his head bent forward. He stared at the unblinking eyes.

'*Please*,' he said, not knowing what he was appealing for. His fingers were numb from the cold and the tears on his cheeks felt like slivers of ice.

★　★　★

The clock said *1.22* now.

Danny Callaghan flicked on the bedside light. He'd managed to doze for a while, then he woke and tossed and turned, and now he reached for a magazine. He turned several pages and began reading a review of a new movie, half-aware of the sense of the words.

Just deliver the van to the church grounds.

He knew that wherever he left the van the chances were that someone would use it in a hit, maybe as a getaway car. Callaghan had no doubt that before the day was done his actions would play a part in killing someone.

Chapter 37

That was some workout.

Karl Prowse found his jeans in the dark. He was tired — in a perfect world he'd just crash out, spend the night here. The bed covers were half on the floor, the sleeping woman lying on her side, naked in the light from the window.

Twice my age, twice my energy.

He was in the shabby little hotel, with the dyed blonde receptionist who'd been every bit as juicy as he'd figured she would be.

Best to go home, get changed in the morning before the big day started. Besides, he wanted to kiss the kids before he left to do the job. You can't ever tell how these things will work out.

Some ride, though.

He stood there, jeans in hand, thinking. Maybe he should stay. Go at it again in the morning.

Nah.

He pulled on the jeans, still staring at the naked woman.

★   ★   ★

It took longer than usual to lock up, cash up and clean up the pub. Novak was yawning when he reached home. No messages on the machine, no notes on the kitchen counter to say that anyone had called. He'd already checked his mobile half a dozen times, but he checked again as he went upstairs.

He eased the covers aside, careful not to wake Jane.

Still no word from Danny.

'I have to deal with this myself.'

'Deal with what?'

'*Please.*'

Maybe it had something to do with Frank Tucker, maybe it was the police. Whatever it was, it felt like something in their friendship had shifted. For the bad, or maybe for the good, but something had changed.

'Don't shut me out. If you need help — '

'Please.'

'Ring me when you can.'

Now Novak left his mobile on the bedside table.

★   ★   ★

Robbie Nugent was walking down Westmoreland Street, a friend on each side, arms linked. They were singing the *Sesame Street* theme. This time of night, revellers were draining away from the city centre, heading for the Nitelink buses. Those who were left were the ones for whom things hadn't worked out — the overexcited young, the drunk and the desperate, the losers reluctant to give up on the night.

Crossing O'Connell Bridge, Robbie unlinked from his friends, took two quick steps and vaulted up onto the parapet. As he walked, he held his arms out on each side and swayed. '*Waaaay*-haaa-ha-*heyyy!*' he teased. One of his friends, hampered by drink, tried and failed to climb onto the parapet behind him. The other laughed very loudly.

Halfway across, Robbie jumped down to the pavement and the three ran together the rest of the way across the bridge and out onto the road, against the lights. Traffic was sparse, but a car coming up the quays made a screeching noise as it braked suddenly, the rear coming around. Robbie half-turned and doffed an imaginary hat to the driver.

They were just past the GPO when a police car pulled up abruptly, nearside wheels on the pavement, the doors opening, a couple of cops getting out. Robbie and his mates began running.

Within yards they'd split up, one friend fleeing up towards Parnell Street, the other turning and running for Henry Street. Robbie sprinted across the road and down a side street, past the Pro-Cathedral. To change his appearance he took off his powder-blue jacket, rolled it into a ball and tucked it under one arm. He took a right and a left and slowed to a walk. He glanced back.

Safe enough.

On his way down Talbot Street he hailed a taxi and told the driver to take him home to Coolock. Before he reached North Strand both his friends had texted him to say that they were free and clear. He texted back. Twenty minutes later he was sitting on a sofa beside his mother, watching *Big Brother* live. Two of the house-mates slumped on separate sofas, sulking silently. The rest were sleeping in the bedroom. The screen showed one motionless scene for a while, then the other, then cut back to the first. Robbie watched, reluctant to go to bed, waiting for something to happen.

⋆   ⋆   ⋆

Sleeping like a baby.

May Mackendrick leaned back and felt a surge of tenderness.

It was one of those too-frequent nights when she'd had trouble getting off to sleep. She lay in the dark, Lar snoring lightly beside her. The snoring didn't bother her. It was as much a part of her night as the darkness and the moonlight from the window.

Lar was lying on his back and she considered his profile.

So peaceful.

Within a few hours they'd know if this was going to work. If it didn't, everything was at risk. In the year after Jo-Jo was killed, when Lar went to pieces, when his health collapsed, she'd stepped in and gently guided him back from the brink. For the next few hours she had no role but to pray.

Heaven and Earth are full of the majesty of Thy glory.

It was something that her mother taught her, the best part of fifty years earlier. You don't need a church to pray, you don't need a prayer book — prayer is just talking to God. All you need are the words in your heart. Think of God in Heaven, say the words silently and sincerely and believe that God will hear them.

I beseech Thee, oh Lord, in the name of all the saints and of the Blessed Mother, to lead us from peril, and into the warmth of Thy eternal love.

Oh most loving Father, refuge of sinners, please keep Lar safe tomorrow. Lord God of Mercy, who takest away the sins of the world, grant us peace, grant us hope, grant us thy blessing. And, please God, send our enemies into the deepest fires of Hell. Amen.

When Danny Callaghan woke he was relieved that the night was over. Then he saw that the clock showed ten minutes to five and he groaned and turned his face into the pillow. It was unlikely he'd get back to sleep soon, and the alarm would go off at seven. He rolled onto his back.

Today.

He was fully awake now, his gaze fixed to the ceiling.

Today, someone will live. Someone will die.

He raised one hand, watched his fingers flexing, did it again and again.

Day Twelve

Chapter 38

You couldn't miss him. Fat man with dark brown hair and a blond goatee beard, wearing jeans and an anorak. Dolly Finn identified the target from a photo. His name was Brian Tolland. You had to give Lar Mackendrick credit. He had everything ready at the war council — names, addresses, location maps and pictures of the targets. Details of who would be where and when. This was more organised than Dolly had thought it might be.

Not bad, Lar, not bad at all.

It was shortly after eight in the morning. The street was a busy short cut for cars seeking to avoid the Simonsville Avenue traffic passing through the Cullybawn estate towards the M50. Nothing else on the street opened for at least an hour. Dolly Finn was wearing a red baseball hat and a bulky green anorak, so he'd remain anonymous on any CCTV cameras he encountered during the day.

He watched the target get out of his white van and take two crates of apples, one atop the other, from the back. He let the crates down, took out his keys and bent to unlock a padlock at ground level. After he pulled up the roller shutter he left the crates of apples inside

294

the shop, then he went back to the van.

The metal shutter was the entire front of the shop. Inside, the remaining three walls all had display counters, with an island counter in the centre on which were an old-fashioned weighing scales and an electronic cash register. The sign above the door said the shop was called The Big Fat Tomato.

When the target carried a double load of orange crates from his van into the shop Dolly Finn came in after him.

'Not open yet,' the man said.

'That's okay,' Dolly Finn said. He pulled down the shutter behind him and when the target turned Dolly squeezed the trigger of his automatic twice and the silenced gun gave a double cough. The first bullet hit the man in the face and knocked him back and down, the second shot shattered some kind of china figurine on a shelf behind him.

The man was lying on his side, making sucking noises. Dolly leaned over and put the muzzle of the gun behind the man's left ear, about an inch from his hair. He squeezed the trigger twice more.

'What matters,' Lar Mackendrick had told the war council the previous evening, 'is that this is done without ringing any alarm bells. We take them down, we cover them up — no one twigs what's going on until we're ready to let Frank know. Then he lashes out, and plays into our hands.'

Dolly Finn pulled Tolland's body behind the island counter. He ate an apple while he waited.

After about ten minutes the metal shutter rattled noisily. Dolly ducked down behind the island counter. After a moment, Dolly stood up. A man in a heavy car coat and a black woolly hat was slamming the shutter back down. When he turned and saw Dolly Finn he said, 'Where's Brian?' Dolly's first shot hit him in the throat. He administered a second shot behind the ear. Then Dolly pulled the man's body behind the island counter. He dragged across several sacks of potatoes and placed them around the bodies. Any nosy parker looking through the letter box in the shutter — nothing for them to see.

When he left, he pulled the shutter down and locked the padlock.

★　★　★

Come on.

Karl Prowse looked at his watch again. He had two jobs to do this morning and if the first target didn't hurry up the odds were that Karl would be late getting to the second appointment and that would make a balls of the whole morning.

If the guy didn't come by the time he'd counted to two minutes he'd move on, do the second job.

Karl felt exposed. Standing a few yards from an old stone bridge, out of sight of the traffic, but visible to anyone who came along the towpath.

Stupid plan.

He couldn't say that to Lar Mackendrick, but it was stupid.

For the hundredth time he patted the bulge in the small of his back, where the gun was tucked into his belt.

'Make sure he's dead,' Lar said, 'before you leave him there. People can take a couple in the chest, even in the head, and survive. And you walk away and a year later they're standing in the witness box, swearing your life away.'

Cillian Connolly jogged there every morning, Lar said. He brought Karl down to the towpath, to show him the gap in the wall under the bridge. 'When you cap him, you stuff him down there — no one's going to find him until the smell gets bad.'

Should be done with it by now.

He watched two middle-aged men come around the corner of the balustrade, down onto the towpath. They both looked with wary curiosity at Karl as they jogged past.

Stupid plan.

'If there's anyone around when he comes, give it a miss. Better to miss him altogether — last thing we want is to set off the alarm bells before we're ready.'

Karl realised that he'd lost count. He looked at his watch again. He'd give it another two minutes.

Stupid plan.

★   ★   ★

After he started the engine, Robbie Nugent exhaled slowly. He sat there, the engine turning over, his hands on the wheel, his eyes wide open,

297

focused on nothing in particular. He was seeing again Perryman's wounds. Small, jagged, black-red holes appearing as if by magic in his bare chest. The silencer made it all the more magical.

Phhttt!

Bingo!

Robbie realised he was gripping the steering wheel tightly and his voice was doing something high-pitched, a long-drawn-out squeal of triumph.

Magic!

No other word for it.

When it started, Perryman backed away from the door of the apartment, a warning finger pointing at Robbie, his mouth open but making no noise. Then he turned and ran and turned again and opened his mouth and —

Magic.

The second guy, the guy coming out of the bathroom, Perryman's boyfriend, he was wearing a Reebok top and shorts. Robbie didn't get as big a charge out of that one. The fact that Perryman was bare-chested, maybe that was what made the difference. You shoot someone and you see some blood on their clothes, that's one thing. You squeeze the trigger and at that very instant a wound appears in his flesh, *exactly* where you want it to be.

No other word for it.

Magic.

Robbie pulled the bodies into the bedroom, manoeuvred them beneath the bed — had to get down flat, far side of the bed, pull like fuck at the corpse's feet. Finished, he looked around — everything kosher. Use the elevator, you maybe bump into a witness, so he went down the stairs to the ground floor of the apartment block and found his car two streets away.

Robbie sought to control the exhilaration. His squealing sound of triumph had become an impatient humming.

Don't fuck it up now.

He eased the car away from the kerb and turned out of the Cullybawn estate, onto the main road.

Like a remote control. Your thumb presses a button and six feet away the channel changes.

Magic.

Killing someone is a big step. You can do a bit of most things and when you're caught they give you a break and you get probation, maybe a fine. Keep doing it, they'll eventually start putting you inside.

Not murder.

Different altogether.

You step over that line once and it's instant big-time. If they get you for that, the bastards tear a huge hole in your life.

That's the downside.

The upside. You go over that line, you've stepped up into another league.

Doing Walter Bennett hadn't seemed like such a big step. That was like giving someone a beating and you take it a little further than usual and he's snuffed. Shooting Declan Roeper — Robbie was embarrassed about that. Shooting a man already lying in his grave — he could tell that Karl was angry and he didn't blame him. Stupid thing to do.

Going after two people with an automatic pistol, taking them out like a pro. That was something else.

Right up into the fucking premiership.

Heading back towards the city centre, staying the right side of the speed limit, Robbie began singing an old Tupac song about when we ride on our enemies. Like Tupac said — you fuck around with us, you get tossed up.

Chapter 39

Karl Prowse looked down at the man's body on the kitchen floor.

Job done.

Tom Richie had staggered a bit, then his legs had given way and he'd reached out and pulled some stuff off the counter. A saucepan clattered on the brown tiles, a plate smashed a moment later, and he was dead by then.

Karl went to the front window and checked outside. Getting into the house had been chancy. He rang the bell and when the target came to the door in his dressing gown Karl quietly showed him the pistol. 'I just need to talk.'

The hope was that the guy would back off, just let him in, so there'd be no need to cause a rumpus and attract attention. Instead, the fucker tried to close the door and Karl had to kick it open and follow him down the hall, swinging the front door shut behind him, then do the business in the kitchen.

Looks okay.

Nothing stirring out front. No neighbours staring at the house, nothing unusual. Job done. At least this one worked out. The first one, by the canal — that was a stupid plan. If he'd waited any longer for Cillian Connolly to come jogging along Tom Richie might have been up and gone by the time Karl got here.

'Tom? You all right?' Woman's voice.

Fuck.

Footsteps coming down the stairs.

Tom Richie lived alone.

Must have got lucky last night.

She came barefoot into the hall. Long hair dyed deep red, about eighteen — which made her a dozen years younger than Richie, lucky bastard. Wearing a black shorty nightdress, sleep in her eyes and her tits hanging out — a ride and a half.

'What if someone walks into the middle of something?' Karl Prowse had asked at the war council.

Lar Mackendrick had said, 'We improvise, we carry on. The important thing is that nothing gets out that might reach Frank Tucker — not until we're ready.'

Karl Prowse shot the woman twice in the chest.

Shit.

The way he'd planned it was that he'd take this Richie guy upstairs and do the business in the bedroom. That didn't happen. Now he had

301

to drag the fucking body up the stairs to hide it under the bed, just in case of casual visitors over the next hour or so. And on top of that he had to carry the bitch upstairs too.

Shit.

★ ★ ★

Five down. Plus the woman Karl had wasted, whoever she was. Lar Mackendrick sipped a coffee in the kitchen. He'd drawn lines through five of the names on his list as the texts came through confirming the kills. One no-show so far. Better percentages than he'd expected.

Halfway there.

Frank Tucker was an impossible target. He lived in an ex-council house on the Cullybawn estate — reinforced doors and windows and multi-camera CCTV made a direct assault out of the question. Frank never travelled anywhere without at least three of his people backing him up.

Lar had identified sixteen of Frank's hard-nosed lieutenants, any one of whom might pick up the ball and run with it if Frank went down. They all had to go.

This morning the most vulnerable eleven were scheduled to be shot. The rest of Frank Tucker's inner circle usually spent their mornings in places where a quiet hit was out of the question. They'd be dealt with later.

Of the eleven scheduled to be shot, five had already gone. Cillian Connolly hadn't come jogging along the Royal Canal, so there was one no-show. Not Karl's fault, and he'd made a good job of Tom Richie. Robbie had dealt handily with Perryman and Cowell. And Dolly had taken out his first two targets.

The important thing was that so far Frank hadn't a clue that five of his hard men were gone. All done invisibly, the bodies concealed for a few hours. Just one target on the list, Fiachra O'Dwyer, would be done publicly. And that would bring Frank out of his shell. He'd be angry, looking to find out who dared strike down one of his people, seeking revenge. He'd call an emergency meeting, and the rest of his inner circle would gather round. By the time he started to wonder why most of his top people hadn't turned up it would be too late. Frank Tucker would be dust.

Restless, Lar went out into his back garden and took a deep breath of cold air. Looking out beyond the harbour to where the mist hung over Ireland's Eye, one hand in his pocket, holding the chequered grip of the Walther P22, Lar could feel the blood singing in his veins.

* * *

At first, Danny Callaghan thought there must have been a mistake.

'I'm here to pick up the van.'

The young woman with the short blonde hair looked at him as though he was speaking a language she didn't know.

Callaghan said, 'This is Karl's house, right?'

She nodded slowly.

She was terribly young. Not yet out of her teens, but the edges of her eyes and the corners of her mouth seemed wilted. The little kid in her arms was bored, the baby in the buggy in the hall was crying. Karl's wife seemed distant from it all, like she'd woken up and found herself somewhere strange.

'Karl said you'd have the keys to the van. I've to pick it up — a white van?'

She still looked puzzled, but mention of the keys gave her something to fix on. She turned and reached over to a shelf in the hall, picked up a set of car keys and gave them to Callaghan.

'What about the garage? Have you got the key for that?'

'It's on the ring,' she said.

Danny nodded. 'Thanks. You okay?'

She said nothing, just stepped back and closed the door.

When he got the van out he went back and locked the garage door. He could hear the baby crying inside the house. He got into the van and he gunned the engine, suddenly needing to be away from here.

★   ★   ★

Coming off the M50 on the west side of the city, Danny Callaghan reached his destination, the grounds of St Ursula's church, in Cullybawn. He took out his mobile, looked at the piece of paper that Lar had given him and began punching in numbers. He could hear a ringing tone at the other end as he glanced into the back of the van, at a large grey blanket covering something in the freight bay. The van was grimy, tattered pieces of cardboard scattered on the floor, along with a few fragments of polystyrene packing material. The phone to his ear, he stood up from his seat, leaned over and pulled at the blanket. Underneath there was what looked like a large beer barrel, set on its side, encased in some sort of rectangular metal cage. The whole thing was bolted to the floor of the van.

'Yeah?'

Callaghan sat back in the driver's seat.

'It's me.'

'You pick it up?'

'Yeah.'

'Where are you?'

'Where you said.'

'Good.'

'Do I just leave it here?'

'Now comes phase two.'

'What does that mean?'

Callaghan looked round at the barrel. It was as though the air around it was suddenly colder, the edges of the container and its casing more stark against the dusty, untidy setting of the commonplace van. Black tape at the rim, holding in place a small white plastic box and a twisted bunch of plastic-coated wires.

Jesus.

'What's in the barrel?'

Mackendrick said, 'Listen carefully to your instructions.'

'What's in the barrel?'

'Danny — '

'I'm getting out of here.'

Mackendrick's voice was harsh. '*Say yes.*'

Callaghan said nothing.

'Say yes, right now — I want to hear you say it.'

'*What's in the barrel?*'

'Listen very carefully. Your ex-missus has a sister, she manages a hairdressing salon in Rathmines. Her name's Lisa. And she has an older brother, a lawyer, he lives in Bray with his wife and his two kids.'

Mackendrick paused, then he said, 'The lawyer's name is Matthew, he's married to Joan. The kids are Karen and Trish.'

'Don't you even fucking think — '

'No point talking unless you calm down.'

'Fuck you.'

'Point is — I've got a list of possible targets. So many, I can't miss. I'm going to give you very simple instructions, and you follow them or you're going to be up to your ankles in blood.'

Callaghan stayed silent.

'It's simple. You're five minutes away from the Venetian House. You park the car there. By the end of the day, this will all be — '

'You can't *do this.*'

'I can reach out any time I want and your ex-wife, your girlfriend, a whole list of people — *pop*, and it's over for them — one, or two or three of them.'

'That's a *bomb.*' Callaghan realised he was whispering.

'It's putting Frank on notice, that's all. No one's going to get hurt. Before anything happens, we phone a warning, they clear the place out and *boom*. Frank needs a lesson — that's all.'

'This is crazy.'

'Discussion is over. Do it now — or take the consequences.'

'Look — '

'Say yes — or I hang up. Say yes — or by tomorrow morning I kill at least two from that list. If you run, or you say shit to anyone, cops or anyone else, I do two more.'

Callaghan rubbed hard at his forehead.

Mackendrick said, 'It's not like you have a choice.'

'What do I do?'

'The Venetian House has a big window, looks like a stained-glass window, some ponce rowing a boat — you drive there right now and you park the van as close to that window as you can get. Lock the van and walk away. Go home, stay home. We'll talk again — but this is the last thing I want you to do.'

'Please — '

'Say yes.'

'Look — '

'*You're killing your ex-missus.*'

Danny said nothing.

'Talk to me.'

'Okay, I'll do it.'

'Say yes.'

Danny's throat was dry. He swallowed and said, 'Yes.'

'Good. You're being watched every second. Anything you do, anywhere you go, we know about it.'

Chapter 40

Lar Mackendrick parked halfway down Ballantyne Avenue. He was driving one of Danny Callaghan's stolen cars, a white Primera. He put the Walther P22 on the passenger seat and took out his list. Dolly Finn had capped another two targets, Karl Prowse had done one more. Another of Dolly's targets was a no-show. Lar updated the list, drawing lines through names. A good strike rate — eight down and two no-shows.

One to go.

Lar was early. At least another — he looked at his watch — half-hour before Fiachra O'Dwyer arrived. Best to be on the safe side.

Ballantyne Avenue wasn't an avenue to anywhere. One end butted up against a railway embankment, with a pedestrian lane leading to a parallel street. At the other end there was a narrow street that led out onto the main road into the city centre. Most of the houses on Ballantyne Avenue were narrow, two-up-two-down, at least a century old. Halfway down the street, where Lar was parked, there were three shops — in the middle of which was the tanning salon run by Fiachra O'Dwyer.

Lar switched on the radio and listened to two idiots arguing about the debt crisis.

He was pleasantly surprised when O'Dwyer arrived after twenty minutes. His green Renault pulled up a couple of yards ahead of Mackendrick's car. Tall, skinny, wearing his usual denim, O'Dwyer hopped out and opened the boot. He took out two Tesco bags, then fiddled with something inside the boot.

'Hey, Fiachra.'

When O'Dwyer turned around, Lar Mackendrick was maybe ten feet away and coming closer.

'Lar.'

'I thought it was you. That's Fiachra O'Dwyer, I said to myself.'

O'Dwyer put the Tesco bags on the ground.

Lar's right hand was close to his side. He moved it slightly, to let O'Dwyer see the Walther.

'Lar — '

'No doubt about it, I said to myself — that's Fiachra O'Dwyer.'

'We have a deal, Lar — you and Frank — '

'Watching the DVD — skinny fucker steps out in front of the camera — laughing at Matty — I didn't see your face, but I've known you long enough. No doubt about it, I said to myself, that's Fiachra O'Dwyer.'

Lar could see it in his eyes. O'Dwyer was considering making a run for it. Lar didn't want this to turn into a chase, so he gave O'Dwyer a moment's hope.

'I want you to take a message to Frank.'

O'Dwyer was breathing fast. He said nothing.

'That's okay, isn't it? It's okay I use you as a messenger?'

'What's this about?'

Lar shot him in the stomach.

O'Dwyer would have fallen to the ground, but the Renault was right behind him and he ended up half-sitting into the boot, his mouth open, his eyes wild.

'Why did you spit in Matty's face?'

'Lar — ' O'Dwyer's voice was a croak.

'What Frank did, I can see the logic in that. But spitting in the face of a man in that position — Jesus Christ.'

O'Dwyer raised his chin, his mouth strained.

'Fuck you.'

'That's the spirit.' Lar shot him in the crotch. O'Dwyer screamed and stood up. His head hit the open lid of the boot, then his legs gave way and he fell to the ground. Lar put a bullet low-down and to one side of his back, aiming for a kidney. Then, when O'Dwyer rolled over in agony, mouth agape, incoherent noises streaming out, Lar leaned down and put another one in his belly, and two more in his head.

The six shots from the unsilenced gun echoed around the street. Lar was behind the wheel, driving slowly, almost at the end of the avenue, when he looked in the wing mirror and saw someone tentatively crossing the street from the tanning salon, towards O'Dwyer's body.

Any time now, Frank Tucker would get the message.

★ ★ ★

Karl Prowse left the clean mobile on the dashboard and used his own phone to call his friend Francie.

'Come on — you've got to be kidding.'

'That's the price,' Francie said.

'Bollocks.'

'He says he can't do it any cheaper.'

The bastards give you a bare-bones price and that gets your juices flowing, then they come up with the extras. A weekend in Manchester, Karl and five friends, a reasonable hotel, tickets for Old Trafford and Saturday night in Sankey's, where you might or might not pull, but you'd end up well wasted, which was the whole point.

'What do you think?'

'I've been looking forward.'

'Me too. Okay, let's do it.'

Karl rang off.

He'd parked alongside the mini-mart across the road from the Venetian House. A good morning's work. Two clean hits, no snags, apart from the bitch at Tom Richie's place and that had worked out. He'd just had a call from Lar on the clean mobile — Fiachra O'Dwyer was history and about now Frank Tucker should be starting to work up a sweat.

This works out — Jesus — if this works out there's no limit.

As Lar's right hand, the opportunities were endless.

And Lar's an old man, not going to be around forever.

So simple. A couple of years back, when Karl

killed a Chink and got arrested and it all fell apart for the cops, that was just temper and he could have spent fifteen years in jail. Stupid. Anyone could do that. This time, this was doing it for a purpose, with a real pay-off.

Karl sat up, thumbs drumming on the steering wheel. Across the road, the white Ford transit van he'd last seen in his garage was slowing down, turning in to the Venetian House car park, Danny Callaghan at the wheel.

★   ★   ★

Get it done. Get out fast.

This time of morning, there were less than a dozen cars in the Venetian House car park. The space in front of the gondolier window was empty.

Danny Callaghan knew about the bad old days in the North, when the IRA sometimes forced civilians, by holding their families hostage, to drive bomb-laden cars to their targets. And then used remote controls to explode the bombs, complete with drivers. That way, the witness disappeared along with the bomb.

As soon as he parked, Callaghan climbed out of the van, locked the door and walked away. He held himself back from running. It would cause disastrous complications if he attracted the wrong kind of attention. When he knew he was safe, out on the main road, he turned and looked back at the van. He had a momentary flash of what the scene would look like with the whole side of the Venetian House caved in, smoke rising from the car park strewn with rubble. He turned and hurried away.

⋆   ⋆   ⋆

The remote control was small, rectangular, made of dark blue plastic. It had a short black aerial at the top, and two switches on the side. One switch was white, the other red. A thick rubber band held the switches in place.

Karl Prowse watched Danny Callaghan cross the road and hail a taxi. There'd be a time for dealing with that smart bastard.

'He's a loose end,' he'd told Lar Mackendrick.

'He's a dog on a leash,' Lar said. 'Any time he thinks he's got the freedom to bark we jerk the leash. We keep him alive until we're sure we don't need him.'

'And then?'

'He's all yours.'

Karl eased the rubber band back from the two switches and slid it off. When he threw the white switch the bomb would be armed. He let a thumb graze the red switch, caressing it with the softest of touches. He made a puffing sound — *phuuuw!*

He put the remote on the passenger seat.

Won't be long now.

Chapter 41

Still nothing.

Novak listened to the ringing tone until the

automated voice invited him to leave a message. He rang off, dropped the mobile on the shelf beside the cash register and poured himself another mug of coffee.

'You okay?'

Jane was leaving for a Christmas shopping trip in town. Novak said, 'Danny's being a pain in the arse. That's half a dozen calls this morning. He never answers.'

'Maybe he needs some space.'

'Maybe he ought to just say that.'

'He'll be okay.'

Jane was wearing a light green jacket over a peasant skirt. Novak said, 'Spring is here already?'

'It's that kind of day. Mind you, it'll probably piss down.'

'You look great.'

She smiled. 'Compliments? What's seldom's wonderful.'

'Don't spend too much.'

Jane had most of the Christmas presents bought. 'As usual, you're the problem.'

Novak sighed. 'What do you get the man who has everything?'

When she had gone he picked up the phone and tried Danny Callaghan one more time.

★ ★ ★

Please, stop.

You'd think Novak would have got the message by now.

Danny Callaghan put the phone back on the

314

bedside table, let the ringtone play on. Too many times this morning he'd checked the screen and seen Novak's name. He'd have turned off the phone long ago if Lar Mackendrick hadn't told him to await instructions.

Lying on the bed, the radio playing softly in the background.

'*I have to deal with this myself,*' he'd told Novak.

Easy to say.

The ringtone stopped.

There were two ways of dealing with this. Do nothing. Lie here on his bed and let the clock tick away until an artificially calm newsreader interrupts the radio programme to report that emergency services are responding to a major incident in Dublin.

The other option was unthinkable.

'*Your ex will get preferential treatment. First on the list.*'

Sickened as he was by the image of carnage at the Venetian House, the thought of Hannah at the mercy of Mackendrick's people filled him with a rage that drove out everything else.

Call the police.

The cops would handle the van, the bomb, they'd go after Mackendrick.

'*There's a whole army of people I can tap into.*'

Horror for strangers versus horror for someone he loved.

When it came, the radio news jingle seemed interminable. The first item was about something in the Middle East.

Nothing.

315

Lar Mackendrick read the text and nodded.

2 arrived for certain – connolly + blount

The job needed someone with the balls to throw the switches, so Karl Prowse was the natural choice. Once Frank Tucker entered the pub, and Karl reported that he'd identified at least another three certainties going in, it would be boom time.

★ ★ ★

Once, twice, three times. A fist thumping.

Danny Callaghan was coming out of the bathroom when the banging started on the door of his flat.

'Danny, open up.'

Callaghan stood just inside the door, his gaze fixed on a scuff mark on the dark blue carpet.

Another three thumps.

'Novak, please.'

'I'm not going away.'

Callaghan unlocked the door and turned back into the flat. Novak came in, shut the door behind him.

'I'm not going away until I know what's going on.'

Callaghan tried to say something but his mouth was dry. He swallowed and tried again. 'I know you mean well, but you're best staying out of this.'

'Frank Tucker? Is that it?'

'No.'

'What, then?'

Danny's gaze fixed on the kitchen counter. On the radio someone was talking about gardening.

'Please. Let it be.'

'It's not woman trouble. I know the signs and this has nothing to do with Hannah.'

Callaghan shook his head.

'Danny, if this — '

Callaghan raised a hand, palm towards Novak. 'Something's going to happen — I can't — it doesn't — *Jesus* — Novak.'

Novak's voice was a whisper. 'There are things that no one should try to handle alone.'

Callaghan raised his head and made eye contact. 'It has everything to do with Hannah.'

★ ★ ★

It took just a couple of minutes to give Novak the outline. 'Mackendrick said he'll give a warning so they could clear the place, but he knew that's what I wanted to hear. It's bullshit.'

Novak took Danny Callaghan by the elbow and leaned into his face. 'It's not a choice — you can't just let it happen. You have to call the police.'

'I can't do that.'

'You have to.'

'It'd be like cutting her throat.'

'*Warn her*, tell her to get the hell away from Dublin until this is over.'

'They'll kill Leon — or one of her friends, they

317

know where her sister works, where her brother lives. And when it's over it won't be over — they said they'll kill Hannah sooner or later, no matter how long it takes.'

'Call her — tell her to get away from here, get her family away — you *can't* sit here and wait for Christ knows how many people to be blown apart.'

'Frank Tucker and his thugs — who gives a shit?'

'And whoever else walks into that pub — '

'It's — the way Mackendrick has it worked — it's supposed to take out the room where Tucker and his people — '

'Jesus, Danny, don't kid yourself — these days, the whole world boasts about their smart bombs, and when the dust settles it always turns out the bombs were as dumb as ever they were and there's innocent blood all over the place.'

'He said — '

'You said it yourself — he said what you wanted to hear. Barmen, waitresses, customers — ' Novak's voice was soft now, his face inches from Callaghan's. 'It's not like you don't know what's the right thing to do.'

Callaghan said, 'I can't.'

'*I'll* do it. An anonymous call.'

Callaghan hesitated.

Novak said, 'Get her out of town, make her as safe as possible — but we have to stop this thing.'

After a moment, Callaghan nodded.

As Novak made the call, Danny Callaghan was tapping out Hannah's number.

Chapter 42

Hannah O'Connor was at lunch in the Ely restaurant in the financial centre. When she saw Callaghan's name come up on her mobile she excused herself and moved away from the table. He spoke quickly in short sentences.

'Jesus Christ — '

One of her three lunch guests, the purchasing officer for a chain of pharmacies that had a lot of printing needs, was looking towards her now, while the other two were still chattering. The cellar restaurant, once a wine store, was a series of rectangular bays, each with several tables, all stone surfaces and echoes. Hannah's *'Jesus Christ'* had carried far enough to alarm the pharmacy guy. She gave him a reassuring nod and moved out into the corridor that ran past the bays.

'Where are you?'

'What have you got me into?'

'I need to know, where are you?'

'In a restaurant.'

'Where?'

'*What have you got me into?*'

'Leave, right now — don't go back to your office, just get out of Dublin.'

'I can't just — '

'This is *serious*. These are *very* dangerous men, they kill people and very soon they'll know I haven't done what they said. *Please*, Hannah, you need to get out. Go to the airport, or get a train — anywhere outside Dublin. Call Leon, Lisa, Matthew — and his family — tell them to take a flight somewhere, check into a hotel — whatever, as long as they drop out of sight.'

'Jesus, Danny — it's one thing to fuck up your own life, but, Jesus Christ — '

'Hannah — '

'I treated you — '

'Don't call the police — they'll know, and it'll make things — '

'I treated you like you're still even half the man I married, but that was a mistake. You fucked up then and you're fucked up now, and you'll always fuck up. I did my best for you — '

Hannah's words echoed down the stone corridor and at several of the bays people were standing, staring at her. As she walked quickly towards the exit she cut Danny off. By the time she climbed to street level and left the restaurant she'd talked to Lisa and convinced her she wasn't exaggerating the danger. 'Do it now, immediately, and ring me when you're settled somewhere. I'm sorry, I'm really sorry.' Outside the restaurant, she made similar calls to Matthew and then to Alex.

Hannah was on the riverfront, looking left and right for a taxi, before she realised she hadn't yet called Leon.

* * *

'How did Hannah — ' Novak said.

Callaghan shook his head.

'It was the right thing to do.'

'I know.'

'The police took the call seriously — they're

320

on their way to the Venetian House. I mentioned Frank Tucker as the target — that got their ears pricked.'

Callaghan nodded.

Halfway through the call to Hannah he'd felt something snap — it was almost a physical sensation, somewhere in the distance between them — and he'd felt an ache and he'd felt something like relief. He hadn't the time or the focus to wonder why. No thought could survive the atmosphere of dread enveloping him. Fear for Hannah and her family, fear for himself.

'We'd better get out of here,' Novak said. 'Pretty soon, Mackendrick's going to want to ask you some questions.'

★ ★ ★

When he heard the siren, Karl Prowse slid down in his seat. The police car overshot the entrance to the Venetian House, did an instant U-turn and fishtailed into the car park. The second police car made the turn first time and when the cops came out of the cars at speed Karl reached for the remote.

Shit.

This is going tits-up.

Only three of Frank Tucker's people inside — no sign of Frank himself yet.

Two policemen went into the pub in a hurry, the other two stood watching the white Ford transit.

A battered Renault Clio came from the other direction, tyres squealing as it skewed sideways and stopped in the middle of the street, blocking traffic. Two of the three plain-clothes cops who came out of the car were carrying Uzis, the third held a very big automatic pistol down by his side. They were all wearing protection vests.

They ran towards the pub.

Karl's thumb found the white switch.

Has to be Callaghan.

He clicked the white switch, arming the bomb.

Bastard.

The ERU guy with the handgun waved at the two uniforms and made a sweeping gesture towards the main road. The two, looking more relieved with each yard they put between themselves and the white van, hurried out to warn off traffic.

Karl put the remote down and reached for the clean mobile.

'Lar?'

'What did I tell you about names?'

'The police are here.'

'Where?'

'The target — some of them have guns — *shit* — '

'They spot you?'

'It had to be Callaghan, that piece of shit — '

'Did they spot you?'

'Too busy. There's just three of Tucker's team inside — do I blow it now?'

'What about Frank?'

'*Shit!* They're out, they're gone!'

'Who?'

At the far end of the Venetian House, close to the boundary wall of the pub, both wings of a service door opened and people scurried down the ramp.

'What's happening?'

Barmen and waitresses in uniform, one of the cops, customers, among them one man that Karl Prowse recognised — Cillian Connolly. Bastard ought to have been tucked in under a bridge on the Royal Canal by now, with a couple of bullets in him.

'They got out, the cops got them out.'

'Get rid of the remote — permanently. And don't accidentally blow the van. Kill any cops and they'll tear the city apart looking for us. Just get out of there. Let me know when you're clear. And no fucking names on the phone, okay?'

★ ★ ★

No panic.

The list of Frank Tucker's people was crumpled in Lar Mackendrick's closed fist. He dropped it on the kitchen table, got himself a glass of water and took a long drink. Then he sat at the table and smoothed out the paper.

Eight dead.

All Frank Tucker knew so far was that Fiachra O'Dwyer was dead and someone had planted a bomb outside the Venetian House. It would take maybe an hour or two of phone calls not answered and appointments not kept before the penny dropped. Then he'd send people around to check on those of his men who hadn't responded.

When Tucker was trying to work out what was

happening he'd no doubt put Lar Mackendrick's name on the list of possibles, but it wouldn't be too near the top. He saw Mackendrick as a beaten docket. He'd be looking elsewhere.

We're not done yet.

Who fucked this up?

'*It had to be Callaghan!*'

Karl was jumping to conclusions, but he was almost certainly right. It had to be Callaghan. Lar picked up his mobile.

★ ★ ★

'What happened?'

'What do you mean?' Danny Callaghan said.

Mackendrick's voice was harsh. '*What happened?*'

'I did what you said.'

'If you made a call and played good citizen the last thing you'll hear is your ex-missus screaming.'

'I did what you told me.'

'Where are you?'

Callaghan was sitting at a table in the Food Hall in Abbey Street, with a half-finished mug of coffee in front of him.

'I'm at home.'

'Stay there. I'll ring you back soon.'

Chapter 43

The television weather woman was promising that the unseasonable mild weather would continue for at least another day. Before that, the lunchtime news had nothing that Frank Tucker didn't know, along with a lot of unhelpful speculation. The television cameras had got to the Venetian House just in time to see an army Land Rover arrive, the bomb-disposal people preparing to do their job. The newsreader said only that the police had no comment on possible motives for the bombing attempt.

'Three possibilities,' Frank Tucker said. He and three of his associates were gathered in his house in Cullybawn. The external doors were steel-lined and the expanding security screens had been drawn across the windows and locked. There were armed protectors upstairs, in the rooms front and back. In a utility room, a man was monitoring the CCTV screens that covered every approach.

'One, it's some snotty little tosser making his move, maybe the Clondalkin mob. Could be, but it's a bit stylish for them. Two, there's always the Eastern Europeans, but I'm in touch there, and they'd rather deal than mix it up. So it's probably number three — the IRA, or one of the spin-offs.'

Cillian Connolly said, 'What about Tommy Farr, Lar Mackendrick — they've got to have a hair up their arses?'

'They're boxed in. They don't have the assets, they don't have the balls, and I'd have heard from their people if they'd been setting anything up.' Tucker shook his head. 'There's Republican head-bangers who've been itching for a long time to find a reason to exist.'

'So, what do we do?'

'We take our time, let the cops beat the bushes and we'll keep an eye on what comes running out.'

★ ★ ★

The building contractor tapped his calculator, paused and looked across the desk at his supplier. 'That's reasonable — when can you deliver?'

'Five working days, tops — probably less.'

'What kind of guarantee can — '

Somewhere down below, there were raised voices and the sound of running.

They were in the top tier of the two-tier prefab that served as the builder's site office. He stood up and was on his way to the window to see what was causing the racket when the door opened and a uniformed policeman stuck his head in. The policeman turned and called, 'He's up here.'

The builder sighed and turned to his supplier. 'Happy days are here again.'

'What's — '

'Send me the paperwork and we've got a deal.'

There were now two cops standing in the doorway. The builder recognised the one in plain clothes. 'How's she cuttin', Henry?'

'A few questions, Ruairi.'

'No problem.'

The builder leaned towards the supplier and said, 'Not to worry — back in the old days the Special Branch did this three or four times a week. Either they're just keeping their hand in or someone's been naughty and they're rounding up the usual suspects. Show them your driving licence and they'll let you walk away.'

He turned to the plain-clothes garda. 'What might I have done now?'

'We're knocking on a lot of doors this afternoon — asking people if they've got any class of a grudge against Frank Tucker.'

The builder shook his head. 'It's a long time, Henry, since I was under the delusion that I had any role to play in sorting out this country's woes.'

'All the same, you won't mind if we check on your comings and goings?'

★   ★   ★

Stella Roeper hadn't seen her husband in three days but she was damned if she'd tell the police that.

'I'm not my husband's keeper. Look around the house, and if you find him tell him I'll be in the front room with my feet up.'

She was long past the fervour of the old days when Republicans greeted police raids and search warrants with defiance or contempt. Long ago the joke was that anyone with connections to Sinn Fein and the IRA had a sure way to get some free gardening done. Just make a phone call to another Republican and whisper that you had some hot material buried in the garden and you could be sure the phone tappers would throw the alarm switch and the uniformed grafters

327

would be along in jig time to dig up your garden.

In truth, it was no joke. They might dig up the garden on occasion, but mostly they'd tear up the floorboards and ransack the living room. The contents of the attic might be dumped onto the landing and every last paperback stripped from the bookshelves and tossed in a heap. It came with the territory, and sometimes they could wreck the house and still miss the gun or two in the false back behind the wardrobe.

Since the end of the Troubles the police had scaled down their anti-terror operations, but Stella Roeper's house remained a regular port of call, given Declan's contempt for the peace and love brigade.

'It's about carrying the torch on, for a new generation,' he said. 'Sooner or later the real thing will start again, as long as the Brits lay claim to a single acre of this island.'

Back in the old days, Declan would disappear without a word, for a night or a week — once he was gone for twenty-three days — and Stella didn't ask any questions. Best not to ask about what you didn't need to know.

There hadn't been anything like that for almost four years.

'A neighbour tells me that Declan hasn't been around for a couple of days. That right, Stella?'

'If she knows that much, go back and ask the nosy bitch where he might be.'

'Declan's a bit long in the tooth for playing soldiers, wouldn't you say, love?'

She looked past him, as though he'd ceased to exist.

'Well, when he comes back, would you tell him we'd be honoured if he'd give us a call?'

The only reply he got was a look of stone-faced resentment.

Stella Roeper was happy that she'd kept the worry off her face.

★　★　★

When they rang the bell and the smart bastard didn't answer, Karl Prowse and Robbie Nugent tried knocking the door in. Robbie hurt his shoulder, Karl kicked the lock several times but it didn't budge. Eventually, Robbie stayed at the door of Callaghan's apartment, just in case, while Karl went down to the car and got a small crowbar. It took him two minutes of prying and grunting to get the door open and thirty seconds to scope the flat and ring Lar.

'Long gone.'

Lar said, 'Plan B.'

★　★　★

The movie was halfway over. Danny Callaghan was in Cinema 6 of Cineworld, in Parnell Street. The movie had something to do with the CIA, but beyond that he hadn't bothered to follow it.

Before seeking refuge in the cinema he'd booked a room in the North Star Hotel, near the train station. All going well, he'd be on his way to Belfast first thing next morning, finding somewhere to hide until he figured out the best move. He half expected Hannah to ring, seeking more information, but nothing happened. No word from Novak, no further calls from Lar Mackendrick. The phone was in silent mode, and he held on to it, hand in his pocket, in case he missed the vibration.

He was coming down to street level on the escalator, having abandoned the movie, when he felt the phone shudder.

'Where are you?' Lar Mackendrick said. 'You were supposed to stay at home.'

'I've just dropped out to get some milk.'

'Liar.'

'Look — what's the — '

'I want you to come and meet me. *Now*.'

'Look, whatever you think was — '

'We've got a friend of yours, name of Novak.'

Fuck.

'Karl wants to kill him right off, I say give you another chance. There's things I need you to do. That okay by you?'

'Let him go.'

'Say yes.'

'Yes — yes — let him *go*.'

'Kimmet's Ale House. Upstairs. You've got half an hour to get there.'

'Okay, I'm on my way — but half an hour isn't — '

'Not a minute more.'

'Please — '

'We've got Novak tucked away and Karl's with him. You call the police again, you do anything

330

stupid, Karl will ring you, just so you can hear your friend die.'

Mackendrick ended the call.

Chapter 44

That's odd.

The shutter was down.

Derry Tynan had been due to arrive at work at The Big Fat Tomato at two o'clock, to take over for a couple of hours. He was ten minutes late.

Maybe the other two had got pissed off waiting and left.

Tynan used his key to open the padlock, pulled up the shutter. He didn't know what to make of the bunched-up bags of potatoes in the centre of the shop. Then he saw a foot sticking out.

⋆ ⋆ ⋆

Karl checked that Novak's wrists were securely tied. He pulled a corner of the tape loose from the bar owner's mouth — last thing they needed was this piece of shit choking on his own vomit. Not while he was still useful.

'You okay?'

'Fuck you.'

Karl kicked him on the hip and was rewarded with a grunt. He smoothed the tape back across Novak's mouth.

Karl was worried. He wanted to believe in Lar Mackendrick, and you had to give him credit

— they'd taken out half of Frank Tucker's inner circle. But Callaghan had screwed things up and by now Frank Tucker would be kicking shins, looking for answers. Lar would need to come up with something special if this still had a chance to work.

★ ★ ★

Detective Sergeant Bob Tidey reached for his mobile.

'Colin?'

'Yes?'

'Bob Tidey. This Frank Tucker thing — it gets worse.'

Assistant Commissioner O'Keefe waited.

'One of Tucker's hard men — Brian Tolland. He runs a fruit and vegetable shop in Cullybawn. I'm down here, and he's got a big hole in his face. One of his mates is lying on top of him. And he's not breathing either.'

O'Keefe said, 'Someone's thinking big. Fiachra O'Dwyer, an abortive bombing — now these two.'

'Anything solid yet?'

'Not for public consumption — an old soldier named Declan Roeper who never bought into the peace process. Quit the Provos, set up his own outfit. We reckoned the Interim IRA were all piss and wind, now he seems to have gone offside for the past few days. Special Branch suspects he has access to explosives — two and two.'

Bob Tidey remembered a case he'd worked on

twenty years back. A local thug terrorised the neighbourhood, smashing windows, stealing cars, running a half-assed protection racket with shopkeepers. The Provos gave him two warnings, then they brought him to a playground one night, held him down. Tidey was canvassing the shopping area the next day and the pensioners had a spring in their step. He'd imagined they'd be frightened and upset by what had happened — instead, they were delighted that the troublesome little shit had got his kneecaps blasted.

'There's mileage in playing the paramilitary social worker game — kneecapping burglars and blowing the heads off drug dealers. A lot of people see it as fair game.'

'They do,' O'Keefe said. 'But when the likes of Frank Tucker start fighting back and no one knows where the bullets might fly — that's when everyone gets religion.'

★　★　★

It makes sense now.

Frank Tucker took a deep breath and leaned back against the bedroom wall. He looked down again at Tom Richie's body. Tom was staring straight up, his mouth open, as though he'd died trying to say something. His eyes were as lifeless as marbles. A line of stringy blood, like red snot, lay across Tom's face, from his nose to his ear. The back of his head was a mess.

Since the bombing attempt, Tucker had been texting warnings to close associates, following up with phone calls. Making and taking one call after another, he'd been aware of gaps in the flow. No answer from Brian, nothing from Tom or Jason or Mick.

He'd come to Tom's house, he'd broken the glass in the front door and it had taken his people less than three minutes to find the bodies upstairs. Tom and some little tart Tucker had never seen before. As they pulled the bodies out from under the bed Tucker's mobile rang and the police told him about Brian Tolland.

On the way here the radio news told him that Emergency Response Units were kicking in doors, mostly those of former members of the IRA.

Tucker nodded to one of his minders. 'I told the police you'd wait here for them.'

Before he left the house, Tucker hunkered down and whispered to Tom. 'Looks like the patriots are eager to die for Ireland.' He kissed the tips of two fingers and touched them lightly against his friend's forehead. 'That can be arranged.'

Chapter 45

The upstairs room in Kimmet's bar had been cleaned but it had a stale smell, as though there'd been a lot of drinking last night and the room hadn't been properly aired. There were small tables around the edge of the room and one long table near the window. Lar Mackendrick was sitting at the long table, the window behind him. There was a coffee pot on the table and an untouched cup of coffee.

Danny Callaghan said, 'Wherever Novak is, let him go.'

'No hurry,' Lar Mackendrick said.

'I'll do whatever you ask.'

'You said that before, then you ratted. You had a job to do. The payment was your life and the lives of your ex-wife, members of her family — all you had to do was deliver a van and keep your mouth shut. Tell me why you couldn't do that?'

'A pub, all those people, Jesus, a *bomb* — come *on* — you were never going to give a warning, we both know that — '

'You put your ex-missus on the block.'

'She's safe — we — '

'She's mine. You sold her to me when you called the cops.'

'You don't know where she is.'

'How long can she hide? Here, or somewhere my people can reach on a cheap flight? A week from now, a year from now? My people will use her for practice. Then they'll open her up, from crotch to throat. She'll never be safe, unless I say so.'

Callaghan said, 'You want something.'

Mackendrick smiled.

Callaghan said, 'I should be dead — instead, you want a chat. You need something.'

'Maybe I'm just a big softy.'

'Maybe you need something in a hurry, and you haven't got anyone else to do your shit work.'

'We need cars — four of them.'

'I got the cars you needed.'

'All ditched. I'd reckoned this would be over by now. Thanks to you, it's not. We need two more cars, and a couple to spare. Rigged so we can use them without any fucking around with the ignition. We need them by first thing tomorrow morning.'

'You need to bomb some more pubs?'

'That was a diversion — a hoax. No bombs now, we just need transport.'

'First, let Novak go.'

'You bring the cars to this street — get them here by seven-thirty in the morning. You stick on clean plates, fill the tanks, park them across the street from here. Put a copy of the *Daily Mail* on the dashboard of each one, so we can identify them. Leave them unlocked.'

'What if they get stolen?'

'When you bring the fourth car you park it, you unlock the other three and you wait in the car, make sure no one messes with them.'

'What about Novak?'

'I'll be in touch and I'll make arrangements for you to collect him. Once we've got transport, it's all over, you can piss off, and take your friend.'

'And my ex-wife?'

Mackendrick moved his head as if stretching his neck. He stared off to one side for a moment, as though he was inspecting something mildly interesting written on a far wall. Then he looked back at Danny Callaghan.

'You screw this last chance — your friend gets

his skull opened. We'll find your ex-missus, as long as it takes. Do this right and I scrub the record — he's safe, she's safe, you're safe, everybody gets what they want.'

Knowing Mackendrick was lying, Callaghan said, 'Okay, I'll do it.'

Mackendrick said, 'You could call the police again — tell them everything — but you don't know where I'm going to be, you don't know where the rest of my people will be. The police show up this time and your friend's dead and there's nothing on this earth will stop us finding your ex and taking her apart.'

'I said I'll do it.'

⋆   ⋆   ⋆

Novak was sitting on a rough floor, his arms around a steel support, his hands bound by a plastic tie, the silver tape across his mouth. He was aching where one of the bastards had punched him a couple of times in the ribs. He licked his lower lip and could taste blood, where another of the bastards had backhanded him. He could hear them talking in the distance.

This was some kind of warehouse. The steel support to which he was bound was one of a line that stretched all the way to the door. It was cold and the place had the feel of somewhere that had been empty for a long time.

There were three of them. Two young guys — one of them sullen, the other nervous. The third was a tall, thin man who didn't say much. No one had said anything about why they'd

337

taken Novak. When he'd asked he'd got the backhand across the face. Had to be the people who had Danny Callaghan by the throat. Maybe this was revenge for screwing up the bombing, maybe it was some new move they were trying. Whatever it was, they had no problem letting Novak see their faces, and that wasn't good. They had no fear he'd identify them later, and there were only so many ways of making sure of that.

Feeling the onset of cramp, Novak moved his legs, bent them under him and leaned against the steel support for relief.

At the sound of a car, the sullen one hurried to the door of the warehouse, opened it a couple of inches and peered out. He turned to the others and gave a thumbs-up. He opened the door wide. A bulky older man came in. He said something to the sullen one, then he walked towards Novak.

★ ★ ★

Driving from Kimmet's Ale House to the Carrigmore industrial estate, Lar Mackendrick suddenly felt a surge of hopelessness. On the lower end of Kilturbet Road he pulled into the Topaz forecourt and parked. His forehead was sweating and his hands were icy.

His confidence seemed to have drained out of him in an instant. Had everything gone right, Tucker would be dead now, his organisation in shreds. Lar would be free to pull together the threads of his own outfit and to recruit the best of the remnants of Tucker's. Instead, his fallback position involved a chancy manoeuvre, against the odds.

There was always the option of copping out.

To where?

Looking over our shoulders for the rest of our days.

No.

The Chinaman's book was in the side pocket of his red anorak. He took it out, the spine creased, the cover worn. The fallback plan was a good one, he believed that. And he still had the element of surprise.

> *Do not repeat the tactics which have gained you one victory, but let your methods be regulated by the infinite variety of circum-stances.*

Whichever way this went, Danny Callaghan was going under the earth. He had his uses, but there was only one answer to his kind of betrayal. By close of business tomorrow, when Frank Tucker was history — please God — Lar would take time to enjoy Callaghan's last moments. The bar owner he'd leave to Karl, but Lar would keep Callaghan as a treat for himself.

The thought gave him hope. He pulled out of the forecourt and waited for a chance to slide into the traffic flow.

Now, in the warehouse on the Carrigmore industrial estate, he stood over the bar owner, leaned down and pulled the tape from his mouth.

'My lads taking good care of you?'

Novak didn't look up. Looking off to one side, he said, 'What have I done to you, for this to happen to me?'

'You know a Danny Callaghan, right?'

Novak said nothing.

Lar bent and grabbed Novak under the chin. He turned the bar owner's head around until they were face to face. Mackendrick said, 'You take it up with him.' He straightened up and walked to the other side of the warehouse, where Karl and Robbie were sitting on a couple of kitchen chairs. Dolly Finn was leaning against an old table.

'Tomorrow, phase two, we kill Frank Tucker.'

Karl said, 'You've gotta be kidding. No way we're getting within an ass's roar of Tucker's house.'

'I never said we would.'

Dolly Finn was looking down at his feet. He said, 'How long do you intend to continue this thing?'

Lar said, 'Okay, we should have been done by now. Shit happens.'

Karl said, 'Frank Tucker's place will be a fortress.'

'We're not going in.'

'Any time he comes out he's going to have an army around him, not to mention the police.'

'He won't come out until this is over.'

Karl said, 'I don't see it.'

'It's simple.'

On the other side of the warehouse Novak was shivering, and not just from the cold. They didn't mind that he saw their faces. And now they didn't mind that he heard every word they said.

★ ★ ★

When Danny Callaghan picked up four sets of licence plates from Jacob Nash he asked if Jacob could get hold of a gun on short notice.

'Are you in trouble?'

'Any type of handgun, as long as I can get it by tonight.'

'Sorry, man — that's way out of my department. Basic tools of the trade, that's me.'

In the late afternoon, Callaghan bought a Stanley knife in a tool shop in Capel Street. When he got to O'Connell Street he went into Clery's kitchen department and bought the sharpest carving knife they had. In an art shop he bought a cutting mat.

At home, he folded the cutting mat twice and wrapped it in tape. It made a sheath for the carving knife. He put it into the inside pocket of his suede jacket and practised pulling the knife out. He had to use his left forearm to keep the sheath in position as he withdrew the knife. The whole thing was clumsy and slow, but it was the best he could do.

★ ★ ★

Karl said, 'What about Callaghan — why isn't he dead yet?'

'I talked to him this afternoon.'

'And he's still breathing?'

341

'We need transport for tomorrow. After that, he stops being useful — you can help me turn off his lights.'

'We owe him — his wife ought to go.'

'Fuck her, too much trouble. When we've got what we need, he's dessert.'

Dolly Finn said, 'How do we take Frank Tucker?'

'The original list I had, there was a man on it named Roly Blount. If Callaghan hadn't ratted, Blount would have been blown to bits along with Tucker. Roly's a smart guy, wicked little bastard. We use him.'

'Pay him?' Karl said.

'Blount will be holed up with Frank Tucker while this lasts. He lives in Raheny. He's got two teenage sons. He has a brother lives around the corner from him. Tomorrow morning, we take the brother, bring him here. We take the wife and the two kids, bring them here.'

'Hostages?' Dolly Finn said. 'How long do — '

'Yes and no,' Mackendrick said. 'The brother we kill immediately. In front of Roly's wife.' He let that sink in. Karl was nodding, Robbie looked worried. Dolly Finn's face was as expressionless as ever. 'Then we use the brother's phone to text Roly, tell him to call back.'

Karl said, 'And we break it to him?'

'We get his wife to do that. She tells him some IRA people have taken her and the kids. And she tells Roly his choices. He kills Frank Tucker — and whoever else gets in his way — and he turns himself over to the police, then he keeps his mouth shut and takes his lumps. Or he can stay on the phone and hear his two kids dying, one by one, followed by his wife.'

Robbie said, 'We're going to kill two kids?'

'It won't come to that — Roly's a tough guy, he'll do the smart thing.'

Karl Prowse was looking at Lar Mackendrick with admiration. Robbie Nugent seemed unsure. He said, 'What age are the kids?'

Lar said, 'It won't come to that, okay?'

Dolly Finn gestured to Lar. 'I need a word.'

When they were about fifty feet from the others, Dolly said, 'I don't like this. You said it would take one day. I didn't reckon on this becoming a career.'

'Karl and Robbie are okay, but this needs someone with real balls and a steady hand. I'll double the money.' Lar was staring into Dolly's eyes, as though he was trying to read something there.

Dolly said, 'Double?'

'Yeah.'

'Double what you owe me, or double the upfront money too?'

'Double everything.'

Dolly said, 'You'll have it ready this evening?'

'Most of it — I'll need to get some more cash tomorrow morning.'

'First thing?'

'First thing.'

'How long more? I mean, I'm anxious to get back to London.'

'Tomorrow — if Roly does what we say, it ends. If not — that's our last shot, you go back to London either way.'

343

Dolly Finn pursed his lips and said nothing for a moment. Then he said, 'No one's going to let his kids die. It'll work.'

★   ★   ★

The car Danny Callaghan was stealing was a Toyota Corolla, parked outside a terraced house with a front garden not much bigger than a window box. It was late, a weeknight, most people long asleep, and it was a cul-de-sac with no through traffic.

It took a minute with the jiggle key to get into the car, then Callaghan punched out the ignition and used a screwdriver to start the engine. Ten minutes later, in another quiet street, he changed the plates. He was wearing a baseball cap so the CCTV cameras wouldn't get anything useful when he filled up at the local Topaz.

It was the second car he'd stolen tonight. Like the first, he'd deliver it to the street across from Kimmet's Ale House. He'd head home for a couple of hours' sleep, then he'd steal the last two cars by dawn.

★   ★   ★

As he turned in his bed, Lar Mackendrick felt his back ache. Too busy these past few days, he hadn't kept up the exercises he needed to keep the aches and pains at bay. By the end of the day, this whole thing should be over. It would take a few days for everything to settle down, then life would return to normal.

Beside him, May was deep into the final chapters of a novel.

It could go wrong tomorrow. If Roly Blount played it stupid it might be necessary to kill one of the kids, maybe the wife — and even then Blount might be stubborn. After that — anything could happen. Lar Mackendrick had only the vaguest notion where he might take it from there. Failure tomorrow meant tapping out. If that happened, the best he could hope for was that the bullshit about Declan Roeper and the Interim IRA would provide some cover while he and May disappeared.

Tomorrow ought to work. Shifting on the pillow, he could see the slim book on his bedside table, the thoughts of Jo-Jo's Chinaman. He offered a moment to his dead brother.

Military tactics are like unto water, for water in its natural course runs away from high places and hastens downwards. So in war, the way is to avoid what is strong and to strike at what is weak.

He could hear May's steady breathing. When he turned to look she was asleep, her book still open on the pillow.

⋆　⋆　⋆

Unable to sleep, Danny Callaghan got up and took the knife and makeshift sheath out of his suede jacket. He wrapped black electrical tape around the sheath. He turned the sheath upside

345

down and its grip on the knife was tight enough to keep it from falling out.

He used the electrical tape to attach the sheath to his left forearm. He put on his suede jacket and the tip of the knife handle was just covered. It felt awkward, but that couldn't be helped.

He put the Stanley knife in the breast pocket of the jacket.

As he worked, Callaghan remembered the conversation in bed with Alex — the casual questions about Hannah.

'I think you've still got a thing for her.'

'Do you think she still cares for you?'

Were they Alex's questions, or did they come from Hannah, from Leon? The briefcase in the closet, where she'd left his jacket — an accident, or was it intended that he would stumble across the affair with Leon? Did someone imagine that he'd make a fuss with Hannah? Or was he making too much of this?

It didn't matter now. Alex might have been prying on Leon's behalf, or it might have been idle chat. Either way, that part of his life was tired, infertile soil. He cared for Hannah's safety, but he realised everything else to do with that part of his life was just habit. And sometimes habits got in the way.

Within a few hours this Mackendrick thing would be over, one way or the other. When Mackendrick's people took the stolen cars they'd have no further use for Callaghan, or for Novak. Whether either of them survived what followed would depend on chance and circumstance. The knives weren't much, but they were better than nothing.

If Callaghan survived, Hannah would still need protecting from Mackendrick. If Callaghan didn't survive, Mackendrick would have no need to threaten Hannah, so she should be okay.

Callaghan reached into his breast pocket, took out the Stanley knife and in the same movement he slid the button forward, opening the blade. He retracted the blade and put the Stanley away.

Then he tried the carving knife. He casually brought his hands together, the fingers of his right hand slipping smoothly inside the left sleeve of his jacket, gripping the handle, the carving knife sliding smoothly from the sheath, slipping from his grasp and bouncing on the floor.

Christ.

Day Thirteen

Chapter 46

The thunderclap that woke Lar Mackendrick was still echoing around the room as he jerked upright in his bed. The light —

The light is on —

Smell —

Gunshot smell —

Lar screamed an obscenity when he saw someone at the foot of the bed, a silhouette against the light.

Someone else near May's side of the bed.

This second man was holding aloft a big, heavy automatic pistol, smoke wafting from the muzzle.

Lar's scream was a frenzied noise as the realisation punched him in the chest and he jerked his head to the right and it was as if something evil sucked all the oxygen out of the world. In that moment, staring down at the mass of shiny dark blood that seeped from May's hair, he knew what the noise was that had woken him and he could feel his heart break.

His scream became a wretched, wavering moan as he pushed his way off the bed, clawing hands reaching for the nearest of the intruders. Something hard hit him on the side of the head and he went down, his chin glancing off the post

348

at the end of the bed. The instant he hit the floor the urge to struggle evaporated. Hands and knees touching the carpet, yet the earth was falling away beneath him. He wanted only to get to his feet, to throw himself onto the bed, to look into May's face, to see her respond. Someone kicked him in the ribs. The pain, the smell of the gunshot, the rush of grief, his stomach heaved. His thumping heart seemed to have expanded to fill his chest.

May —

He was panting. Tried to clear his head. There was something he had to get a fix on.

'Take it easy, Lar.'

Someone was hunkered down beside him.

'No point getting upset.'

'*Cunt!*' Mackendrick jerked forward and up, hands reaching for Frank Tucker's throat. Again, something hard hit his left temple and he found himself face down on the floor, aware that he'd blacked out for a moment. Tucker was speaking calmly. Something about not being a fool. 'It doesn't help, all this roaring.'

May —

Jesus fuck —

Mackendrick's head swayed from side to side, inches from the floor.

He got onto his knees, eased himself upright and inched towards the bed. The blood around May's head had saturated the pillow.

Nothing can change this — this is done —

Over —

For ever —

May.

349

He could taste acid.

Nothing can change this.

Only then, the fear. Not a sliver of doubt that within seconds he would be as lifeless as his wife —

As soon as it came the fear melted. It didn't matter now.

Mackendrick didn't want to know how this had happened, he didn't long for escape or revenge. The world was suddenly too complicated, too confusing, overwhelming. It wasn't his and he didn't want it. In the clearest thought he'd ever known he saw plainly what his life now was — a little thing, lasting only a few more moments, all in this small space and he knew there was just one last thing he wanted to do.

He said, 'May.'

Frank Tucker said, 'You had a good deal, Lar.' Tucker was holding a small Glock pistol. Behind him, Roly Blount had the big heavy automatic.

Lar stood there, tears on his face, his mouth moving silently, spittle on his lips. He wanted only to be on the bed, holding May close, for a few seconds that would last for ever. Frank Tucker was smiling as he raised the Glock and Lar said, 'Could I just — ' and there wasn't any more.

★   ★   ★

Robbie Nugent was up early — awoken by the sounds of his father's pick-up pulling away from the house, the rattle of the ladder strapped in the back. Robbie could hear the washing machine

350

grinding away downstairs. He rolled out of bed. Something unpleasant was pushing its way to the front of his mind. As he left the bathroom, he realised he'd been holding his breath. He let it out, slowly, audibly. Today he might be involved in killing Roly Blount's kids. The thought had an almost physical weight in his head.

'We've no milk,' his mother said. 'I'll go down to Centra in a minute.'

'No bother, I'll get it,' Robbie said.

He was coming back with the milk when he saw them. Parked at the kerb, thirty feet in front of him, two men he didn't know getting out of a black BMW. It was the way they did it, moving together, both looking down the street towards Robbie — this wasn't good. He turned and he ran and he could hear them coming after him.

After several yards he threw away the carton of milk and that got his balance right, his arms pumping, and within a few yards he could feel his stride lengthening. Head down, leaning forward, he knew he was pulling away. He felt a push in the back and a millisecond later he heard the bang and he knew they'd shot him and he was still running.

No pain at all. Just that little push in the back. He didn't know how that could be, but he'd been shot and it didn't hurt. He rounded into Willow Drive — a woman standing back against a garden wall, looking at him with her mouth open — and there was something wrong with his feet, like they were trying to catch up with the rest of his body. He ended up half sitting, half lying and he tried to get up but there was no strength in his legs.

He turned his head and watched the two men come towards him.

★   ★   ★

Karl Prowse's wife said, 'I don't know.'

'What time did he leave?'

All she wanted was for the baby not to wake. She'd been up three times during the night.

'Please, keep your voice down.'

'What time did he leave the house?'

'He didn't.'

The two men knew Karl wasn't here. They'd been in every room.

'He's not here. What time did he leave?'

'He didn't come home last night.'

They said nothing for a while, then one of them said, 'What time are you expecting him?'

She said she didn't know. And after a while they left.

★   ★   ★

Dolly Finn could feel the surge of the airplane engines in the pressure of his back against the seat, the roar of the rush down the runway. He felt the plane lift and soon he was looking down at Dublin. In less than ninety minutes he'd be searching for a taxi at Heathrow.

There was a time when he couldn't have imagined being happy to leave Dublin. He'd left a lifetime's collection of music behind and he'd adjusted to that, too. He'd long concluded that he was a better man for the change. He was looking forward to getting back to London.

The Dublin job was a downer. He had the upfront money, but there'd be nothing else.

'No,' he told Cillian Connolly, 'I'm not looking for money — I'm doing this because it's the right thing to do.'

They met at two o'clock in the morning, in the 24-hour Tesco at Artane Castle.

In the old days, Dolly had worked twice with Cillian Connolly on jobs that paid well. That was long before Cillian hooked up with Frank Tucker's outfit. It took Dolly two phone calls to old acquaintances before he got Cillian's mobile number. Where could they meet? Yes, it was important.

Most of the aisles were half-blocked with caged pallets stacked with packets, boxes and tins. Tesco workers, pale and tired, filled gaps in the shelves. Flanked by sliced pans on one side and Swiss Rolls and Bramley Apple Pies on the other, Dolly Finn told Cillian Connolly what his role had been over the past couple of days. He told him everything about Lar Mackendrick's plans and the people involved, who they were and who did what, why the bombing attempt hadn't worked. He told him about the plan to use Roly Blount's family.

'Lar's easy — you know where he lives. You shouldn't have much trouble tracking down Karl or Robbie.'

Dolly Finn believed there was a time when the smart thing to do was to walk away with whatever you could salvage. They'd missed their chance with the bomb. If that had worked Frank Tucker would be history, Lar Mackendrick would be bigger than ever and Dolly Finn would have a powerful friend. Now the odds were that Tucker would figure out what had happened. The Republican outfits were all well stocked with informers and eventually the police would know that none of the varieties of the IRA were involved.

Too many things might go wrong with Lar Mackendrick's last-chance hostage plan. Sooner or later, Frank Tucker would put Lar's balls in a vice and the names would come flowing. Even in London, Dolly would not be safe.

Much better to sabotage the Roly Blount plan — put Frank Tucker in his debt. Dolly had killed several of his people, but Frank was a businessman. Once Mackendrick's threat was smothered Frank would look at the bottom line, he'd call it quits and Dolly would be safe.

That was what Lar Mackendrick didn't understand. Those years ago, when Dolly got tight with the Mackendrick clan, when he warned Jo-Jo Mackendrick about the threat to his life, it wasn't personal. It was the best way out of a sticky problem for Dolly. This job, it was just business. Good money for dangerous work — and when the shit hit the fan you looked for the least unacceptable outcome.

He heard the plane's undercarriage lock up into place.

Dolly Finn's thumb worked the wheel of his iPod. It had been a while since he'd listened to the soaring tones of Johnny Hodges's sax.

354

Chapter 47

The radio's *pip-pip-pip* at eight o'clock was followed by the RTE newsreader announcing that two bodies had been found overnight in the wreckage of a house fire in Howth. 'Police have confirmed that the fire appears to have been malicious.' The newsreader handed over to the station's crime correspondent.

'Gardai have not named the two dead, but I understand unofficially that they were a man and a woman in their sixties. Sources say the man is known to gardai as a significant figure on the Dublin gangland scene. Preliminary examination, sources say, suggests that both victims suffered gunshot wounds.'

In a stolen car across the road from Kimmet's Ale House, Danny Callaghan sat very still.

Mackendrick?

On the radio, the crime correspondent was saying that the burned-down house was known to belong to a crime figure whose brother, too, had been murdered some years ago.

Can't be anyone else.

Callaghan had delivered the last of the stolen cars to the street near Kimmet's by seven o'clock and found the nearest newsagent. Most of the front pages splashed the gang killings and the attempted bombing. He picked up four copies of the *Daily Mail*, went back to Wakeham Street and left the newspapers on the dashboards of the stolen cars.

Lar and his people were half an hour late. No contact, no calls. And now the news on the radio had to be about Lar Mackendrick.

It changes everything.

Stay calm.

No point trying to work out what had happened. With Mackendrick dead and the others probably scattered, they wouldn't need the cars, they wouldn't need him. They wouldn't need Novak. What were the chances they'd let Novak live? Had they killed him already?

In the night, unable to sleep, running the whole thing through his head, Callaghan had tried to remember the names of the businesses he'd glimpsed when Karl and Robbie had brought him from the warehouse. It was where they'd taken Callaghan when they needed somewhere isolated. It might be where they had Novak.

Nothing else to go on.

McSomething.

Some kind of interiors warehouse — *Mc* — *Something.*

And an outfit selling desks — he couldn't remember the name. A building with something to do with tyres — but all he could remember was a large tattered Michelin poster.

He could find a Golden Pages, spend an hour ploughing through the listings for interiors, for office furniture, for tyres — see if anything rang a bell. If Novak was locked up somewhere, maybe hurt, he didn't have an hour.

★   ★   ★

356

One last time.

It was the fifth time Karl Prowse had told himself that he'd try calling Lar Mackendrick just one last time. Karl had spent the night in the warehouse, dozing fitfully in a too-thin sleeping bag, guarding the prisoner. It was now pushing nine in the morning, and the plan to take Roly Blount's family ought to have been well under way. Still no word from Lar.

Karl used his mobile and listened again as the call went through to Lar's voicemail.

He tried Robbie again. Third time, same result.

Picking up the baseball bat, he crossed the floor to where the fat bar owner was sitting, his hands tied, his arms around the steel support. He shoved the thick end of the baseball bat into Novak's face and pushed. Novak turned his head and the bat slid along his cheek.

'Won't be long now, barman,' Karl said.

One more time. He took out his phone.

★ ★ ★

Novak couldn't tell how much of his shivering was a result of the chilliness of the warehouse, and how much was due to fear.

He'd thought it through, all the permutations. First thing to go was any notion of talking his way out of it. That lump of walking gristle with the baseball bat was looking forward to killing him — it was in his eyes every time he looked down at Novak.

The only question was — would he use the

baseball bat, or would he use the gun?

Novak thought of the possibility of being rescued by the police — not out of the question, but unlikely.

And the way those people talked openly in front of him, there was no possibility they'd leave him as a witness.

It's about taking a breath.

Novak's head was full of his father.

'It's about taking a breath,' the old man had said, all that time ago.

Novak was maybe eleven or twelve, mooching about the house one rainy afternoon. He told his father he was bored.

His father looked at him, one eyebrow raised. Novak was expecting a lecture about how miserable everyone was during the war, how easy his generation had it. Instead his dad said, '*You can breathe, can't you?*' At the end of the day, he said, that's what life's really about, taking a breath. Once you can do that, you've got no end of choices.

'Look at something or listen to something. Go somewhere or play something. If you can't go anywhere, go inside your head and think of something nice. Walk, run, jump, fall over, take a nap, it's all good. Read something, eat something, or put your arms around someone. No end of choices. *Unbore yourself,*' he said.

Novak pushed the past to one side and closed his ears to the muttering of the lump of gristle, who was somewhere at the other side of the warehouse, tapping the baseball bat against something hard.

This time I've got —

His arms, held in place around the steel support, ached. He tried to ignore the pain. Novak pictured his wife Jane and decided that in the time he had, minutes or hours, it would all be about her, about Jeanie and Caroline and Caroline's boys, and the things they'd have done over the next few years if this shit hadn't happened.

★   ★   ★

McCall's.

McCall's Interiors.

Callaghan could see himself leaving Mackendrick's warehouse, noticing the tyre warehouse straight ahead, something about desks on another sign, the dirty logo on the warehouse door — McCall's Interiors.

Callaghan called one of the directory-enquiries companies. They told him there was no listing for a McCall's Interiors.

'McCall's Furniture?'

'Sorry, man.' A young man's voice. He sounded like he meant it.

'McCall's — anything that might be furnishing, interiors, decorating, stuff like that? It's an emergency, please, it's really serious.'

'Doing that now, man — interior designers, interior decorators — ' Behind his voice the clicking of a keyboard. 'Contractors, furniture, curtains — going through the lot — '

'Thanks.'

'Not looking good — not looking — sorry,

man, nothing here.'

'Is there — '

'That was McCall with an M-C. Trying it again with an M-A-C.'

'Thanks.'

After a few moments he came back, sounding like it was somehow his fault. 'Sorry, man — nothing happening here.'

'Thanks for trying.' Callaghan rang off.

The police.

But the police had protocols for everything. They'd want detailed statements, with solicitors involved, upward reporting, superintendents overseeing everything — the police were all about procedure and the procedure would take hours and by then Novak might be lying in a ditch, his eyes as unseeing as Declan Roeper's.

Callaghan's phone rang.

It was the young guy from the directory service. He had a note of Callaghan's number and he'd checked back through records of deleted listings. There was a McCall's Interiors listed up to three years ago.

'Two outlets in Tallaght, one in the city centre — and a warehouse at Carrigmore Park industrial estate — '

He was still talking as Callaghan gunned the car away from the kerb.

⋆ ⋆ ⋆

Karl rang again and again all he got was Lar's voicemail.

Definitely something wrong.

Definitely.

Karl's orders were to wait here until Lar and the others arrived.

Not going to happen.

The sensible thing to do was kill the fat barman and do a fade.

'*We keep him alive until we're sure we don't need him,*' Lar had said.

Karl rang Robbie's number again and a voice at the other end said, 'Yeah?'

'Robbie?'

'Yeah, who is this?'

'I want to speak to Robbie.'

'He can't speak right now — who is this?'

Karl cut the call off.

Cop.

Shit.

If Robbie had been pulled, chances were that Lar too had been arrested.

Karl rang his wife.

'Anyone looking for me?'

'Two fellas.'

Definitely the police.

'They still there?'

'They just asked if you'd been home last night, then they went away.'

'Are they watching the house?'

'Where were you last night?'

'Are they watching the house?'

'No, I don't think so. Why didn't — '

'Pack a bag for me. Just a shirt and jeans, socks and stuff. Pull out — '

'Karl, what — '

'*Fuck sake* — pull out the left-hand side

drawer of the dressing table — can you remember that? The left-hand side drawer — reach underneath. There's an envelope taped to the bottom of the drawer. Put it in the bag with the clothes. Don't open it.'

'Karl — '

'Bring the bag to the corner shop. Buy something — leave the bag with the guy behind the counter, tell him — tell him you have to go out and I'm coming to collect my clothes, I've a job to do down the country, tell him that.'

'Karl — '

'Do it now. I don't have time for messing around.' He ended the call.

Karl turned and looked at the fat barman.

Best thing to do, no question, was plug him now. If he had to do a runner, no way was he leaving this bastard alive.

What if Lar surfaces and we need this bag of shit?

Lar's got lawyers ready for a thing like this. They'd be all over the cops, looking for a loophole. Lar might walk. He might yet turn up, with a plan to pull this off. And that plan might need the fat barman alive.

Okay. No need to panic.

It wouldn't take too long to collect the bag from the corner shop. And if he hadn't heard from Lar by then, come back here, the fat fuck dies and Karl disappears.

He took Novak by the hair, pulled his head back and checked that the silver tape was secure. He smacked the barman's face hard against the steel support and was satisfied to see a bubble of blood come from the fat fuck's nose and run down the silver tape.

As Karl walked away he called back, 'You said your prayers yet, barman?'

★ ★ ★

Callaghan tapped the buttons on his phone and held his breath while he listened to it ring at the other end. When his name came up on her screen, she mightn't even —

'What do you want?' Hannah's voice was cold.

Callaghan reckoned he was a mile, maybe a mile and a half, from the Carrigmore Park industrial estate. He didn't know what he'd find there, if anything, and he needed to know if Hannah was all right. If he'd had time, it was the kind of call he'd have made while sitting at a table, after a couple of coffees and an hour of working himself up to it. He didn't know if he'd ever again have an hour of time to do anything.

'Are you okay?'

'What do you want?'

'I just need to know that you're okay.'

When Hannah spoke, it was as though she was writing the words one by one on a blackboard, big and stark. 'Do not *ever* contact me *ever* again.' And she was gone.

Callaghan put the phone away, an icy wave flooding through his blood.

Somewhere, an earlier part of his life, a source of warmth to which he had stubbornly clung, was finally closing itself down. Among the emotions still simmering from the abortive call to Hannah he recognised regret, and relief. The future, whatever it was, would have to be handled on its own terms.

Always assuming that the future could be measured in anything other than minutes.

⋆ ⋆ ⋆

To be on the safe side, just in case someone came mooching, Karl Prowse had parked his car about forty yards from the warehouse. All the way there, the nagging thought — maybe he ought to just kill the fat bar owner now, take off and not look back. He was reaching for the ignition, still in two minds, when a car came around the old tyre warehouse, just inside the entrance to the industrial estate, Danny Callaghan at the wheel. Callaghan cut the engine, coasted to a stop and came out of the car in a hurry. At Lar's warehouse he gently tried the handle of the smaller door set into the main door. When that didn't work he took something from his pocket and worked on the lock.

Christmas is here early.

Karl waited until the smart bastard went inside. Then he tapped the gun tucked into his belt and strolled back down towards the warehouse.

Chapter 48

The silver tape was off Novak's mouth. Danny Callaghan was leaning over, the Stanley knife cutting the plastic tie and releasing Novak's hands when Novak shouted *'Danny!'* and Callaghan turned and saw Karl Prowse coming at speed, a baseball bat at the ready.

He had time to raise an arm before the bat swung. He screamed as his right wrist took the blow and he dropped the Stanley knife and fell back.

Novak was scrambling to his feet.

Karl dropped the baseball bat and there was a gun in his hand and he pointed it at Novak's face.

'Sit down, hands on your head.'

Novak did as he was told, his legs stiff and awkward.

Karl bent over Danny Callaghan, who was clutching his right arm.

'What you got here, smart bastard?' Karl held the gun inches from Callaghan's head. He reached down, tugged at Callaghan's left sleeve and pulled out the carving knife.

'Not very friendly.'

Karl threw the carving knife towards the far end of the warehouse. Then he picked up the Stanley knife and did the same. He rooted in Callaghan's pockets, found his mobile and stamped on it until it came apart.

'How did you find this place?'

Callaghan turned to Novak. 'You okay?'

'Still here.'

'I'm sorry about this. Nothing to do with you.'

Karl was shouting. 'How did you *find* this fucking place?'

Callaghan turned back to Karl. 'You know Lar

Mackendrick's dead?'

Karl said nothing, his gun hand erratic, pointing this way and that.

'It was on the radio — someone shot him and burned the house down. The police found two bodies.'

Karl said, 'That's bollocks.'

Novak lowered his hands from his head. He held them out towards Karl. 'Look, fella, whatever this is about, holding us here's only going to make — '

Karl shot him.

★ ★ ★

Novak knew he was on his back, he knew he'd been shot. He didn't know if it had happened a moment ago or an hour ago. He could see Danny Callaghan leaning over him, saying something, but he couldn't make it out.

No pain.

A rush, he could feel it in his blood.

This may be —

People get shot, they come back from it —

Uh —

It was as though a broadsword had suddenly cut a wide channel through his belly, tearing his flesh asunder. The pain enveloped him and he looked up at Danny Callaghan and he moaned and it took a moment before he realised he'd made no noise and Callaghan couldn't hear him, it was all going dark.

★ ★ ★

Karl Prowse raised the gun and said, 'Get away from him!' and Danny Callaghan said, '*Fuck off!*' and knelt beside Novak. With every movement, Callaghan's right wrist blazed with pain.

Broken.

Novak was pale, still. Callaghan touched his throat and Novak's pulse was ragged.

'Novak?'

No answer. His eyes were half open but it was hard to tell if he was conscious. His breathing was shallow. He'd been hit in the stomach and blood was soaking his grey shirt. Callaghan reached towards it, then stopped. He had no idea what to do.

He stood up.

'There's no need for this. He's got nothing to do with anything. You're going to kill me — so do it — get the hell out of here, call an ambulance, give him a chance.'

'Why?'

'*Come on!*'

Karl's face was blank. 'Any last words?'

Callaghan braced himself for the impact of the bullet, but Karl was enjoying the anticipation. Killing Callaghan would be a rush, but once he did it the fun would be over.

Karl held the gun as if he was weighing it mentally, showing Callaghan his smile.

Callaghan said, 'You don't even know you're alive.'

Karl pursed his lips, eased the smirk off his face, as though it mattered to him that he be seen to be cool.

Callaghan turned away. He walked over to the sink and ran the cold tap. He watched the water hit the base of the sink, swirl and rush to the plughole. He listened to the sound it made and tried to tune out the pain in his wrist.

He felt Karl's gaze on him and he resisted the urge to turn and face the gun. Despite the sense of horror that enveloped him, he was fairly sure that Karl wouldn't shoot him in the back. He was the kind who wanted to see the face of his victim as the end came.

This is how I die.

Callaghan glanced at the drainer, scarred and dented but clean, like someone had taken trouble with it. Nothing in the sink except a mug, a bowl and a soup spoon. A knife or a fork might have made a difference, but probably not.

No point crying about it.

It's what it is.

He reached down and touched the running water, let the steady, cold flow wash over his hand. He cupped his hand and carried a few drops to his lips.

As soon as he turned around Karl would shoot him and his body would become a vacant container, collapsed untidily on the floor, all life vanishing instantly, like air from a burst balloon. It was important that these moments not be lost to panic.

This is how I die.

Callaghan was aware of the muscles in his stomach and the balance of his poised trunk, the tension in his legs, the pain in his wrist. He stretched his head back, his neck flexing to one side and then the other. His tongue found moisture on his lips. He looked up into the mirror above the sink and he saw his own face.

He turned off the tap.

No need to waste water.

He heard a grunt from somewhere behind and when Danny turned around he saw Novak struggling to get to his feet.

★ ★ ★

Karl Prowse is smiling.

Too fucking much!

The fat barman's corpse has rolled over. One knee pressing into the floor, the upper body jerking into a half-upright position, the dickhead's face white, his mouth hanging open, tongue off to one side.

Karl leans forward, smile widening, as the fat dickhead's corpse strains to speak.

Eyes half shut, blood on his face, red stain on his belly.

A croak comes out.

'Beast . . .'

You have to give the fat dickhead credit.

Every breath he can suck up, every beat he can coax out of that drained heart — dead man, and he's still trying.

Karl looks at Callaghan, standing by the sink, gives him a big smile, then points his pistol at the dickhead's corpse, squeezes the trigger and is immediately rewarded with the flat *tuhhhh* of a bullet hitting flesh and a splotch of red on the dickhead's chest. From a half-sitting position

369

Novak instantly falls straight back, the body hitting the ground with the finality of a door slamming shut.

Karl considers his work for a moment, then aims again at the corpse.

★ ★ ★

The first bullet hit Callaghan in the hip as he lurched towards Karl. The second smacked a hole in the roof as Karl went down on his back, Callaghan's weight knocking him over, Callaghan's left hand desperately reaching for the gunman's right forearm, up near the wrist of the hand that held the gun.

Callaghan's useless right hand trailed off to one side, throbbing with pain. He strained to hold Karl's arm rigid, pushing it down and outwards, limiting the gunman's freedom of movement. He felt the jolt as the gun fired a third time, heard the sound of the bullet smacking into metal.

Callaghan grunted as Karl's free hand punched his side, once, twice.

Locked together by their combined grip, Callaghan's hand and Karl's were like a single twisted limb, the muscles and ligaments knotted together, straining for control.

Then —

Fuck, no.

Callaghan could feel the balance shift.

He was bigger than Karl and stronger, but his body had taken two draining blows. The first from the baseball bat that had shattered his wrist, the second from the bullet wound that was now leaking blood from his side. The pain and the shock were sapping his strength. Callaghan could feel his hand waver. It was as though an invisible weight had suddenly been subtracted from his side of the scales, and Karl had acquired an extra unit of power. The gunman made a *Ya!* noise and made a small jerking movement that brought the muzzle of the gun closer to Callaghan.

Again, Karl's free fist slammed into Callaghan's side.

Callaghan's drained body told him that it didn't have the reserves to regain lost power. It was a matter of time, of distance, angles and waning strength, before the muzzle of the gun would tilt sufficiently to allow the gunman to fire into Callaghan's face.

Callaghan let go of Karl's hand.

The unexpected lapse in pressure stole Karl's balance. Callaghan's foot on the floor and his angled knee gave his upper body the leverage to jerk up and forward, his shoulder smashing into Karl's upper body and pitching him backward. Callaghan, screaming from the pain in his wrist, landed on Karl, slamming him onto the floor.

As Karl's back hit the floor he grunted and Callaghan heard the gun fall and tumble on the concrete.

Callaghan used his right shoulder to pin Karl to the floor. His face was now crushed into Karl's chest. He could smell his sweat.

His right hand useless, Callaghan's free left hand grasped blindly for the gun. He had no idea where it had gone.

He refused to acknowledge the hope that now raged in his skull.

No hope.

Struggle.

When Callaghan had turned from the sink, after Novak was shot, when he'd lurched at Karl, he had already accepted death.

Hope is dangerous.

No hope, no fear. Just struggle.

Callaghan moaned as Karl's punch connected with the wound on his hip.

The gunman's other hand found Callaghan's throat.

Another punch to the wound.

And again.

The hand tightening on his throat.

Callaghan's lungs strain for air, but nothing comes.

No air feeding his voice, no oxygen coming through to his blood, his heart hammering, his flailing hand weakening, his brain racing, his head filling with noise and pressure, a sparking light shooting across his consciousness — behind it everything fading, light seeping away, the stretched muscles in his face relaxing.

'Shit.'

Karl Prowse sounds more contemptuous than angry. He keeps the pressure on Callaghan's throat.

He's looking beyond Callaghan, at the bloody presence two feet away.

There's blood on Novak's face and on his

hands, a quiver in his barely audible voice. 'Let him go.'

Novak's extended hand awkwardly holding Karl Prowse's gun, the muzzle just inches away from Karl's forehead.

Karl punches Callaghan again on the wound. And again.

Novak's voice is a whisper.

'Let him *go*.'

Karl makes a scornful noise and his hand tightens on Callaghan's throat. His other hand stops punching and reaches towards Novak, trying for the gun.

'*Arogancki* . . .'

Novak's voice, soft with regret and pity, is so low that he might be speaking to himself as he closes his eyes, squeezes the trigger.

' . . . *bestie* . . .'

Chapter 49

Novak was still and white, his eyes closed. Danny Callaghan was leaning across him. He said into Karl's mobile, 'Hurry.' Then he ended the call. He was angry with himself for having no idea what to do. To put pressure on either of Novak's wounds might help him or damage him further. The stomach wound was still bleeding, but there was no great flow from the wound in his chest, which might mean that the bullet hadn't hit anything important. Or it might mean the opposite.

Callaghan's left side was on fire, his broken

wrist throbbed. The wounds and the fight and the effort to find Karl's mobile and make the call had drained his strength. He lay on the floor on his back, beside Novak. A few feet away, Karl Prowse was lying on his side, his eyes open and unseeing.

The floor beneath Danny Callaghan was cold, but that was okay — it was soothing, given the blaze of pain that burned through his body. He realised he was looking for patterns in the years of dirt that streaked the inside of the corrugated roof.

Stay awake.

The quiet was intense. He was sure that if he sat up he'd hear the usual distant sounds of city life. He remembered when he was a kid, when his dad took him to the Phoenix Park racecourse, he used to lie flat on the grass and marvel at how the noise of the thousands of racegoers had all but disappeared. Then he'd suddenly sit up and the babble of the crowds was loud again. Down, up, down, up, again and again. He had the urge now to lever his body up, just to prove that his memory of Phoenix Park was real. He knew that if he did the effort would make him vomit.

'You call an ambulance?'

Novak's voice, to Callaghan's left.

'You're awake?'

'You call an ambulance?'

'On the way.'

Novak grunted.

Callaghan turned to his left, saw Novak, his grey shirt bloody in two places.

'How you doing?'

'It's about — taking a breath.'

'Yeah?'

'Long as you can take — ' Novak coughed. 'My dad, long time ago.'

'Take it easy, man — '

'Unbore yourself, he used to say.'

Novak went silent. Callaghan thought he might have lost consciousness again. Then Novak said, 'Some day, my dad said, all that time you kill being bored, some day you'll — '

After a few moments of silence, Callaghan said, 'Novak?'

Nothing.

'*Novak?*'

Novak made a long, low noise — a soft groan that eventually turned into words. 'How long does it take an ambulance to — where are we?'

'They'll get here. You'll be okay.'

'Yeah?'

'Really.'

After a long silence, Novak said, 'Won't be cooking, though.'

'What?'

'No Christmas dinner. We'll have to skip it.'

Callaghan shook his head. 'Not important.'

'Jane, she'll be disappointed.'

'Don't be daft.'

Novak made a sudden wordless noise and said, '*Jesus*, it hurts.'

Callaghan turned his head towards his friend. He couldn't tell if the patches of blood on the shirt had spread.

Callaghan said, 'From what I hear, Christmas

375

in hospital's kind of cool. They make a special effort, the nurses. They make a big deal of it.'

After a moment, Novak grunted something that might have been half a sentence. Callaghan was about to ask him what he'd said, then he looked across and saw that Novak's eyes were closed.

Leave it. Let him save his strength.

Then, his eyes still closed, Novak said it again, louder. 'Next year.' He took a deep breath and let it out. 'Okay?'

'Sorry?'

'Next Christmas — I'll do the turkey, right?'

Danny Callaghan laughed, and the laughter made his wound hurt. He said, 'Next year, sure. I'm counting on it.'

From outside, he could hear the urgent rise and fall of a siren.

Acknowledgements

Many thanks to the publishers for permission to quote from Martin Carter, *The University of Hunger: Collected Poems & Selected Prose*, ed. Gemma Robinson (Bloodaxe Books, 2006).

The quotes from *The Art of War*, by Sun Tzu, are from the 1910 translation by Lionel Giles.

Once again, I'm indebted to Evelyn Bracken, Pat Brennan, Tom Daly, Cathleen Kerrigan and Julie Lordan for advice and support.

We do hope that you have enjoyed reading this large print book.

Did you know that all of our titles are available for purchase?

We publish a wide range of high quality large print books including:
Romances, Mysteries, Classics General Fiction Non Fiction and Westerns

Special interest titles available in large print are:
The Little Oxford Dictionary Music Book Song Book Hymn Book Service Book

Also available from us courtesy of Oxford University Press:
Young Readers' Dictionary (large print edition) Young Readers' Thesaurus (large print edition)

For further information or a free brochure, please contact us at:
Ulverscroft Large Print Books Ltd., The Green, Bradgate Road, Anstey, Leicester, LE7 7FU, England. Tel: (00 44) 0116 236 4325 Fax: (00 44) 0116 234 0205

Other titles published by
The House of Ulverscroft:

STILL BLEEDING

Steve Mosby

After his wife's death, Alex Connor just
wanted oblivion. Only his friend Sarah kept
him going, but she's been murdered. And
whilst the police have the killer, they don't
have her body. The gruesome search for her
drags Alex back into the land of the living —
and the dead. Policeman Paul Kearney is
tracking a killer who's abducting women and
draining them of blood. He's drawn into a
world of dark desires that people will go to
great lengths to hide. Wound together by their
search, if they're to save themselves and the
people they love, Alex and Kearney must go
to a place where normal rules don't apply —
where people trade murder memorabilia, and
a place where life is only the first thing you
lose.

THE STONE GALLOWS

David C. Ingram

After three months in intensive care, DC Cameron Stone could recall his high-speed pursuit of a vice baron through Glasgow that took the life of a teenage mother and her child. And Audrey had left him, taking their son, Mark, with her . . . Unable to return to his old job he works for a private detective, trying to track down a teenage runaway. It's been a bad week. Access to Mark gets difficult. He's roughed up when he finds his runaway, and there's the daubing on his door: 'Burn in Hell Baby Killer.' The only brightness on his horizon is his growing friendship with Liz . . . But things get worse for Stone — somebody is out to destroy him and everything he loves — unless he gets to them first.